THE
EXILE

TOR BOOKS BY C. T. ADAMS

The Exile

TOR BOOKS BY C. T. ADAMS WITH CATHY CLAMP

THE SAZI

Hunter's Moon
Moon's Web
Captive Moon
Howling Moon
Moon's Fury
Timeless Moon
Cold Moon Rising
Serpent Moon

THE THRALL

Touch of Evil
Touch of Madness
Touch of Darkness

WRITING AS CAT ADAMS

Magic's Design

THE BLOOD SINGER NOVELS

Blood Song
Siren Song
Demon Song
The Isis Collar
The Eldritch Conspiracy

THE
EXILE

BOOK ONE

OF

THE FAE

C. T. Adams

TOR®

A TOM DOHERTY ASSOCIATES BOOK

NEW YORK

THE EXILE

A Tor Book
Published by Tom Doherty Associates, LLC
175 Fifth Avenue
New York, NY 10010

www.tor-forge.com

Tor® is a registered trademark of Tom Doherty Associates, LLC.

The Library of Congress Cataloging-in-Publication Data is available upon request.

ISBN 978-0-7653-3687-3 (trade paperback)
ISBN 978-1-4668-2932-9 (e-book)

Tor books may be purchased for educational, business, or promotional use. For information on bulk purchases, please contact the Macmillan Corporate and Premium Sales Department at 1-800-221-7945, extension 5442, or write to specialmarkets@macmillan.com.

First Edition: March 2015

Printed in the United States of America

0 9 8 7 6 5 4 3 2 1

For Dad. I miss you.

AUTHOR'S NOTE

The worlds depicted in this book are the product of my fertile imagination. To my knowledge, the land of Faerie with its courts and cultures as described in this book does not exist anywhere, nor do its magical creatures walk among us. I have not used Spenser, nor any other work detailing the mythos of the Sidhe, Seelie, and/or Unseelie courts. I have, however, used the familiar names of the Sidhe, trolls, brownies, pixies, doxies, goblins, and other creatures.

In this book there is only one Sidhe Court. Various other species, such as the trolls, pixies, doxies, and the goblins, have their own courts and kings who report to the High King, who is the Sidhe ruler. There are other species who either have alliances with the High King or are separate nations altogether. All magical creatures are dangerous to the mortals in their own way, but their malice or lack thereof is completely individual. I considered calling them by different names, but that would have created more confusion and problems than it solved. My apologies if in this work I have depicted any creature in a way that has proven offensive to the beliefs of a reader.

With regard to magic: To my knowledge, the use of magic in this book is *not* based on any religion or philosophy. If it reflects the elements of any religious belief, or runs counter to those beliefs, it was not purposefully done, and I would state again that this is a work of fiction and thus the rules of the "normal" world are not meant to apply.

Finally, I would like to give special thanks to my agent, Lucienne Diver, for her invaluable assistance. To my editor, Melissa Ann Singer, because it is always a pleasure working with you. You make my work so much better. Gru and Anna, I am *so* grateful for your help in making this the best book possible. To Cathy Clamp, my frequent coauthor, I wish you all the best, always.

THE
EXILE

FATE—ATROPOS

(FAERIE)

PROLOGUE

Atropos shivered, despite the weight of her heavy wool cloak. Her bones ached and her joints stiffened in wet weather. It made her move more slowly, which meant she would be out in the rain longer. That soured her mood. She did not want to do this, and cursed the necessity. Normally she'd let one of her other two aspects handle it. With her youth, Clotho could ignore foul weather, and while Lachesis loathed the damp, it didn't incapacitate her. But both of them had history with the king of the Sidhe. Atropos did not trust the younger ones not to be affected by sentiment. So with faltering footsteps, supported by a cane carved of ash, she made her way through the darkened rose garden, following a path strewn with shifting shadows, until she reached a little-known servant's door, tucked discreetly in a corner behind a trellis that bore a thick covering of ivy.

The door was unlocked, as arranged, and she stepped through into a wide, marble-floored hallway dimly lit by a few glowing crystals.

Depending on one's perspective, it was either very late or quite early, barely three hours past midnight. Even the hardiest courtiers had gone to their beds, as had most of the servants. But Atropos knew the king was still awake and at work, and his guards with him.

The man on the door was no fool and no coward. The moment he saw Atropos he knew who, and what, she was. But he stood his ground, a mountain of ebony muscle barring the heavy oak doors with his body, weapons ready, though not actively threatening her.

"I will see the king."

The guard did not meet her milky gaze. Instead he stared over her left shoulder, into the middle distance, as he answered her in a voice that was completely steady, despite the muscle that twitched nervously above his right eye. "The king is not to be disturbed."

"He will see me." Her voice was harsh as the caw of a carrion bird, but the soldier neither flinched nor moved. He was accustomed to death, this one, having dealt it out, and seen it, more often than most. His name, she recalled, was Petros. It was certainly apt. He was solid as a rock—and just about as bright.

Petros opened his mouth to again refuse her, but was saved by the king's command from behind the closed doors.

"Let the crone in."

The guard turned and opened the door for her without further comment.

After the chill dimness of the hall, the warmth and light of King Leu's library was most welcome. Atropos moved gratefully toward the fireplace in the corner nearest the door. Though Leu was seated near the fire, he was not looking into the flames. Instead, he stared at a painting that hung on the wall nearby. To the uninformed, the painting was just that, a perfect rendering of the entry hall of a modern human apartment. Atropos knew, however, that the frame contained something more than a painting. She also knew just how much the image meant to her host.

Leu made her wait before turning to greet her. It was a deliberate slight, and it rankled, though Atropos knew better than to let
that show. She had sought this meeting. She was in his castle, his
place of power. And while all men must bow to the will of Fate,
this was not the time or place to remind him of it. Leu was a king,
and a proud man.

"Why are you here?" He spoke calmly, his eyes gleaming silver
in the firelight.

"I need a boon," she answered sourly.

His elegant, dark brows rose so high they disappeared beneath
a shock of his dark hair, in the front braided tight against his skull
and pulled back in a tail, the back hanging nearly to his knees.
She felt a pang of memory—Clotho's—of the silken feel of that
hair beneath her fingers and sliding over her naked body. . . . The
crone found herself fighting her younger aspect for control of their
shared body. Closing her eyes, she clamped down tight with her
will until Clotho sullenly relented.

"You seek a boon? From me?" Leu gave a slow, feral smile, his
pleasure evident in the anticipatory flash of sharp, white teeth.
"Have a seat," he suggested with belated courtesy, gesturing toward
the beautifully carved wooden chair across from him. "Would you
like a drink?"

Atropos nodded her consent. Resting her cane against the nearby
table she lowered herself onto the straight-backed chair. It was
not a comfortable seat. The carvings dug painfully into her back,
and whatever padding the seat had once held had been worn
down to nothing. She smiled grimly, knowing that the only better seat in the room was the king's; the others were all intended to
subtly discourage everyone else from lingering.

Everything about Leu was subtle, complex, layered. He was a
very physical being, Clotho and Lachesis could both attest to that,
but ultimately his mind was what made him most dangerous—and
the kind of High King Faerie needed. Atropos might not like the

man, but she respected him, and her respect was not earned
easily.

She took a glass of wine from his hand, the liquid so dark a red
it was nearly purple. She didn't worry about poison. He wasn't the
type, and she was immune to most of them anyway. Still, there
was always the possibility of an accident. The man had so very
many enemies.

Leu pushed aside a stack of maps and leaned back against the
edge of the table, quite close to her. Taking a sip from his glass, he
looked down at her and, smiling that dangerous smile, said, "Let
the dickering begin."

1

BRIANNA HAI

Brianna woke before the alarm to the smell of fresh coffee and the sound of her roommate puttering in the kitchen. She couldn't see what Pug was up to, but from the sound of it he was getting food ready for Camille and her kittens. He doted on those cats. Then again, having *been* a house pet at one point in his life he had very strong opinions as to how pets should be treated.

The clock on the nightstand read 5:30 A.M. It was still dark outside, without so much as a hint of dawn on the horizon. Brianna knew she should throw off the covers and start the day, but the bed was warm, soft, and inviting and the past few mornings had been, not cold precisely, but chilly enough to make her old injuries ache. She scratched absentmindedly at the scar above her left breast.

Five more minutes . . . five more minutes wouldn't hurt. But that was a lie and she knew it. Five minutes would become ten, then half an hour, and before she knew it she'd be skipping her workout because she was running late. Missing one workout was

no problem. But once could easily become twice, and soon enough
the habit that kept her fighting fit would go out the window. If
she even thought about letting that happen, Mei would kick
her ass.

You do not want to piss off a dragon, even if she is one of your
better friends. Still, with Mei out of town she didn't feel the least
bit guilty about exercising at home rather than going to the gym.

So Brianna threw off the covers with a groan and rolled out of
bed. Padding down the hall to the bathroom, she tended to her
immediate needs before pulling her hair up into a ponytail and
dressing in a sports bra and black leggings.

Ready to start her daily routine, Brianna took her place in the
clearest part of the living room. She began with stretches and
yoga, breathing carefully and steadily, then moved into her favorite martial arts kata. After that, she stepped onto the treadmill and
punched in the preprogrammed setting: first, a gentle slope, then
increased speed and incline, and finally a gentler cool-down.

As she jogged, she reviewed her plans for the day. Work, of
course. But there was nothing special about that. When her
mother had opened Helena's, it had been a very small, very exclusive shop. It was still exclusive, but the store had grown considerably under Brianna's management; it was a popular venue for local
magical practitioners and did a good amount of online business.
There was always plenty of work to keep Brianna busy.

Busy, but bored.

And frustrated.

The thoughts were unbidden and unwelcome, but also unavoidable.

There was no challenge to her life. Everything was moving
along smoothly. She told herself that this was a *good* thing. She
wasn't having to watch over her shoulder every moment, be suspect
of everything and everyone because relaxing would put her life at
risk. This was positively *excellent*. But she wasn't happy.

A new man would be a nice distraction and she could think of several who'd be happy to oblige. She was, after all, an attractive woman. Oh, in Faerie she was pretty but fairly ordinary, but on this side of the veil, her looks were exceptional. She had luckily inherited her Sidhe father's tall frame and exotic features, but they had been softened by her human mother's lush curves.

Yes, there were always men. But while Brianna had a perfectly normal libido, lately she'd found herself finding fault and nitpicking when she considered possible suitors. That meant that the men weren't the problem . . . and a new lover wouldn't be the solution.

What the hell is the matter with me?

Surely she wasn't . . . homesick?

She shook her head. She did *not* want to go back to Faerie. She shuddered as memories best left buried tried to force themselves to the forefront of her thoughts. There was no good reason for her to go back. Yes, she missed her father. But she did not miss the endless jockeying for power and position or the very real threats on her life.

If she returned to Faerie, even for a visit, everyone, including her father, would think she was putting herself back into the race to become his successor. Ulrich, one of her father's most powerful nobles, would hound her. He was so certain she'd had something to do with his son Viktor's disappearance—and she had, though not in the way he'd thought.

Brianna's siblings, who'd rejoiced when she'd left and mostly ignored her since, would turn on her in a heartbeat. Lucienne would be subtle; Eammon, direct but basically honorable; Rihannon was unstable enough that there would be no predicting what she might do. Rodan . . . Rodan was subtle, capable, and vicious. Brianna couldn't prove it, but she'd lay money that the one or two attempts that had been made against her on this side of the veil had been Rodan's work.

Not for the first time, Brianna wished she knew what was happening back home. Mei, with her trace of human magic, could go back without problems. She would go, and report honestly back if Brianna asked it. But what did it matter to Brianna what was happening there? Her life was here. She'd made her choice. Surely she wasn't regretting it?

She had used a boon—owed her by her father—to leave Faerie when her mother had returned to the human world. Brianna had grown tired of the politics, the backstabbing, and the bullshit— and was more than a little afraid that eventually one of the innumerable attempts on her mother's life would succeed. Helena had lived out the remainder of her life unmolested and happy, and Brianna had been happy with her.

Helena had died years ago. Brianna could go back if she wanted. Her father would welcome her.

Not for the first time Brianna wished there were a seer she could consult. Was this unease hers alone—or her *other* sense giving her a warning? Was something wrong in Faerie? Did her father need her? There was no way of knowing. Because, even if Leu were desperate for her return, he wouldn't ask her to come. He was too stubborn, too proud.

She was still pondering her best course of action after she finished her workout, cleaned up, and headed downstairs to open the shop and face the ordinary business of the day.

———

"Can you kill someone using magic?"

The words made Brianna stop mid-step.

She was on her way through the open front area of the shop. It was pretty, airy, with big windows and brightly lit displays, including glittering crystals and big printed signs saying VIDEO SURVEILLANCE IN USE. A stupid and unlikely place to discuss potential murder—but a surprising number of people had asked that same question over the years. *Damn it, not again!* She sighed. Amazing really, how many people would love the opportunity to end another's life. Well, this wasn't going to be her problem—David was working the counter and he could handle it.

She grabbed the laundry basket of clean towels from the counter in the back room and started up the stairs to her apartment. David was better at dealing with the somewhat murderous than she was: tactful and sympathetic, but firm. Brianna was much too inclined to be harsh and blunt, mainly because she was still angry.

Five years earlier, a young man had come into the shop—an outcast with an air of primal force about him. Within three minutes of his arrival, every customer was gone and Maxine had begged Brianna to take over so she could go on break. Almost as soon as she entered the front room, the man had approached and asked to buy the tools to do the blackest magic available. Cost was not an issue. When she refused to help, he threatened her.

Brianna Hai did not react well to threats. The would-be customer left the shop quickly, with his proverbial tail between his legs. Later, the police investigation revealed that he'd found what he'd been looking for online.

Perhaps because she'd turned him down, the young man's first—and last—attempt at murder by magic targeted Brianna. He wasn't powerful enough to breach the shields and defenses built into the walls and mortar of the shop building, let alone Brianna's personal defenses. And magic, thwarted, bounces back on the caster—with interest.

It was a particularly gruesome and well-publicized death. Coming as it did after the dead man's none-too-subtle boasting to confidants, questions were raised. The authorities, not believing in magic, cleared Brianna immediately. But rumors continued to swirl and the Internet kept the story fresh, and all that led to the kind of inquiries that gave her ongoing headaches.

Grumbling under her breath, Brianna shifted the laundry basket to her left hip. With her right hand she made the swift gesture that would allow her to pass through the wards on her door unharmed. Only when she felt the moving energies still did she pull the apartment key from the pocket of her pants and slide it into the lock.

Once through the door she set the basket atop the occasional table, turned to the painting on the wall, and sank to one knee, bowing her head in the traditional obeisance. She had no way of knowing whether or not her father was watching, but it would never do to show the king of the Sidhe less than the proper honor. After the prescribed ten count she raised her head. The painting was still just that—a painting.

Once it had been nothing more than a landscape painted by Bob Ross, a field of wildflowers in the foreground, a mountain in the distance, the sun shining brightly over all. But that was before her mother had turned it into a private portal connecting Brianna's home and her father's library. Helena had done more than create a doorway between two worlds; she had altered the painting so that the image reflected the king's mood. She'd wanted her daughter to have adequate warning of what to expect on the other side of the veil. It had been an unfathomably subtle and difficult piece of magic. But Helena had been the most skilled practitioner Brianna had ever heard of—on either side of the veil.

Today the painting showed the wildflowers in shadow, with only scattered beams of sunlight finding their way through the clouds above. In the distance, near the mountain, a huge storm was brewing. The clouds were thick and black, with the hint of dangerous green and yellow that spoke of hail; flickers of lightning could be seen.

The unsettling image was not one Brianna had ever seen before. What was going on in Faerie that had her father so upset?

David called from the bottom of the stairs, a welcome interruption. "Boss, the UPS guy is here."

"I'll be right down."

Brianna glanced down at the laundry. She'd come back later to fold and put away the towels. It was a nice, mindless chore that would give her time to consider what might be bothering her father—and what, if anything, she should do about it.

She wondered what was in the UPS shipment—probably the South American artifacts she'd ordered from Raymond Carter. David had some magical ability but was not skilled enough to test these particular items to see if they were as advertised. Besides, she'd been looking forward to this shipment for weeks. Brianna hurriedly locked the door, reset the wards, and headed downstairs.

The moment she stepped away from the wards she felt a thrum of power from below. There was something truly special in that box. Thoughts of her father, nasty customers, and old rumors disappeared in a flash. She was as eager to open that package as a child on Christmas morning. That constant sense of excitement got her through the drudgery and paperwork that was so much a part of running a small business.

Brianna took the electronic delivery tracking device from the UPS man and signed her name with a decided flourish before handing it back. As soon as his brown-clad back was out of sight she pulled a knife from her boot and began cutting through the packaging.

Up close the power of the box's contents was breathtaking, singing along her senses in a low thrum that rang through her body like the vibrations of a tuning fork. When Raymond had called to offer her this merchandise, she'd been half worried that the shipment would contain exotic but magically worthless junk. Normally she would have flown out to meet him, to check the quality. But time hadn't permitted it. She'd been forced to risk trusting him, or pass on the shipment altogether. Now she was glad she had. He had come through for her, better than she'd dared hope. She dug through the packing peanuts with absolute glee, pulling out three separate items. The first two were stones— one infused with magic to attract prosperity; the other, for fertility. They were good objects but not exceptional. The last, an ancient stone knife, held the true power. Touching it stole her breath for a moment. It was . . . magnificent. Worth every penny she'd paid and more.

Raymond Carter might have no magical talent to speak of, but he was the absolute best at procuring quality magical items. Occasionally Brianna wondered how he managed it. After all, he was a very modern American. He didn't believe in magic or psychic phenomena. The only things he believed in were the almighty dollar and his own cleverness, and he had spent a number of years using the latter to make lots of the former by finding unusual items for Brianna.

She was setting the artifacts back in the box when the bell above the shop door rang. Before she could even look up a chill ran down her spine. She turned to greet the woman who stepped through the doorway. Brianna didn't know *who* she was, but she knew full well *what* she was—only the Fae had that level of power, and only a Sidhe would be using it out among the humans in broad daylight.

Sidhe both look like the humans—and don't. The differences are mostly subtle. No pure Sidhe has ever had a pimple or blemish. Most are tall and more slender than the average human. Their ears are ever-so-slightly pointed, their hands long-fingered. But the Sidhe *glow*. It was a power they used to influence others, or as a weapon to overcome another's mind and will.

The woman entering the shop was as beautiful as a warm dawn

after the bitterest of winter nights, every delicate feature perfect, her hair spun gold, her skin flawless cream. Her eyes, the blue of a midnight sky, sparkled with a hint of starlight. Her suit matched her eyes, just as the silver silk blouse beneath the jacket matched that twinkle of starlight. The entire outfit had been tailored to emphasize slender curves and long, silk-clad legs.

Brianna had been raised in the high court of King Leu, but even she wasn't completely unaffected by the woman's glamour. Undoubtedly every human her visitor had passed on the street had stopped, staring dumbstruck in her wake, their eyes gleaming with yearning awe.

Brianna shook her head, clearing the cobwebs. The shine was one of the gifts of the Sidhe, a dangerous beauty that could lure the unwary into betraying all they held dear. Helen of Troy had been an exiled Sidhe.

"Can I help you?" Brianna rose to her full height, keeping her voice neutral and pleasant. Her smile was even sincere. Few of her father's people lived in the human lands. It might be pleasant to speak to someone from back home. And while there had been a time when she'd envied the pure-blooded their shining, that was long past. Her mother's human blood and human magic gave her strengths and skills that a pure Sidhe couldn't match, and enabled her to live comfortably and invisibly in the human world.

The woman, who was studying the granite gargoyle standing between the front door and the picture window, glanced at Brianna for a moment before returning her gaze to the statue. The gargoyle was short and squat, his body as heavily muscled as a Rottweiler with a muscular tail ending in a sharpened barb. His back legs ended in paws with curved claws, his front, in something very close to hands. His face was both wrinkled and elongated, somewhat like a dragon's.

As Brianna watched, the woman held her hand over the statue's head. Brianna felt the subtle surge of power as the newcomer tested the air surrounding the gargoyle, then gave a small, satisfied nod.

"How much for the statue by the window?" the woman asked as she strode over to the counter, high heels clicking sharply against the tile floor. In one smooth move, she pulled the designer handbag from her arm, set it atop the glass display case, and opened it in preparation for payment. She was smiling, utterly confident.

"He's not for sale." Brianna kept her voice neutral and calm. She didn't want to get into a metaphysical shoving match with this woman. She might lose. On the other hand, Pug was her friend, and was not, under any circumstances, for sale.

In the background Brianna saw David hustling the teenager toward the exit, the girl so stunned she moved more like a doll than a human being. The front door bell dinged, bringing Brianna sharply back into the moment.

"I want it." The woman bit off each word, pulling back her shields and turning up the charm until the glare was nearly blinding. If Brianna had been full human she'd have fallen to her knees and worshipped this glorious creature as a goddess— would've done absolutely anything to please her. Which was, no doubt, the point.

The polite smile Brianna had been wearing vanished. She spoke softly, but clearly, putting a touch of force behind each separate word. "He is not for sale."

The blonde's hand froze above the credit card she had set onto the countertop, her eyes widening. She gave Brianna a measuring look, taking in every detail of the shopkeeper's appearance: the knee-high leather boots with silver bat-shaped buckles, the black suede trousers, the black brocade and lace top with a sweetheart neckline that accented curves that were not delicate enough to be Sidhe. She stared for a long moment at Brianna's face, with features that were delicate, but not quite delicate enough. The coloring, too, could be Fae, or not: milk-white skin, waist-length hair that was true black with blue highlights.

"Who *are* you?" the woman hissed. She said *who*, but it was clear to Brianna that she meant *what*. No ordinary mortal could have withstood her, and they both knew it.

"Who are *you*?" Brianna glanced at the credit card on the countertop and saw the letters of the woman's name blur, shift, and reform. One moment the card read Ivy Woods, then Brooke Rivers, then Heather Meadows. Pure illusion, but as solid as the floor beneath Brianna's feet. Impressive. Unethical, too, but the woman facing her obviously wasn't the type to sweat that sort of thing.

The woman didn't answer. Instead, she turned up her power, creating a pure, brute force meant to crush Brianna's resistance. It was breathtaking and cruel, and the Sidhe didn't even appear to be working up a sweat.

It was real work for Brianna not to show how badly that lash of power hurt, but she managed. Despite pain that burned across sensitive nerves beneath her skin, she managed to sound utterly blasé. "I'm the owner of this shop, and the granite gargoyle is not for sale. We do have several plaster versions of similar design—"

The woman's hand shot out like a snake, trying to grab Brianna's arm. Touch would make the spell much stronger and more effective. Brianna stepped back, out of reach, and put up her best shields—just in time, too, as a blow of pure magic and will slammed into her defenses like a sledgehammer. The impact didn't stagger her, but it came close. Damn, the bitch was powerful. Brianna was already preparing her return strike, but before she could release it, Pug leapt into the space between the two women.

He landed with a crash. Sixty-five pounds of granite was more weight than the top of the display case could bear. Glass exploded outward—not toward Brianna. She'd had enough warning to redirect her shield. But the Sidhe bitch hissed in pain as blood from multiple cuts stained the silk of her suit.

Her power flared blindingly. Through watering eyes Brianna saw the wounds healing, the glass slide free of the woman's body to fall tinkling onto the floor.

"You insult a guest." The woman's voice was an ice-edged razor.

"No. This is a public shop. You asked for what you got. Now I suggest you leave."

The situation balanced on a knife's edge. Brianna waited for the woman to say the words, to call for a true duel. She could see that the Sidhe wanted to—rage blazed in those midnight eyes and her bloodied hands were clenched in fists. Gritting her teeth, the blonde hissed, "This isn't over," before leaving in a blur of furious speed.

"Wow! What was *that* all about?" David's eyes were a little too wide as he stared at the shattered glass on the floor and the gargoyle busily licking up the pool of blood.

Brianna sighed. "Sidhe bullshit." She glared down at the gargoyle but held her tongue. He had, after all, earned a reward. Besides, there was never any point in admonishing Pug. He did what he did, and that was the end of it.

David said, "I got the kid out of the shop before Pug jumped. She didn't see anything."

"I know. I'm surprised you were thinking that clearly, all things considered."

He grinned. "One, I wasn't the one she was focusing on. Two, I'm gay. Cut the attraction factor considerably."

Brianna shook her head. He was so wrong. Sexual preference means nothing to Sidhe power. The woman's magic *should* have overridden everything. That it didn't made her wonder, yet again, if someone in the Antonelli family tree was more than human. Not that it mattered. Unlike most of the Fae, Brianna really didn't have any problem with it one way or the other. She saw and experienced more prejudice, brutality, and cruelty on the other side of the veil than she had ever run into here.

"Boss, you're fading out on me," David observed.

"Sorry." Brianna smiled at him and forced her mind to focus on the here and now. "Just thinking."

"And not about anything too pleasant, judging from your expression."

"Perceptive, as always," she admitted. It was one of his best and most annoying qualities and was probably part of why her mother had hired him five years earlier.

Then, David had been a rebellious sixteen-year-old with an unhappy life. His father didn't approve of the fact that his son was gay. Kids at school had been giving David a hard time. Life, in general, had sucked. His father had insisted he get a job to "keep him out of trouble," but David had been turned down everywhere he'd applied—not surprising given his disaffected, sullen attitude.

He'd walked through the door of Helena's and Helena Washington had hired him on the spot, to his and Brianna's surprise. David had come a long way since then. Gone was the gangly teenager, replaced by a man. Six feet tall and muscular, with dark brown curls kept just long enough to frame a face dominated by luminous dark eyes and a very kissable set of lips that were smiling more often than not. He had grown into himself. He was confident about his abilities both as the assistant manager and as an artist. And well he should be. He had brains and talent by the boatload.

Today he was dressed in black leather pants with short black suede boots. His tight black T-shirt showed off every rippling muscle as well as the clear outline of nipple rings beneath the thin cloth. The edge of an elaborate Asian-style tattoo peeked out from beneath the sleeve of the shirt.

"Why don't you go in back and get online, see if you can find someone willing to deliver a replacement display case on a rush basis," Brianna suggested. "I'll clear up the mess and put away the new stock."

"Right." As David turned to walk through the door to the office and storeroom Brianna almost stopped him to ask what he'd said to the girl to get her to leave. She stopped herself. David didn't need her second-guessing him. He was good at his job, knew the drill. She was just being paranoid. The Sidhe bitch had shaken her. Brianna had lived long enough in the human world, away from her enemies in Faerie, that she'd let down her guard. It wasn't a mistake she'd be making again. And it reminded her all too clearly just how dangerous it would be for her to go back home.

2

It didn't take long for David to find a glass vendor willing to do an emergency repair. Once he had, she left him alone in the front part of the shop. He could easily manage any customers who came in and deal with the delivery, installation, and stocking of the replacement display case—including two of the new items. The knife, however, was going in the safe in back. Brianna might part with it sometime in the future, but for now, she preferred to keep it for herself. A knife like that would be a formidable weapon, operating as it did on both the physical and magical.

Considering the morning's attack, Brianna wondered if she should replace her regular boot knife with the new arrival. The blade of the stone knife was long and narrow—too long by far to be legal to carry. While the police didn't harass her, they did pay *very* close attention. She tried not to break human laws without good cause and she didn't want to use magic or illusion to mess with anyone's mind unless it was absolutely unavoidable.

Brianna continued mentally debating the issue as she looked

around the back room. The front of the shop was all about appear-
ances and customer comfort. The place was well lit, with the goods
tidily displayed on shining glass shelving. Sparkling crystals, soft
fabrics, and gentle music added to the pleasant atmosphere.

The back rooms were her personal work area and had been re-
modeled a few years ago to her specifications. The main area was
large and open, taking up the back half of the first two floors of
the building. The long wall that divided this space from the shop
itself was covered with shelving that held hundreds of books, rang-
ing from modern paperbacks to very old, very dangerous, leather-
bound volumes. The latter were kept on the highest shelves, hidden
behind locked doors, a very effective guarding spell, and an illusion
that made it almost impossible for them to be seen.

Spell components were stored along the eastern wall, in a cabinet six feet long and twelve feet high. The cabinet's "drawers" were
clear plastic tubs; the smallest, in the top rows, were six inches
wide and tall but twenty-four inches deep. The bottom bins were
twenty-four-inch cubes. All were filled with various spell components. The cabinet ended at the door to the staff bathroom, which
was right next to a tiny kitchen.

A perfect circle had been inscribed into the main section's floor
while the concrete was still wet. Once it had dried, Brianna and her
mother had painted it with designs that incorporated the circle,
making it look decorative. In fact, it was a circle of power and
protection—which was why the work table stood in the center of it.

This was Brianna's place of power, where for years now she'd
done her magic work. Here, she was safest—and strongest. Still, it
would be foolish to let that go to her head. No Fae ever made an idle
threat; nor would one willingly take "no" for an answer. Ms.
Woods/Rivers/Meadows would be back, Brianna was certain, and
the next time, she'd be fully prepared and loaded for bear.

She looked at the knife sitting on the table in front of her. It
was a pretty thing. The blade was hand-chipped obsidian, the hilt

bone. Both the pommel and the joint of blade and hilt were encrusted with rough-cut turquoise and bloodred garnet. Picking it up, she checked the weight and balance as she ran through familiar knife-fighting motions. It felt good in her hand—almost too good, as if the knife were calling to her, as if it had a will of its own.

That, more than anything, decided the issue for Brianna. She moved quickly over to the safe hidden in one of the kitchen cabinets and punched in the access code. Only when the knife was safely locked behind steel and wards did the pressure that had been building within her ease.

That was worrisome, and definitely worth some research. Now that she realized just how dangerous that knife was, she knew better than to put it on sale; and she'd be on guard against its lure.

In the meantime, she had other, more pressing dangers to deal with. Locking the door between the front of the shop and this back room, she returned to the table. Sitting on her usual stool she focused her energy, cleared her mind, and gathered her strength. In a few moments the stress and distractions of the morning drained away. Slowly her muscles relaxed and a sense of calm purpose filled her, peace and strength rising within until her body hummed with contained power.

There were formidable protections built right into the building. Those spells were old, complex, and stronger than anything Brianna could manage on short notice. They made a solid base for her to build on. It was important that she, Pug, David, and Maxine were thoroughly protected. She didn't worry about Mei. The dragon could, and would, take care of herself.

So, she needed something that would protect not only the inhabitants, but her apartment as well as the shop and its contents. She did not want to duel this woman, whoever she was. But risky as that would be, it would not be nearly as dangerous as having the denizens of Faerie believe her weak. Brianna knew she was being watched. She was her father's daughter, and a royal. Of course she was watched.

So I need to give them something to see. Preferably something impressive enough that no one will mess with me.

It was a tall order, but worth the effort.

She spread her hands atop the work table. She knew every scar that marred the surface beneath her fingers—a burn here, where a stone had exploded from the stress of a spell, a faint claw scratch there. She scanned the wood with her other sense, checking to be sure nothing would interfere with the work she was about to perform. Magic flowed through the wood, humming flawlessly beneath her fingers. Excellent. She would not need to cleanse the table before beginning. That was good. The work she was about to do would demand enough energy without adding one more thing.

Opening her eyes, she glanced around, trying to figure out exactly what supplies she would need, in what quantities, for the protections she was going to build. Perhaps she should ask Pug. . . .

He appeared as if her thoughts had conjured him, climbing down from the rafters with nimble proficiency. He was graceful, in his way. Surprising in a creature made of solid granite.

"Thank you for earlier," Brianna said with a smile.

His claws clicked against the concrete floor as he came to join her.

"You were doing fine without me," he growled.

Brianna blinked a little in surprise. He was not prone to giving compliments.

"Thank you." Brianna appreciated his faith in her but wasn't sure he was right. Damn, that woman had been powerful.

He gave a brief nod and leapt onto the tabletop. It was a testament to the strength of the wood and the furniture's solid construction that he could. "Were you thinking talismans or runes?"

"Talismans for David and Max," she answered. "Runes for the four corners of the building's foundation and the four corners of the roof."

She reached around him to collect a pencil and sketch pad. With deft strokes she drew out her plans so he could see them. It would take a full day to create that many artifacts, but she was hoping to build a full web of protection around and within the walls of the building, and she wasn't about to leave her employees vulnerable. They were her responsibility . . . and her friends.

Pug nodded his approval.

"I don't suppose you'd wear a talisman if I made you one?"

Pug snorted with derision and rolled his eyes. It made him look utterly ridiculous, but she didn't laugh.

"You're the one she was after," Brianna pointed out.

She was pushing and he didn't like it. Without a word he jumped down from the table and stalked across the floor to the storage shelves. Gargoyles were among the smallest of the stone trolls, larger only than the rocs. Still, he had the gift of all the trolls, a natural affinity for rocks of all kinds. He'd be able to pick out the best pieces to use for this to work in a matter of seconds where it might take Brianna more than an hour—and she still might get it wrong.

Pug didn't speak, but his barbed tail waved irritably back and forth as he crossed the room. The noise of stone grinding on concrete made Brianna grit her teeth, and she forced herself to ignore the slight grooves his tail was wearing into the floor.

"I'll think about it," Pug finally said.

Brianna blinked slowly, glad that he couldn't see her reaction. Pug was one of the toughest and most courageous beings she'd ever known. The fact that he would even consider wearing extra protection made it clear that she wasn't the only one worrying about the blonde. Brianna chewed at her lip with her teeth—something she hadn't done since childhood. "I wish I knew who she was, and why she was exiled."

"You could contact your father," Pug said as he climbed up the heavy metal utility shelves like a monkey.

Brianna groaned. She couldn't help it. Her father was Fae to the core. If she wanted information, she'd have to barter for it and she couldn't think of a thing he'd want that she'd give willingly. Of course, that was pretty much the point. The price had to be a *price*, after all. "I'd rather not. I'll check with Mei first, show her the surveillance video. She's older than I am. She may know this woman."

Brianna rose, retrieved the large stepladder from where it leaned against a wall, and set it up by the bookshelves. While she could do an adequate protection spell from memory, it was likely she'd find a better one in one of the secure books—something that she could adapt to use both her human and Fae magic.

"If she doesn't, her father might. But whatever it takes, you need to find out."

"Why?"

"I tasted her blood."

"And?" Brianna asked from the third step of the ladder.

"She's incredibly powerful, but it's more than that. . . ." The gargoyle paused as though searching for the right words. "She tasted wrong . . . tainted, as if something had fouled her blood."

Brianna risked a glance over her shoulder at him. Pug was looking at her, his expression more serious than she'd seen in years. "Do you have any idea what could do that?"

"No, and I don't like it."

"Neither do I." Brianna paused, choosing her next words with great care. "Earlier this morning I was thinking of Faerie, wondering what was going on, whether I should go visit."

"No." Pug's voice was firm. "Bad idea—very, very bad idea."

"I know . . . but this . . . what happened . . . it makes me wonder if my other sense is trying to tell me something."

The gargoyle went still, his expression pensive. "You don't have your mother's gifts of foresight," he began, "but you're not a null, either."

"I wish there was an oracle. . . ."

Pug turned away, so she couldn't see his face, but there was something furtive in the movement. "Pug?"

He turned to face her again but his features gave nothing away. "Ask Mei to go. If she won't check on things for you, I will check with my brother. But you should stay here unless they give you no choice."

"What makes you think they won't?"

He growled. "I'm not a null, either."

His words were not at all comforting. Then again, she hadn't been looking for comfort. She needed information in order to protect herself and the others. When Mei returned from her trip, Brianna would see if she was willing to cross the veil for a visit. In the meantime, Brianna would deal with the more immediate threat.

She turned her attention back to the bookshelves. Eventually, she found what she wanted, in an ancient grimoiré. The writing was faded and the language difficult enough that she reread it twice, still standing at the top of the ladder, to make sure she understood it well enough to use the spell.

She met Pug back at the table and set to work. It took two full hours until she was satisfied with David's talisman. She slid the glowing stone, still hot to the touch, onto a plain silver chain from her jewelry stock. Once it had cooled a bit, she gave it to David, telling him to wear it next to his skin at all times.

It was late afternoon by the time Brianna finished all of the pieces to her satisfaction. She was exhausted, plus sore and stiff from sitting in one position too long. But she knew she'd done good work—she could feel the power thrumming from each individual stone. Once she set the runes in place, the building would be a formidable magical fortress.

It hurt to drag her weary body from the stool. Looking from

the books stacked on the table to the ladder Brianna couldn't help but sigh. She was so damned tired. Even thinking about replacing the volumes on the shelves seemed to take too much effort. But she didn't dare leave these particular books sitting out. In the wrong hands they'd be dangerous.

As if he'd read her mind, Pug reappeared in the doorway. "I'll clean up. Put the stones in the safe and get some rest. You look like something Camille dragged in from the alley."

Brianna shook her head in weary negation. "I need to get the runes laid."

Pug's jaw thrust forward stubbornly. "Can you honestly tell me you have the energy to set the spell properly right now?"

If she said yes, she'd be lying, and they both knew it.

"Go take a nap. I can stand guard for a couple of hours."

Brianna opened her mouth to argue, then thought better of it. She really was exhausted. Feet dragging, she locked the runes in the safe next to the stone knife. That done, she ducked into the store just long enough to give Max's talisman to David. He'd give it to Max when she came in and pass along the instructions on how to wear it. Then she went upstairs to her apartment.

Brianna automatically bowed at the painting without really seeing it. Rising stiffly, she stared at the hall in confusion. It said much about her level of fatigue that it took her almost a full minute to realize what had changed. First, Camille had moved her kittens from the box downstairs into the laundry basket full of clean towels. And the basket had been moved from the occasional table onto the floor, replaced by a sculpture.

It was a stunningly beautiful piece: black marble carved into the shape of a pair of lovers entwined. Every detail was absolutely perfect. An art appraiser would undoubtedly say it was worth a fortune—not that anyone would ever see it. The thing positively reeked of Fae magic and was probably a gift from her father.

Brianna looked for a note or card and spotted a piece of folded and sealed parchment pinned under a corner of the base.

Ignoring the small bundle of black fur determinedly attacking her left boot, she carefully extricated the note without touching the statue itself. The wax seal bore the mark of the Sidhe monarch's signet ring. No one but the rightful ruler could get, or use, that ring. It was tied to him or her and would respond to his magic alone.

"Oh, shit."

Brianna turned at the sound of Pug's voice coming up the stairs behind her. "Is that what I think it is?"

"A gift from my father." Brianna's words were slightly slurred from exhaustion, her movement slow as she showed him the card.

"Ah."

Brianna stared at the statue and wondered what His Royal Majesty was up to. It was an ungracious thought, but not unwarranted. Her relationship with her father was . . . complicated. Leu was, foremost and always, the king. He loved his daughter; she never doubted that. But his first duty was to his subjects, a duty he took very seriously.

He was also proud, stubborn, and until Brianna's mother came into his life, Brianna doubted anyone had ever dared disagree with him, let alone asserted their will over his in any matter, large or small.

It was Helena's streak of defiance that had both attracted and repelled him: that and the Fae's long-standing fascination with humans. Brianna had been told that Faerie had been very different in her grandfather's time. But he had died in an attempted coup along with the rest of the family long before she'd been born. Only Leu had survived, by a trick of Fate.

Under Leu's rule Faerie closely resembled the human world. But the differences, while not always obvious, were profound and deadly. Those were the dangers that had trapped or killed the unwary for generations.

Brianna knew that, while she physically resembled her father, in many ways she was very much Helena Washington's daughter. She was stubborn, willful, and had never excelled at the intrigue that was a major part of palace life. That frustrated her father to no end and even though she had left Faerie, she knew that he— and others—still included the fact of her existence in their plots and plans. The king also believed that he knew what was best for her, Brianna knew; she was certain that he watched her and watched over her. She suspected that he even occasionally manipulated circumstances from behind the scenes.

Leu was king, and he was Sidhe, and their customs made for very complicated relationships. This gift was a prime example.

"A love and fertility totem." Pug kept his voice carefully neutral. Brianna didn't know if he was managing her, or worried that HRM was studying their reactions.

"Yes. It is."

"Did you touch it?"

"No." But she wanted to, desperately, which meant that dear old daddy had targeted the spell directly at her. Damn it. If she touched that statue, the next "suitable" male she ran into would fall into irresistible lust with her, they'd bang like bunnies until she was preggers, and then . . . well, then his part of the spell would be over and she would have a baby to contend with. Brianna was not knocking babies. They were cute. Adorable even. But she was definitely not ready to be a mother. And despite her father's blood in her veins, she was human enough to want a *relationship*, not just a sperm delivery. Maybe even a *marriage*. And that was a concept so completely foreign to her father's people that they didn't even have a word for it. Among the Fae, monogamy was considered perverse, baffling, and unnatural.

"Back away from the statue," Pug advised. "Go down the hall.

Rest up. When you've had a chance to sleep you'll be better able to figure out what to do about this, and find a suitable return gift."

It was excellent advice. So why did Brianna have such a hard time putting her father's note on the table, slipping her hands into her pockets, and walking away? *Magic.*

3

NICK ANTONELLI

"Antonelli, my office, now." Captain Brooks was a no-nonsense, hard-core cop who'd come up through the ranks, earning his position through hard work, long nights. Like many in his line of work he had failed marriages behind him, and an uncertain future once he retired. But that was the future. Now he was the captain, and the boss. The job was his life. And nobody, but nobody argued with him when he used that tone of voice.

Nick followed him down the hall to a small, square office dominated by a single worn desk buried under teetering piles of manila file folders. Large windows looked out on the "bull pen" where the officers Brooks supervised sat. Behind the desk stood bookshelves that were filled with worn textbooks on criminal investigation techniques, forensics, anatomy, and weaponry, along with old three-ringed binders that held God and the captain alone knew what. The only personal touches were some old faded snapshots of his children and grandchildren, and a pair of bowling trophies.

Two chairs faced the captain's desk. One was already occupied by a blond man with sharp features and cold blue eyes. Nick had seen him before—around the federal courthouse when he was waiting to testify. He was a fed, a Fibbie. He greeted the man with a brief nod before taking the open seat beside him, all the while wondering what in the hell was going on.

Captain Brooks sat. Leaning back in his chair he made the appropriate introductions. "Nick Antonelli, this is Special Agent Jesse Tennyson. Special Agent Tennyson, this is Detective Nick Antonelli. Agent Tennyson is here to ask you a favor."

"A favor?" Nick didn't bother to hide his skepticism. In his personal experience the feds didn't politely ask for favors. They demanded what they wanted—and they generally got it.

Tennyson gave Nick an assessing look, taking in every inch of his appearance in that single glance—much as Nick himself had done a few seconds before. Nick knew what he saw, a big man, his hair a little longer than average, its coffee-brown curls touched by just a hint of gray. Hazel eyes stared unflinchingly at the world, dominating a face with a strong jaw, high cheekbones, and deep dimples. He looked hard, tough, the kind of man casting directors would seek for a "made man" in an '80s-era De Niro movie, but with a better suit, perfectly tailored to emphasize broad shoulders, a narrow waist, and conceal the shoulder rig that was a daily part of his uniform.

"Your brother is David Antonelli."

Shit. Hell, damn, fucking shit. Do not tell me David is involved in something the feds are investigating. "Yes."

"And he works for Brianna Hai."

"Yes."

A slight smile tugged at the corner of Tennyson's mouth. He could tell that Antonelli wasn't happy about his line of questioning, and it amused the hell out of him.

Glad one of us is having a good time, Nick thought sourly. *David, what in the hell have you gotten yourself into?*

"We've been looking at Brianna Hai in regard to a couple of unsolved cases—but we're having a hard time getting close to her. She has a very small, and extremely tight-knit circle of acquaintances.

"And you want to use my brother?"

"No. He's close to her, but not one of her confidantes."

Nick sat up straighter.

"We want to use you. Hai doesn't socialize much. She works at the shop, works out at the gym, and occasionally does a little modeling for a local artist. We've determined that the best way to get close to Brianna is at the gym where she works out—the Ju-Long Gym and Dojo. But it's not open to the public: private membership, by invitation only. We're hoping that you can convince your brother to wrangle you and your friend Jesse an invitation."

"It won't work. David knows I work out at our uncle Phil's, always have."

"Your uncle Phil is going to close down for six weeks to do some remodeling," Tennyson said mildly.

"I see." He did, too. The feds were apparently serious enough about this to convince Phil to shut down.

"In exchange for your help in this, we will keep your brother out of it as much as we possibly can."

Nick looked over at the captain who was giving his best neutral expression. There was nothing to read there.

"Just an invitation?"

"That's all. Just get me in the door."

He didn't say *then stay out of my way,* but it was implied. "When is this supposed to happen?"

"The sooner the better. Can we count on your assistance?"

Nick thought about it for a moment. David would be pissed if he ever found out Nick had used him like this. But if Hai was dirty, Nick wanted her off the streets—and David out of the line of fire. This was his best bet at achieving that.

"Yeah. I'll make the call when I get off shift."

"Good."

Tennyson rose, then Nick and the captain. Reaching into his pocket Tennyson pulled out a business card. "Here's my card. My cell number is on the back. Call me when it's done."

Nick took the proffered card. Pulling out his wallet he slid it in behind his driver's license, where it wouldn't be obvious, but he'd be sure not to lose it. "Right."

———————

"What was that all about?" Juan pressed the button to unlock the doors of their unmarked car. A gray Ford, it was a midsize sedan, and as ordinary as white-bread toast. That was, Nick supposed, the whole point. An unmarked car was supposed to be unnoticeable. Still, it had an engine to it—and Ted, the station mechanic, kept it running smooth.

The car beeped, and the lights flashed at the same time as the doors unlocked.

Juan Sanchez wasn't just Nick's partner, he was his best friend. They'd been working together for a few years now. Each trusted the other with his life on a daily basis. It was tempting to just tell him. After all, Nick knew his buddy could keep a secret. But honestly, he didn't want to talk about it. Hell, he didn't really even want to think about it. So he just shook his head and climbed into the passenger seat.

"Where are we headed, anyway?"

"Juju left a message on my cell. Say's he has something big for us. Wants to meet with us down at the railroad yard."

Juju was one of their CIs, a confidential informant. Fifteen years old, the kid was from a tough neighborhood. He lived on the fringes, not fitting in, and not nearly as tough as he thought he was, or probably needed to be. He'd given them good information once or twice in the past. More often, he tried to get money from them while providing vague and useless crap. Nick didn't like him. Then again, as Juan kept reminding him, you don't have to *like* him to use him. "The railroad yard? Seriously? Can't he just meet up with us at the mall, or a restaurant like everybody else?"

"I know. I know. But you know how paranoid he is, and it's not like I could argue with a voice mail." Juan turned the ignition, and the car's motor came to life with a roar.

"Think this time he actually has something worthwhile?" Nick asked.

"Only one way to find out."

4

JU-LONG

It was a perfect night for flying. The skies were clear as midnight glass with diamond stars sparkling. A snow white half-moon shone bright, shimmering reflections glinting off the river below. The air at this altitude was cold, the mist from the dragon's breath dissipating in the wind of his passage as he made lazy circles, not hunting, just flying for the sheer joy of it. It felt so good to be away from the stifling corridors of the palace, from the crush of Sidhe with their poisoned smiles, constantly jockeying for some advantage. On nights like this he wondered if the price he paid to save the last of his kind was too high.

But that was stupid. What was done was done and best to be done with it. He snorted at the memory of one of his mate's favorite sayings. He missed her—particularly on nights like this. He'd been alone a long time, and while the shining Sidhe women were beautiful, most were too cautious to take a dragon to their bed, and thus far none of those who were willing had caught his fancy.

He shook his head to clear it of unwelcome thoughts. It was far too fine a night to waste brooding. Filling his lungs with air he let out a blast of fire, just for fun, before executing the kind of tricks that he'd used to win Marissa all those years ago.

He was pulling out of his third consecutive barrel roll when a streak of blinding lightning thundered through the air a few miles away, moving from the ground to the sky. The crack of thunder that followed was loud, even at this distance. On the ground it would be deafening.

That was not natural lightning—not on a night like this. Ju-Long straightened his body, streamlining it into an arrow that shot through the air in a blur of speed at the first beat of his powerful wings.

It was over before he landed. King Leu stood just outside of a ring of standing stones in a circle of scorched earth and the shattered bodies of half a dozen fried and blackened pixies and one dead guard. Scorched pixie dust filled the air around the king, blackened multicolor glitter settling sadly to earth. And while his attackers had obviously perished Leu hadn't escaped unscathed. There were tears in his dark gray tunic, and a single bloody scratch marred his cheek where one of his attackers had tried to take out his left eye. His expression was one of utter disgust. Still, he stood on the narrow path that passed through the wide swath of water that surrounded and protected the sacred circle.

"Your majesty." Ju-Long landed neatly, dropping onto one knee on the path before the king. His form shimmered, changing from beast to man-shape in the time it takes to blink. He was clothed in the illusion of a full guard's uniform and his magic made it real even to the touch. "May I be of service?"

"I'm fine, thank you," Leu answered curtly. Then, taking a deep breath he mastered himself. Ju-Long could actually see the king forcing himself to be calm, setting aside the formidable anger at having been forced to defend himself against his own small subjects.

He raised his voice, speaking to an audience that, while hidden, was undoubtedly present. "The Pixie King rules his own court at my pleasure. Occasionally I'm forced to remind them of that."

"I suspect the new king or queen will bear it in mind, having been given such a firm reminder."

"We can but hope." He sighed. "Walk with me, Ju-Long. I had intended to pray alone, but your company is always welcome."

Leu led them down the path between the nearest pair of stones, the lintel of which was far overhead.

"I thought I was the only one who still came here." Ju-Long spoke carefully. The king had good reason to be angry, and while he seemed in control at the moment, caution was definitely called for.

"Not quite. My duties don't allow me to come often—and the nobles would use it against me if they knew I came at all. They believe the stories of the oracles are myth. Faerie is not alive. It is a place, not a being."

"They are wrong."

"Oh, yes. She is not like us, but she is definitely alive. I've felt it." Leu made a gesture with his hand and the ground heaved, a pair of boulders bursting up through dirt and grass. He sat on one, motioning for Ju-Long to take the other.

"The first time was the night Valjeta and her people attempted their coup. I *felt* the rest of my family die; and when I was the last, the only one left, I felt the power of Faerie slide into me. It's . . . difficult to describe. The closest I can come is that I was the cup, and her power and knowledge flowed in for me to hold and use."

"You said the first time. There were others?"

"I brought each of my children here on the night of their birth. I felt her react to them . . . testing them to see if they were—"

"Worthy?"

"No, more than that, and less. The king or queen must be capable of holding the power, controlling it. It doesn't even have to be a Sidhe—although we're the ones with the most magic."

They sat in silence for a moment. If Leu wanted to talk, Ju-Long would listen. But he would not push. Not tonight, when his king, his friend, seemed so haunted and fey.

"Valjeta and her people are gathering up their forces. They're preparing to move against me. I can feel it. The storm is coming. I've tried to prepare, but I very much fear we won't be ready. My people don't believe much in Faerie, or in me. My children—"

Ju-Long shifted on his stony seat, acutely uncomfortable. He had strong opinions about most of Leu's children—thoughts and opinions best kept to himself.

Leu gave Ju-Long a sharp look, but didn't pursue it further. "You came to me when your people had been hunted to extinction, when you and your children were the last three dragons left. You swore to serve me. And I swore to protect your lives, so that dragons would not vanish from the skies of Faerie."

"I remember."

"When the time for battle with Valjeta comes I cannot guarantee your safety. To keep my oath I will have to send you across the veil."

"I have human blood, human magic. I can cross. But you will need your dragons. When the time comes, I will release you from your oath."

"We'll see." Leu gave a sad smile. "Valjeta cannot win. Faerie will perish. She needs the ruler as much as the ruler needs her and she cannot use a broken vessel like Valjeta. Fate tells me I am to die at her hand—but she doesn't say when. Nor am I certain she's right. Atropos likes to pretend that our lives are set in stone by the oracles and her weavings, but I know better. If they were I'd have died with the rest of my family in the coup, and Faerie would have perished with us. I will fight tooth and nail to survive and protect my world and my people. Still, I must also prepare for what will happen if she is right. When the time comes I must choose a worthy successor; one that both Faerie and the people will accept."

Ju-Long schooled himself to remain still. Straining his ears he heard the sound of soft footfalls on stone. Men were coming. They were moving in stealth, but he could tell there was more than one.

His expression alerted Leu, whose features had grown harsh with anger. At a signal from the king, Ju-Long rose, sliding silently into the shadows as Leu's magic lowered the stones that had been their seats back into the ground.

There was a flash of sparkling light and the silence that had descended on them was cut by the shrill war cries of a dozen pixies. Sidhe voices, male and female, shouted virulent oaths. Magic flared, and by its light Ju-Long caught sight of a group of three attackers.

They wore light armor, with no insignia. But their features and coloring were of those from the far northlands, territory held by Sidhe nobles who gave lip service to a king they viewed as weak while they secretly plotted against him. Ju-Long gathered his power, preparing a magical strike against the man in the lead, but before he could loose it the pixies struck again.

The fight was brutal, bloody, and remarkably quick. The pixies swarmed, diving at the intruders, attacking their eyes with weapons and magics. Off-balance and blinded, the first Sidhe stumbled into the man behind him. Both staggered. The man fell and the woman's boot slipped off of the stone where she'd been standing. She regained her balance, one foot in the shallow water, water that moved in silent, gentle ripples outward—then in larger, faster ripples moving inward.

With a whispered word from Ju-Long power flowed out from his left hand, encircling the third Sidhe, raising him from the ground as it kept him frozen immobile, until he hung fifty feet above the water's surface. A swarm of pixies circled him, their wings buzzing with the sound of a thousand angry wasps. They circled, but none were foolish enough to touch. They could smell dragon magic—and the dragon was powerful enough to destroy them all with little more than a thought.

Ju-Long left the man suspended, but fully conscious and aware, let him watch as his companions were wrapped in long, fibrous strands of what looked like seaweed, and dragged inexorably to the water where, if they were lucky, they would drown before the Philae stripped the flesh from their bones.

They weren't lucky.

The water thrashed, turning black in the moonlight as the Sidhe bled, shrieking hideously each time their heads broke the water's surface.

The entire thing took only a moment or two, but it seemed much longer.

Leu and Ju-Long stepped out from the shadows behind the standing stones, standing on the path. With another whispered word, air and water coalesced into a shimmering force that lifted both men until they stood before their captive. The pixies moved away—though not far off, waiting and watching to see what was in store. Below, the water became deceptively smooth, its glassy surface giving no hint of the creatures hidden below.

"We have a few questions for you." Ju-Long's words were deceptively pleasant. "If you answer them your death will be quick, and relatively painless."

"I won't." The man's voice was strangled and breathy with fear, despite his words of defiance.

Ju-Long smiled. "I was hoping you'd say that."

5

NICK ANTONELLI

It was broad daylight, and a warm day. So why was his skin crawling with goose bumps? Nick and Juan were on foot, making their way over uneven gravel through a maze of tracks and railroad cars decorated with multicolored graffiti. The bang of cars coupling and screech of metal on metal served as background noise. Gravel dust and grease scented the air.

"Did he say *where* in the railroad yard?" Nick snarled. He was losing patience with this. Already on edge and irritable from this morning's meeting, he was not in the mood to be led on a wild goose chase by a paranoid informant, and his dress shoes were not comfortable for hiking on uneven ground.

"No." Juan sounded disgusted, though whether he was aggravated at Juju for getting them into this mess, or Nick for being an ass was anybody's guess.

They'd nearly reached the fringe of abandoned buildings at the edge of the yard and still they'd seen no sign of him. Coming around the end of a long row of identical black tank cars both men saw a bloody male body sprawled on the ground. Drawing their weapons, they moved forward to check for life. Adrenaline sang through Nick's veins as he used the cars for cover, his eyes scanning the area, looking for movement.

There was the shifting of shadows behind the glassless second-floor window of one of the ruined buildings that lined the yard. Light glinted off of metal in the window frame.

"Juan!" Nick shouted to his partner as a hail of bullets rained down on them from a weapon set on full automatic. The roar of gunfire and Juan's screams of pain joined the cacophony of the trains, all of it overpowering the series of well-aimed shots fired from Nick's Glock.

"Officer down": the two words that officers everywhere dread most. Every day they risk their lives to serve a public that can be mistrustful and downright hostile. Those two words over the radio brought instant, massive action to bear. In minutes the railroad yard was swarming with cops and emergency personnel. Two gangbangers were caught fleeing the scene. The third was as dead as Juju.

Juan was alive, if barely, thanks to Nick's first aid and the efforts of the EMTs. But he was badly injured, and God alone knew if he'd survive the surgery to repair the damage of multiple bullet wounds.

Nick had discharged his weapon in the line of duty, had used deadly force against a fourteen-year-old kid. It had been necessary. He'd do it again in a heartbeat. But it was going to be a complete cluster fuck . . . already was come to that. The press had arrived with the cavalry, and they were already casting racial overtones on the situation. He'd heard them doing it as he sat inside the back of a cruiser waiting to give his statement. He'd

already handed over his weapon and been tested for gunshot resi- .
due by the techs.

Nick hadn't killed the kid because he was black, white, green,
or purple. Hell, he hadn't even *seen* the kid well enough to tell
what color he was. He'd seen the gun, and movement, and he'd
fired in response to gunshots. But the truth wouldn't keep him
from being pilloried in the press.

But that didn't matter. All that mattered right now was that
Juan make it.

Closing his eyes, Nick said a quick prayer for his friend. *Whatever the fallout, I'll deal with it. Just please, God, please let Juan live.*

Nick wanted, needed to go to the hospital, to be with Maria and
the family, to show his support. Instead, here he sat, in the back
of the cruiser, with all the time in the world to worry about his
best friend and think about just how fucked he was.

6

KING LEU OF THE SIDHE

Leu stripped off his filthy garments, letting them fall to the bathroom floor. Leaning down, he turned the taps so that gloriously hot water sprayed from the showerhead. Teo, his body servant, would be arriving any minute to "wake" him. He would be horrified to see his king doing such mundane things as taking care of his own bath and laying out fresh clothing for the day. But while Leu liked the little human, and was inclined to indulge him, today he was simply not in the mood.

The interrogation had been necessary, but very messy: with good reason, of course. Time had been limited, and neither Ju-Long nor Leu would have wasted it. Just invading the man's mind would not have been enough. They needed him to be injured badly enough that, when he was allowed to "escape" Valjeta's other supporters would welcome him back with open arms. And he needed to believe it had been a normal interrogation, without dragon mind control—or they would kill him and a precious intelligence asset would be lost.

It was definitely necessary, but not by any means pleasurable. Nor was Leu looking forward to his first task of the morning—notifying the guard's loved ones of her death in service of the king.

He sighed, climbing under the water's spray, letting it sluice the worst of the filth and gore from his body. He'd love to take a bath right now, long enough and luxurious enough to soak away his aches and pains—physical and mental. That wasn't happening. There was no time. There was never enough time for pleasure anymore.

Leu heard a light tap on the bathroom door. It cracked open to reveal the prominent nose of an elderly man of Polynesian descent, his caramel-colored skin deeply wrinkled, his dark eyes old and possessed of considerable wisdom and compassion.

"Your majesty?"

"Teo." Leu turned. Pointing at the pile of clothing on the floor, he said, "Burn those. Do it personally. Make sure no one sees it done." Grabbing a bottle of liquid soap he poured a bit into his palm before rubbing it over his body until he was covered in fragrant lather.

"Of course."

"And send a message to Segall. We need to reschedule my appointments for the next week I am going hunting."

Segall was his secretary, a clever, hard-working individual who toiled quietly behind the scenes to make sure that everything in Leu's life ran smoothly. Most of the time he even succeeded.

"I will. I have a message for you from him as well."

"Oh?"

"The first of the three statues finally arrived. It is perfect. The spells are quite potent. He's arranged for it to be delivered to Brianna. The artist claims he is nearly finished with the other two—you should receive them in a matter of weeks."

"I'll believe it when I see it." Leu snorted in derision. "All three statues were supposed to be done years ago."

"I know. But he really does do beautiful work, worth waiting for. I'm sure you'll agree when you see it in Brianna's apartment."

Leu smiled at Teo. He knew he was being managed, but the old man did it so well. It occurred to the king that he'd been taking his friend for granted, which simply wouldn't do. "When was the last time you took a vacation?"

"It has been a while, but I don't mind. We've been busy."

"Well, as I'm going to be gone hunting, I won't be here to need your services. I think that would make this a perfect time for you to go on another one of your expeditions to the other side of the veil." Leu stepped under the spray, rinsing soap from his body. "Shall I tell Brianna to expect your arrival through the portal? Or would you rather I chased down someone with human magic to send you somewhere else?"

"Your majesty is too kind, but there is much to be done here, even when you are away."

"Nonsense, you've earned this and more." Leu's smile was warm, and more real than it had been just seconds before. Teo really did deserve a holiday, and Leu wanted him out of the way if, as their interrogation victim of earlier suggested, the palace would come under attack soon. Teo was human, and fragile, and, thanks to his frequent trips to the human side of the veil, he had aged. He was no longer the brash young man who Leu'd saved from being murdered by a jealous husband. Time might have stopped for him in Faerie, but on Earth it passed on inexorably, leaving its mark on Teo each time he set foot on her soil.

Brianna, too, would age, though more slowly thanks to her Sidhe blood. Unless she chose to return home to Faerie his daughter would eventually look older than siblings hundreds of years her senior—older even than her father come to that.

He poured shampoo in his palm and began working it through his hair. Brianna was a concern. This might not be the best time for her to use the statue. Then again, any time was a good time for a baby. And really, she had no excuse for not having provided him with a grandchild long ago. She was human, far more fertile than her Sidhe half siblings. She could have done. She'd simply chosen not to. She would resent being manipulated, having him force her hand. But she'd get over it . . . eventually. And coming back to Faerie with a baby would soften the Sidhe nobles' hearts toward her. That was a good, and very necessary thing.

It was also necessary that he deal with Ulrich and his obsession with his son Viktor's disappearance.

"Yes, a hunt is exactly what we need." Leu was speaking more to himself than his servant, but Teo answered.

"I'll have Segall make the arrangements," Teo assured him. "Who will be joining you?"

Leu turned off the shower. Stepping out he took the towel Teo extended to him and began drying himself. As he did, he considered the answer to Teo's question.

7

ASARA

The king was in a very odd mood, Asara thought as she looked across the fire at where he sat eating bison roasted in the camp pit. They'd hunted and killed the beast that very morning. The king's teeth gleamed red in the flickering firelight. The chill breeze played with the front of his ebon hair; his long braid disappeared into the blackness of his leather tunic. He seemed wild, and more than a little dangerous.

Looking at him now, so unlike the crafty political creature she'd always known, Asara felt disconcerted. She couldn't remember Leu ever having led a hunt in all the many years she'd known him. Still, he'd been good at it, and was obviously having a good time laughing and joking with Ulrich and the three nobles he'd invited along. Wine and strong drinks flowed freely as they tossed six-sided dice in a round shield taken from one of the king's personal guards.

Ulrich threw back his head and laughed, his craggy features breaking into a fierce grin that made Asara shudder. Leu was joking . . . with *Ulrich* of all people—a man whom Asara would have sworn on the truthstone was not capable of anything resembling mirth. Asara thought she knew Ulrich well thanks to the many years she had spent turning him ever so subtly against Leu's human daughter. Ulrich's now-obvious and growing dislike of the child had driven a wedge firmly between the two men, but tonight there was no sign of it. Like old friends, they joked, drank, and gambled—another thing that the king simply did not do.

Asara had known Leu her entire life. When she was still quite young, she'd set her cap for him and used her pale blonde beauty to lure him to her bed. She'd been his mistress on and off ever since. She had even borne three of his children. She would have sworn she knew everything there was to know about the man.

But something had changed. *He* had changed. There was a wildness to him, a recklessness that reminded her of the tales she'd been told of his youth—before she'd been born, when he'd been just another prince of the list, no more likely than any of the others to ascend to the throne. And yet, beneath the apparent mirth, she perceived a razor's edge of desperation. She felt it in her bones, like the first frost that presages the cold of winter, and shivered beneath her fur cloak from a chill that had nothing to do with the weather.

"You seem pensive, milady." Ju-Long stepped out of the shadowed darkness. Squatting down, he held long-fingered hands out to the flames, basking in the warmth.

Asara forced herself to smile, to play the politician. Ju-Long was the king's spymaster. Of average height, his eyes hazel, hair a nondescript shade of light brown, he could, and often did, blend invisibly into a crowd. And while he was invariably pleasant and excruciatingly polite, he could make her skin crawl with a single glance.

The sign of a guilty conscience? Unlikely. A conscience was not a burden she'd ever been forced to bear. She'd been born cold and life at court hadn't warmed her. She felt no need for love, had decided long ago that she wasn't capable of it. The absence had never bothered her. From what she'd observed, love was a weakness that was all too easy to exploit. Lust, on the other hand— that she quite enjoyed.

"I am surprised by this outing, and the king's mood." Asara chose her phrases carefully. Lying was for weaklings, so she spoke the truth, but selectively.

"No man can be expected to meet with Fate and remain unmoved by the experience."

"Fate?" Years of practice at schooling her face and voice stood Asara in good stead. She didn't splutter or give any outward appearance of shock.

"You didn't know? Atropos visited the palace the other night and met with our king. She begged a boon of him."

"And what did our king get in return?"

Ju-Long met her gaze, his expression impassive as always. "That is the question I was going to ask you."

Asara was saved a response, for at that moment Leu rose from his game. With a rueful sigh but a cheerful grin, he pulled a leather pouch from his tunic and tossed it into the shield, where it landed with the muffled clank of coins. Turning, he caught Asara's gaze. He gave her a wink; then, with an exaggerated yawn, excused himself and left for his tent.

She followed almost immediately, leaving Ju-Long without an answer.

Kenneth, one of the king's guards, opened the tent flap without comment, letting her past the web of wards that made the silk dwelling impenetrable to weapons, resistant to fire, and invisible to anyone more than one hundred yards away. The king's traveling home was as safe as magic could make it—safe from everything but treachery. Leu's father had been murdered in a nearly identical tent, with the same protections. Asara wondered if that memory had made Leu uneasy, caused his strange mood.

She stepped into a large open pavilion dimly lit by a single glowing crystal in a lamp hung from the center tent pole.

Leu stood directly in her path, his face shadowed.

"Why are you here, milady?" He spoke softly, so softly that no sound would carry outside the tent, but his voice was cold, the words dropping soft as snowflakes between them. Asara knew in that moment that, like a snowstorm, this conversation could prove deadly.

"I believed that you wanted me, sire." Asara kept her eyes down and used his rank, not his name, because in this moment, however private, he was the king: not her lover, not the father of her children. He was Leu, King of the Sidhe, High King of all the Fae.

"Asara . . ." Her name was a soft hiss on his lips. "I am not speaking of this moment and you know it. You presumed to join this hunting trip, uninvited."

Asara's eyes widened in honest shock. It had been many years since she'd needed an invitation to join Leu anywhere.

His expression was serious as he met her gaze. "You are far too skilled a courtier to make such a basic mistake." He raised his hand and with a touch gentle as a feather across the skin, brushed his thumb across her cheek. "I have indulged you too much, and for far too long. Your games normally amuse me enough that I tolerate them. But . . ." He used his index finger to raise her chin, so that her eyes met his. Normally beautiful swirling silver, tonight his eyes had the shine of steel and the gray of storm clouds. "There is no more time for such things. The hour is late, and I will do what must needs be done."

Asara schooled her expression but her body betrayed her: pride stiffened her spine. He might be king, but she was not a woman to be trifled with.

Leu's gaze darkened, his features hardening into an unreadable mask. He pulled his hand away as if dropping something filthy. His next words were spoken loud enough to carry clearly through the thin silk to the guards and the nobles outside the tent. His tone was neutral, cold—and that was somehow worse than the heat of anger. "Lady Asara, you will leave immediately for the palace, where you will remain in your quarters to await my pleasure. Make no mistake. This is no request. It is a royal command. Go."

She left, her face flaming, heart filled with humiliation, confusion, and a building fury. He'd dismissed her like a whore—or a serving wench. Yes, Leu was the king. But after all these years, to deliberately make a spectacle of her in front of nobles who would gladly and happily spread word of it; to force her to spend days riding home, since without an escort or Leu's explicit permission, the king's gates would be barred to her . . .

This crude, unpolitic dismissal was very unlike the sophisticated man she knew. What had happened to him when he met with the Fate? Atropos was the crone, the cutter of the threads of life. Had she shown Leu his death? Such a sight could change a man, Asara knew. But Leu was no coward. He had never feared for his own life in all the time she'd known him.

Asara found herself hoping Leu wasn't due to die. She might not be capable of love, but she'd cared for him, enjoyed their time together. She would miss him if he were gone.

Still, all men die. Even kings. If his time was coming, there were things she needed to do—preparations to make to assure that it was one of her children that followed him onto the throne. As she untied a pair of horses from the string she began formulating a plan.

8

BRIANNA HAI

Brianna woke to bright sunshine. A small ball of long, black fur with wide green eyes was kneading its claws into the blanket by her head. It took a minute to clear the fog of sleep, but she could smell coffee, and bacon cooking. Someone, David from the sound of it, was humming off-key. Brianna sighed. The man couldn't carry a tune if his life depended on it.

"Are you awake yet?" he called cheerfully from the kitchen.

"Getting there." She moved into a sitting position, careful not to disturb the kitten, who'd curled up and taken to purring like a motorboat.

Brianna was still wearing the clothes she'd fallen into bed in. They weren't even particularly rumpled, evidence that she'd been too tired to move much in her sleep. That explained why she was so sore and stiff. A body is not meant to stay in one position for so long. Someone, probably Pug, had managed to get her boots off, because though Brianna didn't remember removing them, they were sitting neatly on the floor at the foot of the bed.

"Not that I'm complaining," she called out as she rose clumsily to her feet, "but what are you doing here and at"—she glanced at the clock—"six thirty in the morning?"

"Pug phoned me. And he let me in."

Brianna was dumbfounded. Pug had used the telephone? It was a startling concept. Yes, he was more intelligent than most humans, and he had seen her make calls, but how the hell had he managed the buttons with his claws?

"Anyway," David continued, "you need to hurry up if you want any bacon. I brought fresh homemade bread, milk, and honey like he told me, but I figured the human part of you would want meat. I didn't realize that gargoyles are such suckers for pork." There was a hint of reproach in his voice. Pug must be with him.

"I'll be right there. Save me some."

She went to the kitchen by way of the bathroom. A glimpse in the mirror told her she looked as bad as, or worse than, she felt. Her skin was almost gray from fatigue, even after more than twelve hours sleep. By the time Brianna made it into the living room and over to the breakfast bar there were only four slices of bacon left on the platter.

"Thanks for coming. I appreciate this." Brianna sank onto the nearest stool and Pug moved to a perch farther down, giving her elbow room. David put a plate laden with food onto the smooth granite surface in front of her, followed by a tall glass of whole milk and a bear-shaped bottle of honey.

"No problem." He gave her a sunny smile. "It was the least I could do, considering you wore yourself out working on an amulet for me." He fingered the stone hanging from the chain at his neck. It glowed in the sunlight, and even in her exhausted state Brianna could feel the hum of its power.

"Did Max get hers?" Brianna lifted the honey bear and began squirting the warm golden liquid onto the slices of bread on her plate.

"Not yet." David shook his head. "She called in sick last night. I covered her shift."

Brianna groaned around a mouthful of food. She liked Maxine, she really did. A sweet, middle-aged, earth-mother type, she was almost painfully honest, but she was not the world's most dependable employee and the computer sometimes baffled her. Brianna considered firing her about once every three months, and always wound up giving her one more chance—in part because she couldn't seem to find anyone else who'd be any better.

"I don't mind. I didn't have any plans anyway." He sighed gustily. "The fireman and I have reached a parting of the ways."

Pug rolled his eyes; Brianna felt like doing the same but managed to control her reaction. David was young and good-looking, and seemed to have a constant stream of dalliances, none of whom seemed to last more than a month or so. It was no surprise to hear that the fireman's tour of duty was over.

"Anyway," David said, shooting Pug a look, "I'll give Max her necklace as soon as she gets in." He smiled. "And I have an idea about a return gift for your father."

Brianna blinked somewhat stupidly. "How did you know about that?"

"I've been researching fairy legends. I read that if you get a gift, you have to give as good a gift or better or you risk insulting the giver." He looked at Brianna with wide, nervous eyes. "Is that wrong?"

"No, it's absolutely right." She set down the now-empty glass of milk, which David promptly replaced with a full mug of coffee. She was starting to feel better. Not terrific, but better. In a few more minutes the food would kick in and she should actually be able to face the day. "And you do *not* want to insult any Fae—but particularly the Sidhe."

"Why particularly not the Sidhe?"

"Because they're the most temperamental," Brianna supplied.

"And the most dangerous," Pug answered.

Brianna wasn't so sure about that. The goblins were wicked fighters; pound for pound, even the smallest of the stone trolls were tougher than the Sidhe; pixies and doxies might be tiny, but they fought in swarms and their bites could cause suppurating wounds that festered the flesh off of a body. There were dragons, and other, worse things that would rather eat you than look at you. Brianna couldn't think of a single creature native to Faerie that wasn't dangerous to a mortal who had been lured to the far side of the veil. But the Sidhe had the most magic, and were by far and away the sneakiest and most tricksy. As the current high king, her father was the most dangerous of all. Which thought brought her neatly back to the problem at hand.

"What did you have in mind?" Over the lip of her mug, Brianna watched David roll up his sleeves and start cleaning up the mess in the kitchen.

"I think you should get in touch with Ed. He's got some absolutely amazing paintings."

An undeniably gifted painter, Ed was an art school classmate of David's. He was also the single most egotistical and annoying human being Brianna had ever had to cope with. At David's behest, she'd modeled for some illustrations Ed was doing for a fantasy novel. By the third session it had taken all of her self-control not to throttle the little bastard and put all four of them out of their misery.

When she didn't say anything, David gave her a meaningful look. "I know he's an ass. But he's a talented ass, and you need something special for your father. Do you really think you're going to get anything else on short notice without paying an arm and a leg?"

"Probably not. But it might be worth the money. Truly."

David's usual good-natured grin returned. "I'll go with you.

He'll behave better if I'm there. If we hurry, we can get there before he goes to class and be back in time to open the shop."

"You really think he has something that would work?"

David smiled knowingly. "I know just the thing. Trust me." He made a shooing gesture with his hands. "Go get changed. I'll finish in here."

He was being unbelievably bossy, but Brianna was too tired to argue. Besides, she *did* trust him.

It didn't take long to shower and brush her hair and teeth. Ducking into the bedroom, she dressed quickly, choosing black jeans and a black T-shirt with a silver floral pattern on the front. She pulled her hair up in a simple ponytail, pulled on socks and a pair of black running shoes, and was ready to go.

David was waiting in the living room. Pug had vanished. At her questioning look, David said, "He said he was going to guard the shop since you haven't completed the protections yet."

"Ah. Let's get moving." She gestured for him to precede her. They rounded the corner into the entryway with him just a fraction in front of her. Without even intending it, Brianna's hand started to reach for the statue.

"Don't even *think* about it, Hai. Put your hands in your pockets."

He said it without turning around. Now *that* was just weird. Still, he was right. Brianna stuck her hands in the pockets of her jeans, spared a quick glance to make sure the cats had food and water, and the two of them were out the door, leaving her father's magic safely behind.

Emerging into the shop, Brianna glanced up and spotted Pug in the shadows, on one of the metal rafters. She didn't like leaving Pug by himself. He'd fed on enough blood yesterday to satisfy a stone troll of his size for several days and she knew he would protect the store against any enemies vulnerable to stone, claws, and teeth. But he was what the woman had been after. If she came back, she'd no doubt bring reinforcements and they'd be ready to take on a gargoyle. Pug wasn't stupid, but Brianna wondered if he had enough sense to stay away from things he was no match for. She thought he did. Still, after his act of heroism yesterday . . . she was oddly reassured when he met her gaze and gave her a very obvious wink.

She mock-glared up at him, growling a warning. "If there's any trouble, make sure you don't bite off more than you can chew."

He smiled in response, deliberately showing her all three rows of wickedly curved teeth. His meaning was clear. He could bite, and *chew*, a damned sight more than she was giving him credit for.

"Fine, fine." Brianna grumbled as she punched in the series of numbers that activated the alarm system and followed David out the front door.

It was a five-block walk to the building that housed Ed's studio. Even in the city, surrounded by concrete, Brianna could sense the turning of the season. The first bite of autumn was in the air. Tonight would be the first frost. In a few days the leaves of the carefully cultivated trees that lined Commerce Square would transform from summer green, to crimson, gold, and warm brown before falling into the gutters.

Commuters were lining up outside the nearby Starbucks with their briefcases and cell phones. Brianna kept scanning the area, looking for . . . something. She had a strange sense of foreboding, a general sense of unease that made her twitchy.

"What's the matter? I've never seen you like this." David's eyes narrowed, his expression serious.

"No, I don't suppose you have," Brianna admitted. She smiled, but the expression felt artificial. Something was wrong, or about to go wrong.

David stopped, standing stock-still in the middle of the sidewalk. "Damn it, Hai! Stop being so friggin' secretive! Haven't I earned the right to know what's going on?"

His dark eyes blazed, his hands clenching in fists. It was obvious he was well and truly pissed. She hadn't meant to anger David. She loved David like a brother—hell, *more* than any of her brothers—but he was full human, and despite all the time they'd spent together, there were some things he didn't understand about magic and the Fae.

"It's just a feeling—not even enough to be a premonition."

He stared at her for a long, silent moment, willing her to tell him everything. Unfortunately, she already had. Finally, he gave her a sour look and said, "You truly have no idea what's wrong?"

"No."

He bit his lip and ran one hand through his hair, turning it into a tousled mess. "Well, doesn't that just suck." His smile wasn't happy and his eyes scanned the area for trouble.

Brianna grinned, relaxing fractionally. She couldn't help it. David would probably never know how much she appreciated his absolute trust in her abilities. Anyone else she knew would have argued—claimed she was being paranoid. Not David. David just believed her. "Yeah, well, whatever it is, we'll deal with it. But let's not dawdle, okay?"

"Not a problem."

They turned off the main road, onto a narrow side street. In less than two blocks the neighborhood transitioned from marginal to bad. Instead of curtains at the windows, there were tattered sheets or blankets. Neatly trimmed lawns gave way to mud and weeds. Debris and trash filled the gutters. A sagging fence was liberally tagged with graffiti. A battered old Plymouth rested on cinder blocks.

Two blocks more and they reached a narrow, three-story building of cracked red brick. The entrance was at the top of a set of concrete steps, the door flanked by rows of rusted mailboxes.

Each box had been crudely labeled in whitish paint with an apartment number. A few sported peeling name labels.

Brianna's skinned crawled in response to hostile stares. They were being watched, sharp eyes peering out from behind ragged cloth in many windows.

David took the steps two at a time. The outer door was unlocked and he held it open for Brianna. Inside, the scent of stale urine hit her like a blow and she realized it emanated from a homeless man snoring in one corner. Heading for the stairs, Brianna felt a stirring of energy and turned back, only to see the man shambling out the door.

"Boss?" David was waiting for her, halfway up the first flight of steps.

"Nothing. Never mind." Brianna waved him forward and followed, but couldn't keep herself from a backward glance before hurrying to catch up.

Ed and George's apartment was on the top floor of the building. A corner unit, it was perpetually cold thanks to all the windows, but filled with wonderful light that Brianna assumed was useful for a painter. As they made their way up the final set of stairs, Brianna could hear an argument in progress. George's basso profanities were punctuated by Ed's shrill nasal whining. Great. Just great.

Perhaps in response, another tenant on the third floor had cranked up the volume on his television until Brianna could clearly hear every word of the sermon being broadcast. She recognized the voice of the great Reverend Ralph, who had been expounding on evil for years. Today he was harping on the sins of the flesh and the corruption of popular culture. Periodically the audience would respond with a rousing, *"Amen."*

David gave Brianna a long-suffering look and raised his hand to pound on the door to Ed's apartment. Neither combatant noticed right away, so David kept knocking. At last the argument broke off and Brianna heard the heavy stomp of booted feet approaching, followed by the metal scraping of locks being pulled back.

The door opened a crack, showing half of George's unshaven face, bisected by a narrow, brass, safety chain. "Waddaya want?"

George glared at them. He lived under the oft-spoken presumption that if he didn't keep constant watch on Ed, the other man was going to run off and bed anything that moved. It wasn't an attractive attitude, and Brianna wouldn't have tolerated it in Ed's place. But Ed seemed to accept it. She sometimes wondered if perhaps he even encouraged it, manipulating George, making him jealous.

Brianna was half tempted to just turn around and leave, but she could tell from David's body language that he wasn't about to let George's bad attitude get in their way.

"I called earlier. Brianna wants to buy one of Ed's paintings."

George growled an incoherent response, then closed the door. Brianna heard the chain being shifted before the door opened again, revealing George lumbering away. A few seconds later she could hear him slamming pans and dishes in the kitchen.

"Sorry about that," Ed said as Brianna and David stepped into the apartment, but by the look of him, he didn't seem particularly sorry. He was twitchy, his spindly body moving in sharp, uncoordinated jerks that told Brianna he was wired on something. His natural paleness was more pronounced than usual and there were shadows like bruises under his preternaturally bright eyes. His dark hair was a mess of tangles, his jeans baggy and paint-stained.

"I've pulled out some of my best for you to look at." He gestured wildly at a large group of canvases leaning against the far wall. They ranged in size from only a few inches across to huge pieces that took up nearly half of the long bare brick wall they leaned against.

The place was a mess. The entire living room area had been taken over by Ed's painting supplies and canvases in various stages of production. The bedroom, visible through the open door at the end of the hall, was a mess of rumpled sheets and laundry piled haphazardly on the floor. While she couldn't see the bathroom, she'd had enough previous experience here not to want to.

Shaking her head, Brianna walked over and began flipping through the paintings, trying to ignore the negotiation going on behind her. David had offered a price, Ed was arguing for more, and George, God help her, had returned from the kitchen and was trying to serve as the voice of reason. The whole exercise was pointless if she didn't find something worthwhile.

The first few canvases were disturbingly odd. They were brilliant; the images haunting, dreams and nightmares captured in pigment. But looking at them, Brianna had to suppress a shudder. They probably deserved to be hung in a gallery, but she wouldn't want them in her home. Nor were they suitable for her father.

She heard soft footsteps behind her, and half turned to find Ed at her elbow. George and David had retreated to the couch and lowered their voices.

"The first three are my most recent work," the painter said.

"They're quite remarkable," she admitted, "but I'm looking for a gift that needs to be a little more—"

"Traditional?" Ed suggested.

"Exactly." Brianna smiled, trying to take the sting out of the rejection.

He nodded. "Try the ones further back." As he reached past her, perhaps intending to move some of the canvases out of the way, his hand brushed against hers. Brianna felt a shock, like an electric current, that made her jerk back. In that instant Brianna knew that her magic had sensed something *wrong* about Ed; the zap was a warning.

"Ouch. Damn! That hurt." Ed glared at her.

A moment later George edged his body between Ed and Brianna. Brows lowered, he asked, "What's wrong, Ed?"

"Nothing—I just got a shock. Must be static from the rug."

Brianna couldn't imagine there was enough nap left on the threadbare carpet to generate a good charge, but George relaxed visibly. He didn't leave but his posture became less aggressive.

"Brilliant, isn't he." His tone challenged Brianna to argue.

"Definitely," Brianna agreed. "I just hope I can find something right for my *father*." George or no George, if she didn't see something suitable, she wasn't pulling out the checkbook. Nor did she intend to waste much more time on this. She and David needed to get back to the shop in time to open.

"Here." Ed pulled out the third painting from the back. "What do you think of this?"

With an aggrieved sigh, George moved aside so Brianna could see the whole piece. The moment she did, the breath caught in her throat. She was completely awestruck.

It was a woodland scene. Done in photorealism, the soft sunlight of an early summer morning filtered through leaves of every color of green imaginable and speckled a forest floor. It drew you in, as if you were walking into the painting, and into the woods until Brianna almost expected to hear the notes of the songbird perched among the branches, see the rabbit bolt when her footfalls came too close. It was amazing, each plant, each animal, every leaf and blade of grass was so perfectly depicted that Brianna could almost smell the loamy earth, hear the birds in the trees.

It was glorious, exquisite and amazing. Her father would treasure it. Ed could name whatever price he wanted. If Brianna could afford it, she'd pay it.

Ed stared at her, a knowing smile twitching at his lips. He was smug, but he had good reason to be. "This is the one."

"Yes. It is," Brianna agreed, her voice hushed.

"I'll give you a break on the price because you modeled for me." He sounded both cocky, and oddly, sad. Brianna wondered if he was sorry to part with it. Were his paintings the children of his mind and talent? Was it hard to let them go? She'd never had such a gift, so she would never really understand.

"Thank you."

His eyes met hers, the look acknowledging that something more serious than a mere purchase was going on. For the first time, Ed and Brianna actually understood each other.

"When is that book coming out anyway? I'll want to get a copy," Brianna asked.

Ed smiled, and again it had that hint of wistful sadness she didn't quite understand. "I asked and the author sent me autographed copies for you and David. George, could you get the books for me while Brianna writes the check? They're on the nightstand."

George didn't argue, stomping out of the living room area without comment. Taking the hint, Brianna pulled her checkbook and pen from her back pocket. David gave her the figure he and George had settled on. It was a hefty amount, but that painting was worth every penny. Who knew, if it didn't go to drugs, it could buy the boys a house—with lots of windows and perfect light. The thought made Brianna smile.

9

The painting hadn't looked that big in Ed's living room. It wasn't until Brianna and David were carrying it that it became apparent just how awkward an eight-by-twelve-foot canvas could be. It wasn't heavy, but it was large and ungainly. It had been hard getting it down the narrow apartment stairs; the real challenge, however, came at street level. Who knew that it would make the perfect sail, catching the slightest breeze and attempting to drag the two of them into traffic—to the spirited accompaniment of horns and cursing?

Brianna was in good shape. She knew David was as well—after all, you can't carve marble or move magical artifacts made of stone unless you were reasonably fit. But after the first few minutes Brianna could feel the strain in her shoulders and arms. Too, once they started they couldn't exactly stop and put the canvas down.

It didn't help that the used grocery bag that held their new hardcover books kept slapping against Brianna's legs. By the time they had traveled two blocks she was well and truly sick of the entire process and they hadn't even reached the halfway point.

A vehicle pulled to the curb ahead of them and a gravelly voice filled with amusement called out, "Hey, bro, you look like you could use some help."

Peering around the edge of the canvas, Brianna got her first in-person look at David's older brother.

Brianna had seen pictures and heard a lot about Nick from David over the years. He was a few years older and different enough in age and personality that they hadn't been that close growing up. Now, as adults, they were developing a real friendship. According to David, his brother was stubborn, hard-headed, and a world-class smart-ass, but otherwise a good guy and a damned fine cop. One thing Brianna counted in his favor was the fact that of all the Antonellis, he alone had never given David a hard time about his sexual preference.

Brianna's eyes widened when she caught sight of him, her pulse speeding slightly. The pictures she'd glimpsed on David's cell phone had definitely not done him justice.

Oh, my.

10

NICK ANTONELLI

God, Nick was tired, completely exhausted. He wandered down
the hall from the intensive care unit to the little waiting room
with its uncomfortable molded plastic chairs and bank of vending
machines. A television overhead ran incessantly. Looking up he
was disturbed to see a clip of himself rushing into the hospital.

Turning toward the nearest machine, he took a look at himself
in the glass. Yep, he looked just as bad in person. His work clothes
had been taken into evidence, so he'd changed into the rumpled
and ratty sweatpants and T-shirt stuffed in the gym bag at the
bottom of his locker. He hadn't bothered to shower, either—and
there were speckles of dried blood here and there that he'd missed
when he'd done his lightning-quick wash-up.

Juan's blood: Juan, who was out of surgery and clinging to life
in the ICU down the hall, his family gathered, pale and intense,
praying or quietly crying as they waited for news of whether he
would live or die.

Nick found himself blinking back tears. It would've been

better if it had been him. He didn't have a wife, a brand-new
baby. And while his parents and David would mourn, it wasn't the
same. Damn it anyway! Rage at his own helplessness, instant and
intense, rolled through him, making him want to hit something,
anything. Closing his eyes he reined in his emotions, waiting
until his ragged breathing had steadied before opening them.
When he did he was surprised to find he was no longer alone in
the room. Juan's mother had come in behind him. He could see
her reflection clearly in the glass of the vending machine.

Inez Sanchez was not a young woman. Tiny, she was less than
five feet tall. Her silver hair was pulled back in a tight bun and lac-
quered into place with enough hairspray that not a single hair had
come loose, even after all these hours. She wore an old-fashioned
housedress with purple flowers and a hand-knitted sweater in an
improbable shade of lilac. Widowed young, she'd raised five children in a questionable section of the city. It was a testament to her
that not one of them had wound up in trouble and all of them still
attended both her Sunday dinners and mass on a regular basis.

"You need to go home. You need rest." She spoke English, but
not perfectly, her accent thick, even after all her years in the
United States. She wrinkled her nose. "And you need a shower."
The words were sharp.

Nick turned to face her, unsure of what to say. He opened his
mouth, but before any words could come out she launched herself
across the short distance between them, hauling him into a fierce,
rib-cracking hug. "You saved him. You saved my Juan. God bless
you."

Nick clung to her, vision blurred. "I'm so sorry."

"No. You did good. You saved him."

"If only . . ." Stupid, useless words.

She pulled back, pointing a bony finger into the middle of his
chest. Speaking slowly, and very clearly, all traces of accent gone,

she said, "Stop that!" Then, more normally, "It was not your fault."
She poked him hard in the solar plexus.

Maybe not, but he sure as hell felt like it was.

"You need sleep. Go home. Rest. You can come back later.
We'll be here."

"But—"

"Go home."

He managed to leave the hospital without talking to any reporters, but they didn't make it easy. Still, when he reached the
third floor of the hospital parking garage his truck was right
where he'd left it. It was easy to spot, a big red 4x4, parked between a shiny new BMW and an old beater of an Oldsmobile.

He hit the button to unlock it and climbed behind the wheel,
shivering a little. The temperature had dropped with the sunset.
Starting the engine, he turned the defroster all the way to high so
that it would clear the fog from the windows as it heated the
cabin.

Leaning right, he flipped open the glove box to see if there
were any cigarettes. Nothing. He'd given up smoking long ago, but
sometimes, when he was really stressed . . . of course, there weren't
any. Maybe he'd stop by a convenience store on the way home.
Then again, maybe not.

He hadn't expected to sleep, but he had. There were nightmares,
but he only half remembered them. They couldn't hold a candle to
reality anyway. Juan had been shot. Nick was on forced leave
pending investigation into the "incident."

Nick rolled over, grabbing his cell phone from the nightstand
to check the time. It was 7:30. On any other day he'd have been
up for hours, done his run and had breakfast, be dressed and on

his way to work. It was a routine. He liked routine. Other people might find it boring. He felt it gave his life structure.

He hit a number on speed dial and heard ringing at the other end of the line. Juan's sister Yolanda picked up the phone on the first ring. Apparently she'd been the one chosen to stay with the baby at Juan and Maria's house. "Hello."

"Yolanda, it's me."

"Nick. Hi. I'm so glad you're okay. And thank you. Thank you from all of us." There was a lot of emotion packed into her words, her voice sounding strained as if she were fighting tears.

Nick flinched. He so didn't feel like he deserved thanks.

"Your mom sent me home last night. I figured I'd call and check in before I head back to the hospital, find out how he's doing. I know they can't use cell phones in the ICU, but I figured somebody had to be at the house taking care of the baby."

"That'd be me. Juan's hanging in there. The docs say they're hopeful, that it's a good sign."

Nick closed his eyes and said a quick prayer of thanks.

"You okay?"

"I wasn't shot."

"I know. But are you *okay*?" Yolanda put obvious emphasis on the last word. "It wasn't your fault, you know."

"You don't know that."

She snorted. "Yeah, Nick, I do. You love my brother. You'd never let him get hurt if you could help it. We all know that. You're practically part of the family."

"Thanks, Yo." Nick forced the words past a lump in his throat.

Whatever she would've said in response was cut off by the sound of a baby crying in the background.

"Baby's up. I've got to go," Yolanda said. "Nick, stop blaming yourself. Just . . . *stop*, okay. Juan wouldn't want that and you know it."

She hung up before he could answer.

Nick had showered before falling into bed the night before, so he didn't bother this morning, just brushed his teeth, dragged a comb through his tangled dark curls, and pulled on a clean pair of jeans and a tee, with a denim work shirt over the top in case it was still chilly out. Grabbing wallet and keys he dashed down the stairs, intending to grab some breakfast at a drive-through and head back over to the hospital.

He was heading down Commerce when he spotted a pair of idiots who were trying to carry a massive painting down the sidewalk. The damned thing caught every breeze like a parasail. Traffic was at a near standstill as people slowed to watch the spectacle and to make sure they could stop if the fools managed to get blown into the street. As he got closer, Nick realized he *knew* at least one of the morons. It was his brother, David.

Family, ya gotta love 'em.

Nick pulled the pickup to the curb and climbed out.

"Hey, bro, you look like you could use some help."

"Nick!" Relief was evident in David's voice. "And you've got the truck." He lowered the canvas and rested it atop the toe of his booted foot to keep it clear of the sidewalk.

The other end of the painting settled down as well and a woman peered around the edge of the canvas. He recognized her from photos in her old police file and his heart sank. It was Brianna Hai, big as life and twice as gorgeous. Jeans and a T-shirt clung just tight enough to show dangerous curves. Her skin was amazing, pale and flawless, but it was her eyes that got to him. They were a misty silver, shot through with sparkles of charcoal and fog and every other imaginable shade between black and white. A person could get lost looking into those eyes, which were framed by the longest, blackest lashes he'd ever seen. Without a bit of makeup or apparent effort, she was the most heart-stoppingly beautiful woman he'd seen in years, and completely unaffected. It wasn't that she didn't know. It just didn't matter to her. That impressed him almost as much as the cut muscles in the arms holding the canvas. He told himself to cool his jets, that the woman in front of him was serious bad news. His body wasn't inclined to listen.

Shit, shit, shit.

She smiled, flashing deep dimples, her eyes sparkling. Nick found himself smiling back at her, despite his better judgment. And yet, despite her obvious attractions, a big part of his mind was on Special Agent Tennyson and the fact that the sumptuous woman in front of him was his key to admittance to the dojo.

David began making introductions. "Brianna, this is my brother, Nick. Nick, this is my boss, Brianna Hai."

"Hi." Nick extended his hand. She took it, her handshake firm, businesslike.

David stared at him for a long moment, his expression worried and uncomfortable. Nick could almost hear the gears grinding as his brother debated whether or not to ask the inevitable question.

"I'm okay. I'm on the way to the hospital now to check on Juan."

"Juan?" The lilt in Brianna's voice made it a question.

Nick took a deep breath to steady himself. "I don't know if David's told you, but I'm a cop. Yesterday I was involved in a shooting. My partner is in the ICU."

"Oh. I'm so sorry. Don't let us keep you," Brianna said.

"No. It's okay. This will only take a couple of minutes." He gave them a rueful smile. "I consider it a public service. You guys are causing a traffic problem."

"It *is* a little awkward," she admitted with a wry grin that made Nick's pulse speed.

Nope. Not interested. That woman is nothing but trouble, Nick reminded himself as he moved around to the back of the truck. Letting down the tailgate he climbed inside, rearranging the miscellaneous items that had collected in the truck bed to make room for the painting. Meanwhile, David and Brianna moved into position to begin loading it.

"David's told me a lot about you," Brianna said, making small talk to keep the silence from becoming awkward.

"Uh-oh." Nick gave a forced laugh. "Don't believe everything you hear. David's prone to exaggeration."

"Am not!" David protested.

"Are too."

Brianna laughed, her eyes sparkling. "Oh, you're definitely brothers."

Once the space was ready, Brianna and David passed the canvas up to Nick, who carefully moved it into place at an angle so that it would fit diagonally across the bed. "I wish I had a tarp. I'd hate for this to get damaged."

"I'll ride in the back with it," David offered. Suiting actions to words, he climbed up into the truck bed next to Nick.

Nick shot his brother a sour look. That was illegal, and they both knew it. Then again, he couldn't think of another safe way to get the painting to wherever they were going. It was just so damned big.

"We're only going to the shop, it's not that far," David assured him.

He was right. It wouldn't be far. But he still didn't like it. Even so, Nick didn't argue, just gave a grumbling growl and jumped down. A quick visual check told him that closing the tailgate wasn't an option, which didn't improve his mood. Still, his only comment to David was, "I'll take it slow."

He opened the truck driver's door as Brianna was climbing into the passenger seat, and heard the local news rehashing the shooting . . . again. *Shit!*

"I'm surprised you didn't hear about the shooting on the news." Nick pressed the button to turn off the radio before turning the key in the ignition and starting up the truck.

"I've been busy. Still, from what you said I assume you defended yourself and saved your partner. If that's true, you didn't have a lot of choice." Her voice was so unemotional that she could've been talking about the weather. Nick looked away from the traffic long enough to glance at her. To his astonishment she looked as calm as she sounded. It wasn't that she wasn't interested— she simply wasn't passing judgment in any way. That was the last thing he expected.

"I didn't," Nick said.

"I'd wager the reporters have never been on the wrong end of a weapon." There was wry humor in Brianna's voice.

"Probably not."

"Then they're not going to understand." She gave an eloquent shrug.

"Nope." Nick didn't say more than that. Frankly, he didn't know what *to* say. Her attitude, while welcome, was also a little disturbing. People were not normally that casual about a shooting death. He wondered if maybe the feds were onto something in their suspicions of Brianna Hai.

That reminded him, he was supposed to be arranging an in for the Fibbies. "You obviously work out. Do you belong to a gym?"

"Yes. Why?"

Nick kept his voice oh-so-casual. "I usually work out at my uncle's place, but he's closing down for a few weeks to do some remodeling. I'm trying to find a place that my buddy and I can work out 'til Phil opens back up."

"Ah. Well, I can ask Mei. We'll have to see what she says. What's your buddy's name?"

They'd reached Helena's. Nick pulled the truck into the loading spot in front of the door and climbed out. "Jesse Tennyson."

"Is your friend a cop, too?"

David answered before Nick could. "Has to be if he's friends with Nick. My brother doesn't know how to talk to anyone who doesn't carry a badge."

"Hey!" Nick protested.

"What? You know it's true. You talk to anyone but a cop and it's like you're carrying on an interrogation." Dave winked at Brianna and continued, "He scared the crap out of so many of my boyfriends I've stopped introducing them to him."

Nick let down the tailgate as Dave moved the canvas upright. The two men unloaded the painting while Brianna went toward the door, digging in her jeans for her keys. Before she reached it the door swung open, revealing a confused-looking older woman.

"You're not upstairs?" She sounded shocked. "But then who . . . what . . ."

With the door open Nick could clearly hear sounds from above: pounding and a high-pitched screech that resembled fingernails on a chalkboard.

Even Nick's unusual conversation with his brother's boss hadn't prepared him for what came next. Hai shoved the woman aside and dashed into the shop, moving as fast as any cop Nick had ever known.

Dave let out a curse and nearly dropped his end of the painting. The urgent expression on his face made Nick hustle him and the unwieldy canvas into the shop. As soon as the thing was safely set down, the Antonellis took off after Brianna.

Heart pounding as he followed his brother through the shop and up the stairs, Nick automatically reached for his gun— which wasn't there. He faltered for half a step before the rest of his cop instincts took over and he straight-armed David, forcing him to drop behind him as they neared the top of the stairs. Nick needed to see what they were dealing with, assess the situation before they jumped into something they couldn't handle.

It sounded like a pitched battle of some kind was taking place. He heard deafening, whistling screeches, some kind of animal growling, at least one human cursing . . . and the unmistakable sounds of people hitting one other. Then there was the smell . . . a cesspool would smell better, all of it overlain with the meaty scent of blood and torn flesh.

Hai stepped backward, into Nick's line of vision. She raised the plastic tote bag she'd been carrying and swung it like a weapon at a blur of green that was speeding toward her head. Whatever was in the bag was heavy; when it connected, Nick heard a heavy *thunk* followed by the crunch of bones breaking. Whatever she'd struck shot away from her and an instant later, the wall shuddered from an impact and one of the shrieks was abruptly cut off.

Nick moved forward cautiously, feeling his brother close behind, until he had a better view—and then froze in shock. *Things* were flying around the room. They looked something like bats—if bats came in multicolored green with red eyes and had wide, froglike mouths filled with rows of razor-sharp teeth dripping with pus-yellow venom. On the floor, beside a dead cat, was what a gargoyle statue would look like if stone lived, moved, and used language that would make a marine blush.

"*Shit! Doxies!*" David yelled in Nick's ear as he tried to shove past his brother; Nick wouldn't let him. Hai and the gargoyle were doing just fine without him. There were only two of the batlike things left and neither David nor Nick were armed.

Realizing the odds had shifted, the larger of the two . . . doxies . . . executed a pinpoint turn, narrowly avoiding the seeking claws of the gargoyle, and dove straight *through* a painting hanging on the wall. The last creature tried to follow, but was neither agile nor quick enough. The gargoyle caught it with a lightning-fast grab and was preparing to crush the life from it when Hai shouted, "Don't kill him. We need answers!"

The doxie's screaming had nearly shattered Nick's eardrums, but it fell silent as the gargoyle stopped short of crushing it. It wriggled in the thing's clawed fist as blood ran red down the mottled stone of the . . . statue's . . . arm.

"He won't talk," the gargoyle growled.

"He won't have to," Brianna answered. Stepping carefully over the crumpled bodies and blood-slicked floor she used her index finger to scrape the fresh blood from the gargoyle's arm. Tracing patterns in the air, she spoke softly in a musical language that Nick didn't recognize.

The air shimmered, as if from heat, and something like a hologram appeared, floating in the hallway. A breeze, heavy with the scent of rain-fresh grass, cleared away the stench of death and blew the woman's hair back to reveal a face harsh with concentration. Through the . . . portal . . . Nick could see a group of ten to twenty doxies on the ground, many injured, grouped around a white plastic laundry basket filled with squirming, hissing kittens. The doxies were screeching at one other, obviously angry and arguing.

"What are they saying?" David asked.

"They're arguing about who is supposed to be giving the orders and whether to send for reinforcements. Apparently the prince had been in charge, and they're afraid to tell their king that they left him behind."

The doxie in the gargoyle's grip began fighting again. He shouted something and the doxies in the vision looked up and around, as though they'd heard.

Brianna swore and dismissed the image with a wave of her hand. She glared at the captive creature. "We don't *have* to keep you alive. I've got the information I need now."

The doxie hissed, spitting foul-smelling gunk onto the floor in front of her feet. It began eating through the wood like acid. The gargoyle tightened his grip in response, until the creature couldn't move and was struggling to breathe.

"Don't kill him yet," Brianna said. "If he's the prince, he may be useful as a hostage."

"What's the plan?" David pushed past Nick and went down on one knee beside the cat's corpse, his body quivering with anger. Nick could see tears shining in his brother's eyes, but the younger man's voice was absolutely steady.

"Pug and I will go after them," Hai announced.

"I'm going with you," Dave said. As Nick began to overcome his shock, he realized that his brother hadn't been surprised by anything—not the doxies, the living gargoyle, not even his boss doing battle. Little that had happened in the last few minutes had made sense to Nick. But Dave—he clearly knew the score.

"The fuck you are." Nick's voice cracked. He wanted to sound tough, unfazed. He wasn't.

"David—" Brianna started to argue.

He didn't let her finish. "They broke into your home. You can't let an insult like that pass unanswered. And you need to know who set you up. Besides, Camille was as much my cat as yours and Pug's. Those kittens are mine, too. I'm not going to stay here and do nothing while you go after them. And don't tell me it's dangerous. I *know* about doxies. I've been studying, I've been talking to Grandma Sophie."

"Grandma Sophie?" The words popped out of Nick's mouth unbidden. "What the hell does Grandma Sophie have to do with this?"

Dave gave him a startled look, as if he'd forgotten his older brother was there.

"Nick, look," Dave said, speaking quickly. "There's more to reality than you know. There's magic, and doxies, and faeries, and a whole 'nother world. Grandma Sophie was part of it. She taught me. She would've taught you, too, but you weren't interested." He turned to Brianna, speaking urgently, eyes blazing as he argued his point. "I'm coming with you. You're already outnumbered and they may be sending for reinforcements. And you can't go in with guns or edged weapons, that would be an act of war. Your father would have your head. I can help—even if it's only by carrying the kittens while you fight."

Nick stared at his brother. This was a side of David he'd never known, never even suspected. And yet, looking back, he realized there had been half-remembered conversations, things his grandmother had said and done that were just not . . . normal.

"Let him come," the gargoyle growled.

"If he's coming, I'm coming." The words popped out of Nick's mouth without thought. David was his baby brother. Nick wasn't about to let him go into danger without going along as backup.

Brianna made a disgusted noise and threw up her hands. "Fine. Come. But *I'm* in charge. You'll do as I order, without question or hesitation. *Is that clear?*"

"Yes, ma'am," David agreed. Nick just nodded. It made sense. She knew what they were dealing with, after all. Besides, judging from her little exhibition a minute ago, there was a lot more to Brianna Hai than her admittedly gorgeous exterior.

She glared at them both, then started issuing orders.

"David, go to the bedroom closet. Bring sunglasses, neck scarves, and heavy jackets. Also, bring me the cat carrier. We'll take our prisoner with us. Nick, Pug, stay here while I get some things from downstairs. I'll be right back."

Nick did as he was told, contenting himself with staring at the gargoyle and its captive, and wondering what the hell was really happening, because this, this just wasn't right. He tried discreetly pinching himself, just to make sure he wasn't dreaming. He wasn't. Which meant he was standing in the middle of a pile of dead fairies, looking at a very live gargoyle.

Holy shit.

"You must be David's brother, Nick."

The gargoyle's voice sounded . . . gravelly. Nick had to fight down a burst of hysterical—and very unmanly—giggles at the thought. It was just so . . . appropriate.

"I'm Pug. How're you holding up?"

"I'm a little shell-shocked, but I'll be okay," Nick lied. He wasn't okay, and didn't see any signs of getting that way any time soon. Reality had taken a left turn a few minutes ago. He was still hanging on, but it was by his teeth and toenails. David, damn it, seemed to be just fine.

"Good." The gargoyle nodded.

Nick was saved from further conversation by his brother's return. David had brought everything Brianna had ordered, along with a small padlock—like a luggage lock—to secure the cat carrier's door.

David and the gargoyle . . . Pug . . . caged the doxie. The gargoyle said something in a foreign language and Nick felt heat, saw a glow briefly surround the cage. Clamping his mouth shut on the startled exclamation that came to his lips, Nick began wrapping one of the scarves around his throat. He buttoned his overshirt and pulled on a pair of shades.

When Brianna came back, she was carrying a pair of tennis racquets and a white, mesh laundry bag that shimmered in the sunlight in a way that made Nick's eyes water behind the dark lenses of his sunglasses.

She thrust one hand at him and opened her fist to reveal a necklace—a stone threaded onto a long silver chain. "Put this on. Make sure it's touching skin." Without asking any of the questions that leapt into his mind, Nick took the pendant and slipped it on, tucking it under his T-shirt. The stone felt oddly warm against his skin.

"I thought that was for Max?" The lilt in David's voice made it a question as he snicked the padlock shut.

"I'll make another one for her tomorrow. Right now he needs it more. You've still got yours?"

"Yes, ma'am." David reached beneath the neck of his shirt and withdrew a pendant similar to the one Nick had slipped on.

"Good. Bundle up and put on your glasses. Remember, doxies work in swarms, they primarily go for the eyes and throat to disable the victim before they take them down and eat them."

Eat them? Nick's stomach roiled and he glanced at David, protective instincts on full alert. His brother's face expressed a determination Nick had never seen from him before. Suddenly his

THE EXILE 91

"little" brother looked older, and far more dangerous, than Nick could ever have imagined.

Hai looked at the brothers, her expression grim. "David, you're on rescue." She handed him the laundry bag—which Nick abruptly realized was a net. "Your job is to get the laundry basket and the kittens. The net's been bespelled to entangle and capture anything that flies toward it, so as long as you have it, anything that attacks you *should* be captured before it can hurt you."

She offered Nick one of the tennis rackets, handle first. "I want you to guard David's back. If you have to slam them into trees or rocks, do it. A hard enough impact will put them out of the fight. They'll most likely heal . . . eventually." Seeing his raised eyebrow, she added, "It's not an edged weapon so hitting anyone with it won't be considered an act of war."

Nick wasn't sure that explained anything, but what was one more note of madness in a morning like this one? *Were* there other mornings like this one?

Slipping into a leather jacket, Hai zipped it up all the way, then turned up the collar and began wrapping a long scarf around her neck. Grabbing both the second tennis racquet and the caged doxie with her left hand, she gestured with her right. The air in front of her shimmered and parted.

The gargoyle stepped between her and the portal. He looked at her steadily, with a grim expression on his stone face, and said, *"Pudorum tui invoco."*

With those ceremonial words he invoked an honor debt. Brianna blinked. "You didn't need to do that."

"Yes, I did. Now you can honestly tell your father you had no choice." Pug's narrow smile still managed to show too many teeth. "Let's do this." He turned and stepped through the doorway that hadn't been there a moment before. David was right on his heels. Taking a deep breath, Nick followed, stepping into the unknown with Brianna Hai at his back.

11

The four of them stepped into the middle of the doxie camp. Before the enemy could react or sound the alarm the gargoyle was on them, teeth and claws cutting down the small, deadly beings like a scythe mows through wheat. Never would he have believed a creature made of stone could move so fast. David ran straight at the group guarding the kittens, howling a war cry that scattered the doxies like startled birds. Unfortunately, that didn't last long. Seconds later they were grouping into two separate formations to dive-bomb him from opposite sides. Brianna, meanwhile, was swearing like a sailor as she swung the tennis racquet for all she was worth.

David turned toward one set of attackers, trusting his brother to take the other. The net Brianna had created opened wider than Nick would have thought possible, with a noise like a vacuum it sucked four or five of the incoming doxies inside; a few survivors zoomed away to regroup. Nick shook himself and turned to take on the creatures coming from the other side, swinging his tennis racquet in a frenzy of forehand and backhand strokes. At first he tried to aim, but there was no time, or point. The doxies were everywhere. So he just kept swinging, feeling a shudder through his arm each time the racquet made contact with a scaly body.

Despite his best efforts, two or three of the nasty, screeching things got close, grabbing at the glasses protecting Nick's eyes and clawing and biting at his neck. Their claws and teeth fouled in the thick yarn of his scarf. He could smell their fetid breath. The acidic saliva burned his skin after eating through the thick denim fabric of his outer shirt.

"I've got them!" Nick barely heard David's shout over the shrieking of the enraged doxies. He turned to see his brother running toward Brianna, bent over the laundry basket he was carrying. Reaching down, Nick grabbed the net with his left hand. Stuffed with doxies, it was too heavy to lift, so he dragged the awkward bundle over the rocky ground as he made his way toward Brianna who stood in the midst of a pile of stunned doxies. All the while, Nick kept swinging the racquet. His right arm felt like lead, his head was pounding from the din, but he didn't dare slow down or pause. The damned things just *kept* attacking.

David stumbled in front of him but stayed upright. Only a few more feet and they'd be home free. Beyond David, Nick could see Brianna standing behind the gargoyle, her hand raised to split the air and make a doorway.

In the next instant her expression changed to a look of shock and horror just as Nick heard, no . . . felt, something behind him. He turned to see a huge rift in the air. Pouring through it were hundreds of doxies, led by one the size of a Labrador retriever. Obviously male, his scales were mottled green and black and his wingspan looked to be at least six feet.

Oh, shit. I'm going to die over a litter of kittens.

The big doxie flew straight at Nick, and despite the screeching that filled his ears, Nick swore he heard the leader shout, "Charge!" in good old American English.

He couldn't run without exposing David and the kittens. The tennis racquet would be useless against something that size, so he dropped it and did the only thing he could think of. He opened the net.

The impact when the huge flying doxie hit him knocked Nick to the ground. Somehow he managed to keep a grip on the net, holding it open and facing up into the screeching deadly swarm.

The stone pendant flared, burning hot against Nick's skin. The mesh became furnace-hot in an instant, searing his fingers and palms. He screamed in agony and tried desperately to tear away the talisman or drop the net, but he literally couldn't release his grip.

His ears popped and Nick felt the air around him shudder. The air pressure changed and there was a whirl of wind, as though the bag in his hands held a tornado, sucking in the oxygen he was trying to breathe and the airborne doxies with it. They struggled desperately against the inexorable current, trying madly to veer off.

There was no way the bag should have held the king, let alone this many of the creatures, yet doxie after doxie was sucked inside.

The net was a growing, crushing weight, pinning Nick to the ground. He saw stars, felt consciousness fade. Then, nothing.

12

KING LEU OF THE SIDHE

It was a glorious morning. Leu rose with the sun, watching as dawn burst over the horizon in a glory of pink and gold, as the deep blue of night grudgingly gave way, as the last of the stars faded from sight.

The hounds bayed in the distance, their calls followed by the thrashing of brush being trampled. Body tensing, he raised his spear. He waited, ready, holding his horse steady with silent commands of body and mind.

The boar that burst from cover was a huge male, its shaggy black coat scarred from battle. Wicked tusks flashed as the animal turned sharply on two hooves, trying to gore the lead hound, which leapt nimbly aside at the last instant.

It was all the opening Leu needed. He flung the spear with all his strength; the weapon whistled through the air and struck the enraged beast with a meaty *thunk*, burying itself deep in the beast's muscled chest.

The boar squealed in agony, turning its hateful red gaze to the man it correctly identified as the source of its pain. It struggled, trying to attack, even as deep crimson heart's blood gouted from the wound and stained the ground red.

It fell.

The king's huntsman dismounted first and checked to be sure the beast was dead, but Leu knew it was. The huge boar's sides had stopped heaving. His horse, too, had quieted; though not much pleased by the scent of blood, it had been trained to war as well as to hunt.

"Excellent throw, your majesty," Ulrich said as he brought his horse up until he was nearly beside the king. Nearly. They were not, after all, equals. Ulrich's horse was not unlike his rider; big, gray, strong, and rangy, it had a mind of its own and required a strong hand to control him. "It has been some time since we hunted thus, but you have lost none of your skill."

"My thanks. From you that is quite the compliment." It was true. Ulrich was a great outdoorsman. There was no finer hunter, and few better warriors, among the Sidhe. This was the reason Leu had called for a hunt—so he could speak with Ulrich away from Asara. Leu knew well that oft as not it was his mistress's honeyed barbs that fueled Ulrich's rage at Brianna. Knowing what he now did, Leu needed to reconcile with Ulrich, for the Fae would soon need all of the old man's skill at arms and military tactics.

Ulrich bowed his head slightly, acknowledging Leu's compliment.

"The beast is slain," the huntsman announced. There were cheers from several throats, and calls of congratulation, which Leu acknowledged with a smile and nod.

"We ride back to camp. This day's hunt has ended so early that methinks another day or two in the field would not be found amiss." Smiles greeted this announcement. Riders formed up, waiting for Leu to take the lead, leaving the huntsman and his assistant to deal with butchering the carcass.

"Ride with me, Ulrich." Leu gestured to the space immediately beside him. "I would speak with thee privately."

At his words the others fell discreetly back, although the guards remained close enough to be able to defend his majesty should it be necessary, their eyes ever watchful.

"As my king wishes."

They rode together through the thick brush at the outer edge of old wood forest. Leu gathered his thoughts, choosing how best to approach this man who had once been his friend, and was now not quite his enemy.

"I met with Atropos the other night."

Ulrich's brows rose, his eyes widening, but he made no comment.

"She needed a boon. I granted it in exchange for information." Leu grimaced.

"Am I permitted to ask what you learned?" Ulrich asked. His speech, usually so direct, was guarded.

"My enemy lives. She's found a way to break through the veil. The attack will come soon."

"That is ill news."

"You believe it so?" The question had a barb in it.

Ulrich didn't flinch. "You are a good king. You have always done well by Faerie. I do not agree with all you have done, but it is not my place to judge your decisions—or your taste in women."

Leu threw back his head and laughed. Ulrich was not a subtle man. Besides, he had a point. Leu's women were notoriously difficult. Truth be told, he liked a woman who could keep him on his toes, who had power of her own and was capable of commanding respect on her own merits. But that did make things . . . lively on occasion.

Ulrich continued. "You are my king. You have my full support. My quarrel is with your daughter only."

"And if she becomes queen after me?"

Silence except for the thud of hooves on mossy ground. Leu sighed. He'd expected as much. Ulrich was as proud and stubborn as Asara in his own way.

"If she is proved innocent of your charges?" Leu asked.

"I don't see how that would be possible." Ulrich's voice was a low rumble. He was so certain . . . so very certain. Leu was not. Parents oft underestimate their children, but she had been so very young when Viktor had disappeared, and so very smitten with him.

Ulrich turned, meeting the king's gaze directly. "*If* she is innocent, and becomes queen, I will support her."

It was not what Leu wanted to hear, but it would have to be enough.

At a nod from the king Ulrich fell back to ride with the others, leaving Leu alone with his thoughts.

Ju-Long returned to the camp just after the midday meal and went directly to the king's tent.

"Well?" Leu asked as he acknowledged the spymaster's bow. "What is it?"

"Your majesty, we have a problem."

13

BRIANNA HAI

"Would you care to explain to me how I came to be called to a battlefield to negotiate a peace treaty between Moash, King of the Doxies, and *one of my subjects?*" Brianna's father didn't raise his voice, but the heat of his anger moved in a blistering wind across her back as she knelt with her forehead pressed to the one of the white marble squares of the floor of the throne room.

David, Pug, and Brianna had been transported—under guard—from the battlefield to one of the king's gates, and from there to the throne room. Nick had been carried away on a stretcher—Brianna hoped it was for treatment of his injuries. She was worried about him, but she couldn't ask without making things infinitely worse.

She tried to think fast, to quickly come up with the right words to explain. Apparently she wasn't fast enough, because the king's voice lashed out like a whip.

"You would keep your king waiting?"

"Of course not, your majesty." Brianna's voice was muted, careful not to cause offense by word or tone. "I was simply unsure where to begin." She didn't dare look up. Didn't move. She might be his daughter and, according to her half siblings, his favorite, but Leu wasn't her father now, he was the High King, and she'd dropped a major diplomatic incident into his lap.

Taking a deep breath, Brianna started at the beginning and prayed that nothing she said would make things any worse.

"I was coming home from purchasing a gift for you from a human artist and walked in on the tail end of a doxie raid. Apparently a war party had come through the painting that links my apartment to your study to steal a litter of kittens. I'm assuming it was for their fall festival." It was an educated guess there. The fall festival was only a few days away and was one of three main holidays for many of the lesser Fae. This year's celebration would be particularly grand as it would honor the twenty-fifth anniversary of Moash's investiture as king. It was well known that fresh roast kitten was his favorite dish.

"That's not possible." The king's rage had gone from hot to cold. Brianna could hear it in his voice. She suppressed a shudder. "The painting portal is specially keyed. It can be used only by you and me."

"When I arrived some of the doxies fled through the painting," Brianna replied. "I assume they came in the same way. But when we followed, we found ourselves in a field, not the palace."

The silence in the room had weight, as if the air had thickened. After an interminable moment the king spoke. "Kenneth." Brianna heard the booted footfalls of the Chief Captain of the High Guard move past her, toward the throne. There was a rustle of fabric; Brianna's past experiences told her Kenneth had dropped to one knee to await orders.

"Take two each of your best investigators and magicians. Check the princess's human apartments and the portal. Bring whatever evidence you find directly to me."

Brianna heard the captain's murmured, "Yes, sir," despite the muttering of the various nobles who'd wrangled a spot in the audience. She remained silent while he rose and walked past her and, she assumed, out of the room.

"Continue your tale," the king said.

"The doxies had killed the mother cat, who was the prized companion of Pug the gargoyle."

The king snorted in acknowledgment of that. Like everyone else, he knew that gargoyles developed almost insanely devoted relationships with their cats. He probably thought it was silly, but he was too much the diplomat to say so.

"Pug called on an honor debt, and I was required by duty to try to save the kittens, although frankly, I might have done so anyway. I did not like that the doxies had been able to raid my home."

"No more do I," her father admitted. "And if my carelessness is a cause of this, I will owe you a debt."

Now that his anger was no longer directed at her, Brianna risked a glance upward. Dressed in a simple green tunic and trousers with black trim that matched his boots and in no way distracted from his regal air, Leu was pacing back and forth on the dais.

"Go on." His eyes met hers and Brianna returned her forehead somewhat guiltily to the floor. Still, she managed to adjust her position so that she could see a little bit of what was going on while maintaining her obeisance.

"We came as individuals, intent only on stopping the raid and retrieving the kittens. In order to make sure that our actions were not seen as an act of war, we brought no bows, guns, or edged weapons with us. Nor did I cut my hair."

The king paused in his pacing, and she could sense his approval.

"Instead we dressed to protect ourselves, and brought weapons that were only meant to capture or wound."

"The enchanted net." He returned to the throne and took his seat, draping one leg over the arm of the carved marble chair in a provocatively casual pose. "Honestly, daughter, I would never have believed you capable of that level of magic. A net for one doxie, perhaps as many as ten. But hundreds, including King Moash himself? Has your power grown so great in the human lands?"

"I wouldn't have thought so."

"Interesting." He waved his hand in an indolent gesture. "You may rise."

"Thank you, your majesty."

Brianna would have liked to rise gracefully to her feet before so many witnesses, but that was impossible. She'd been prostrate long enough that her body had grown stiff. Still, she managed to stand without assistance and kept her head bowed, not even daring to glance at Pug who stood at her left side. The king might be feeling less furious, but she wasn't out of the woods yet—not by a long stretch.

"You're welcome." Leu gave his daughter a long, assessing look. "Tomorrow we will meet with the ambassador from the doxies to negotiate and sign a suitable treaty. Tomorrow night there will be a state dinner followed by a ball in honor of the agreement. Until then, Gwynneth and a set of guards will escort you and your . . . *guests*"—he glanced at David, who was standing miserably in the middle of a tight grouping of guards—"to Abracham House for the night. The other human is already there, receiving treatment from my personal healer. All prisoners are to be turned over to the seneschal, who will provide food and housing in addition to any needed medical care prior to exchange and release after the treaty signing."

He turned to address Pug. "I have received a request from the Diamond King that you attend him and his court at sunset. I will not offend a fellow royal by detaining you from such an appointment." His tone was dry. King Leu of the Sidhe had never quite gotten over having to acknowledge as a fellow royal a creature who'd once been his mistress's pet. Brianna doubted he ever would. Still, he was too much a king to let it interfere with the performance of his duties. "I suggest you leave now."

Pug bowed and backed down the main aisle leading away from the throne. Like all courtiers, he would not show his back to the king.

As Leu turned to Brianna, she caught a momentary glimpse of an unguarded expression. He was exasperated, but also proud. "Brianna, you may go."

Brianna bowed deeply from the waist. "Thank you, your majesty." She made sure her voice showed that she was, indeed, grateful.

Abracham House was the manor that had served as her mother's prison for the long years Helena Washington had been under house arrest. It was impossible to perform active magic within its walls. Brianna was going, under guard, to a very nice, well-appointed jail.

But David and Nick were going to be there with her, and her father had arranged to have Nick treated by the best healer in the kingdom. The seneschal would take responsibility for the injured and captured doxies and for Camille's kittens, all of which Brianna would have found nearly impossible to do. She just hoped the negotiations and rituals of appeasement could be done *quickly*. If King Leu were irritated enough, he might well choose to change the way time ran in Faerie. Then it might be weeks or months—or more—before Brianna and her companions were allowed to return home.

She stood quietly, waiting as Gwynneth made obeisance to the king and gathered twelve warriors to make up the escort. There was an equal mix of male and female and none of those selected were familiar to Brianna—they'd probably enlisted after Brianna left Faerie. In Gwynneth's place, she'd have made similar choices, but there was a certain ominous feel to marching out of the throne room and past the throng in the halls in the midst of a grim escort.

Guests of the king were allowed to use dog carts to travel between the various buildings of the royal encampment. Prisoners walked. David and Brianna were marched down the cobblestone road that led through the palace gardens and manicured lawns, past the dryad's tree, following a familiar route toward Abracham House. Brianna hadn't seen it in more than a decade, but even from a distance she could see that it hadn't changed. As ever, it looked more like a walled estate than a prison. Surrounded by well-tended lawns, the building was a three-story mansion of grayish-tan stone. The simple, mostly rectangular structure design was symmetrical, with two towers connected by elaborate loggias on both the first and second floors.

French doors led into the main building, which had a beautiful open-air courtyard in the center. Every stone was perfectly fitted; the ornamental carvings on each column were a work of art. Brianna knew that every one of the manor's seventy rooms were exquisitely appointed. It was a cage, but a well-gilded one.

David turned a worried face toward her. "Do you think Nick's okay?"

"The king said he sent his best healer. That means Morguenna, and she's studied human anatomy and medicine." She tried to sound reassuring, though her own stomach was in knots. She wouldn't be able to relax or concentrate until she heard for herself that Nick was all right. He had come here under her protection, and she'd failed him. If he died, Brianna would never forgive herself.

"It's all my fault. If I hadn't insisted on coming, he wouldn't have joined us, wouldn't have gotten hurt." David's voice was tight, as though he were fighting tears. Perhaps he was. Nick had certainly been badly injured when they'd pulled him from beneath the crushing weight of the bag full of doxies. But he was alive, and if it was possible to heal him, Morguenna would do it.

"Don't think like that. You did what you thought was best. Nick is a big boy. He knew it was dangerous."

"Yeah, but he figured it was cop dangerous, not magic dangerous."

There wasn't much she could say in response. Fortunately, they had reached the elaborate, wrought-iron gates.

"Brace yourself," Brianna warned her friend. "This is going to hurt."

She was rewarded with a puzzled look, but as soon as David's feet hit the first stone beyond the gate he stumbled. If a guard hadn't been there to catch him, he would have fallen. Brianna wasn't surprised. Anyone with the least magical sensitivity couldn't help but react. There was a sense of absence, a *wrongness* burned into each and every stone of the walkway, every inch of the grassy grounds. It not only sucked at a person's power, leaving them helpless to work any magic, but sapped the will to do anything at all.

For Brianna, passing over the fitted stones of the nearly one hundred stairs leading up to the house was like passing back in time, back to the unhappy years of her adolescence spent in a perfectly appointed prison. As she passed through the arched walkway Brianna shuddered from a chill that had nothing to do with the coldness of the stone. Flinching inwardly at each blow of Gwynneth's mailed fist on the oaken front door, she wished her father had sent her anywhere else.

Brianna had no doubt the king knew this, of all places where captives were kept, would bother her the most. It was a petty cruelty, and showed more than any words could just how angry with her her father was—and not just because of the doxies. At least not entirely. No, Leu still hadn't forgiven Brianna for leaving, for choosing to cross the veil with her mother and live among the humans.

Even that might have been forgiven, because the king knew full well how much Brianna had loved her mother. But Helena Washington was long dead and gone, and still Brianna preferred the company of humans to life at court. To her father that was a

slap in the face, an insult that he might never completely forgive and would never forget, no matter how much he loved his
daughter.

The door swung slowly inward; Brianna expected to see the
majordomo who had run the prison household since it was first
built. Instead, she was greeted by her half sister Lucienne.

Standing in the foyer of Abracham House, Lucienne looked even
more beautiful than Brianna remembered. Her floor-length gown
of shimmering layers of sheer metallic gold fabric left little to the
imagination as it whispered around a body that managed to be
both slender and lush. Lucienne's thick red-gold hair hung in perfect curls down to her knees. Her skin was smooth cream, without
the hint of a blemish or the freckles so common in human red-
heads. Her eyes were the green of new spring grass, flecked with
gold. They would have dominated her delicate heart-shaped face
even without the artfully applied makeup she wore.

Of all of their father's mistresses, Lucienne's mother had been
far and away the most beautiful—and dumb as the proverbial
post. Brianna had met many a rock with more brains. Though Mara
hadn't known it, it had been a sad day when she caught the king's
eye, because while Asara, Leu's primary mistress, was not subject
to human jealousy, she would never tolerate a true rival, or risk
that anyone other than one of her children would someday take
Leu's place on the throne.

Asara was discreet. Mara's death had been officially deemed an
accident, but if every Sidhe in Faerie who believed that gave Brianna a dollar, she still wouldn't have enough to buy a cup of coffee
at Denny's.

"Lucienne!" Brianna didn't bother to keep the surprise from
her voice. While she had always gotten on reasonably well with
Lucie, she couldn't imagine why her sister was here.

"Greetings, Sister, and congratulations on your victory." Lucie swept into a low and graceful curtsey that gave David an

unobstructed view of her formidable cleavage. "I would beg a private word with you," Lucie continued.

Beg, my ass, Brianna thought. None of her siblings had ever begged for anything in their lives. Still, she managed to keep her expression utterly bland, falling back into the habits of court as if it had been minutes, rather than years, since she'd last been in Faerie.

Lucie rose with a graceful gesture, motioning for Brianna and the others to come in—as if there were a choice. Still, if she could be gracious, so could Brianna. She manufactured a smile and walked through the front door and past her sister.

David followed at Brianna's heels, and she was pleased to note that he didn't seem to be paying undue attention to Lucienne, despite the fact that she was shining like a star and that her outfit, while perfectly acceptable in Faerie, would be considered indecent back in the human world. Lucie raised an eyebrow at that, a flicker of annoyance passing briefly over her lovely features. Brianna, however, was quite pleased. Whatever latent talent David had for resisting Sidhe shining was holding, which would provide him a measure of safety even when Brianna wasn't present.

Once Brianna and David had stepped across the threshold, the guards' duty was done. At a gesture from Gwynneth, the men rose to attention, bowed in unison, then turned and marched off. It was odd . . . very odd. She was, after all, a prisoner, and while she was an acknowledged member of the royal family, she wasn't a potential heir. Confused, she stood staring at their retreating forms for a long moment.

Lucie closed the door firmly behind the guards. Turning to Brianna, she said, "Like your escort, I've no doubt our father will find, *once again,* that you've done absolutely nothing wrong. When he does, he'll appreciate that someone thought to greet you and see to your comfort." She was acting both smug for having thought of it and resentful about the perceived necessity.

Brianna sighed. Though Lucie pretended that she was as stupid

as Mara had been, Brianna had no doubt that her sister manipulated things so that most thought her survival—despite her
mother's death and their siblings' machinations—stemmed from
phenomenal luck.

She'd liked Lucie. At one time she'd thought they were close.
Until one night, in her cups, Lucie confessed that one of the reasons she'd been deliberately nice to Brianna was that it brought
her favor in King Leu's eyes. The words had stung, badly. Fool
that she was, at the time Brianna had been naive enough to think
Lucie actually liked her. Instead, Lucienne was one of the many
Sidhe who believed Brianna to be their father's favorite child.

She sighed again. She was tired. Too weary to want to play
stupid political games. "Well, it was kindly done, whatever the
reason. Thank you."

Lucie gave an equally gusty sigh and cast a disgusted look in
her sister's direction. "Gods, but you are such a saint. Do you have
any idea how annoying that is?"

"Pardon?"

Lucie's patience evaporated, and she snapped, "Bri, will you
grant me an audience or not?"

"Lucie, you don't have to ask. You outrank me." Brianna didn't
bother to hide her confusion. "If you wanted you could order me
to strip and do handsprings and I'd have to do it."

Lucie gave an unladylike snort of amusement. For just a moment Brianna saw a flicker of friendliness, but it disappeared so
rapidly she decided it must have been her imagination. "Only for
a day and a few hours. When the list comes out at sunset day after
tomorrow you'll be on it. I won't. There's limited space you know.
Your victory over the doxies has moved you above Rihannon and
dropped me from the list altogether."

Oh, shit.

Brianna's knees didn't give out, but she couldn't hide her shock
and dismay. The list was exactly that—a list maintained by the

oracles of the potential heirs of the High King that would be acceptable to Faerie. At regular intervals the oracles sent runners from their home in exile with the current list. But rumor moves faster than the fleetest messenger and news of changes to the list always seemed to leak before the actual announcement.

The last thing, the *very* last thing Brianna wanted was to be considered in line for the throne. Plenty of people, including some of her siblings, hated her enough to wish her dead already, without any added incentive.

In addition, Brianna truly believed she would be a bad choice. She had never understood people well enough to succeed at politics. Worse, if she ever were chosen, there'd be civil war. At least half, maybe more, of the people would refuse to follow her based on her mother's history alone.

"You honestly don't want it." Lucienne stared at her, eyes wide with shock. "You always *said* you didn't, but I never really believed you. After all, how could you *not?*"

"Easily." The word popped out of Brianna's mouth without thought.

Lucienne's laugh was as rich and sweet as poisoned honey. "Diplomatic as always."

"Just one more reason I'd be a disaster on the throne." Brianna shook her head. "I don't believe this. Your sources must be mistaken. The oracles would never consider me."

"Oh, there's no mistake. Trust me." She would've said more, but fell silent at the sound of footsteps approaching from the main hall.

David managed to stay silent in the background, but he was shifting restlessly from foot to foot, obviously worried. He opened his mouth to speak into the silence, but the newest arrival beat him to it.

Morguenna appeared, blonde and elegant in her rose-colored healer's robes. At her heels was the majordomo, in his usual

impeccable navy uniform with a double row of polished gold buttons. He bowed low enough that his silvered braid trailed onto the
floor. "It is good to see your grace again. How may I serve?"

"Hello, Saturnino." Brianna gestured toward David. "Could
you please escort my guest to his brother's room and see to their
comfort?"

"Of course, milady." Brianna didn't think he could bow lower,
but he managed. "Will you be taking your former rooms?"

Brianna caught herself before she could sigh yet again. It occurred to her that she seemed to be doing that a lot, and needed to
stop—she was showing all too clearly what she was thinking and
feeling. Not smart under the circumstances. "I suppose so," she
agreed. As the majordomo led David through the archway toward the main staircase a thought occurred to her. "Saturnino?"

He stopped in his tracks. "Yes, milady?"

"Make sure that no one does anything that might influence my
friends' ability to leave Faerie when the time comes."

"Of course, milady."

Brianna shook her head. Three miladies in less than two minutes? Saturnino had never shown that level of deference to her before. Which meant that not only was Lucie right, but the news of
her elevated position had already leaked to the general public. This
was so bad . . . and there wasn't a damned thing she could do
about it.

14

Lucie and Brianna sat on opposite sides of a stone picnic table easily capable of seating twelve, sipping tea that Brianna recognized as having been made from plants grown in Helena's old greenhouse. The courtyard smelled of late-blooming flowers; afternoon sun kissed each leaf of every vine that climbed the pillars of the covered walkways. Against the plain stone backdrop, the leaves seemed to glow with every conceivable shade of green.

Before Brianna and her sister had adjourned to the courtyard, Morguenna had briefed her on Nick's condition. He wasn't as gravely injured as Brianna had feared. The healer had been able to take care of the worst of his wounds using magic before the rescue party reached Abracham. Once here, the spells laid into the foundations prevented the healer from working any active magic, but Morguenna felt that the potions she had created, which he would have to take at sunrise and moonrise for the next three days, would be all that was needed at this point. If Nick followed orders, he could expect a full recovery. She'd explained that she would give the same report to King Leu and then left for the palace.

Lucie had suggested she and Brianna have tea outdoors: tea, because she knew Brianna liked it; outdoors because it would be more difficult for the servants to spy on them. Not impossible, there was no way to manage that. But at least they would have some privacy, so Brianna agreed.

Lucie poured the steaming liquid into delicate white china cups decorated with an ivy pattern. Fragrant steam rose over the gilded rims and Brianna took a deep breath of the peppermint-scented mist. Immediately she felt her shoulders start to relax.

Lucienne spoke, keeping her voice low. "First, I wanted to warn you. Rodan has paid the best bards to come up with ballads celebrating your victory. He plans to have them played at the dance tomorrow night."

Brianna managed not to splutter her tea, but it wasn't easy.

Her sister continued, "Of course, if you act embarrassed, the doxies will have cause to call insult."

"Which is exactly what Rodan is hoping will happen."

The redhead smiled before taking a sip of tea. "You're better at this game than you used to be." She meant the words as a compliment, but to Brianna, all it did was highlight how bad she'd been at it before.

"I'd almost have to be," she admitted. "I couldn't do much worse."

Lucie gave a musical laugh and set down her cup. "I've missed you, Bri." She gave a rueful grin. "I didn't expect to. But after you left, I kept thinking about that last night, when I drank more than I should, and said . . . well, you know as well as I do what I said." She sighed. Her regret sounded real, but she'd always been a fine actress. Brianna looked into her sister's eyes, searching for the truth of what she was feeling, and couldn't be sure.

"I thought you were pretending to be my friend because of politics, in case I wound up on the list, or on the throne. I swear, it never occurred to me that you might actually be trying to be my friend. We're royals. We don't have friends. We have toadies, servants, and rivals. Not friends." There was no bitterness in Lucie's words, not even resignation. These were the facts of her world.

Brianna shook her head, to show her disagreement. "I do."

"I know." Lucie gave her a sad smile. "I envy you that. Just as I envied you your mother."

That was news. Brianna had loved her mother, adored her even, but Helena had been difficult at best, and her relationship with King Leu had been tumultuous enough to keep the entire kingdom walking on eggshells.

"Don't look at me like that." Lucie pointed a manicured nail at Brianna. "Your mother loved you for exactly who you are. And she insisted on your having a life and an identity besides being Leu's daughter."

"She was also a convicted criminal."

Lucie reached across the table to pick up one of the delicate pastry puffs that Saturnino had brought for them as a snack. "No one's perfect." She popped the treat delicately into her mouth, closing her eyes at the exquisite taste. When she'd swallowed, she continued. "And she was a *clever* criminal. They had to convict her of the lesser crime."

While at the king's order, no one had told Brianna the whole story, she had looked up the file when she'd joined the guards. Until shortly after Brianna's birth, the veil had been wide open. Any Fae, or any human with enough magic, could and did cross at will. The Sidhe, in particular, took advantage—which was how all those human tales of stealing babies and kidnapping beautiful women came about.

Helena Washington did not approve of this. She continually

argued about it with the king—arguments overheard by half the kingdom. She wanted him to forbid it. He refused. She warned him that if he didn't put a stop to the traffic, she would.

And when he did nothing, she acted.

One afternoon when Brianna was still a toddler, the veil slammed shut. Faeries caught on the human side were trapped there. Sidhe on the Fae side couldn't go through without a talisman that used *human* magic. Humans who were above the age of consent who knew how to cross—and wanted to—could come and go as they pleased . . . but they couldn't take anyone with them, and *no babies*.

It was no wonder the nobles had wanted Helena dead. The Sidhe adored babies of all kinds, but most particularly fat, healthy, human babies, whom they spoiled rotten given half a chance. Brianna had seen the sternest and most fearsome members of her father's court go gaga over the offspring of the humans living on the Fae side of the veil. She could only imagine their rage at being cut off from the greater source.

Helena was questioned, extensively, but refused to answer. She refused to say anything at all, despite direct orders from the king. So they convicted her of insubordination, defying a direct order, and obstruction of an investigation. The nobles wanted her executed. It was practically a miracle that Leu had been able to satisfy them with house arrest.

Brianna felt Lucie watching her. Her sister was giving her time to think, time for the information to sink in thoroughly. When she decided Brianna was ready, she continued, "Our best mages tried to find the 'ground' she used to tie down the spell."

That made sense. If they could find the anchoring point, they could trace the magic to its source, and possibly unravel it.

"What happened?"

"They couldn't. It was as though the anchor was everywhere in Faerie. And it moved." The admiration had changed to awe. "I can't imagine how she did it."

Neither could Brianna, and she'd known her mother as well as anyone short of her father. What Helena had done had earned her the everlasting enmity of the Sidhe, but her daughter didn't doubt she'd thought it was worth it. Brianna would bet she'd fully expected to be murdered for her pains—which meant she'd built it to outlast her own death. And it had. Amazing. Absolutely amazing.

Not for the first time Brianna wished heartily that her mother were alive again. Brianna missed her so much. A tiny woman in stature, Helena had possessed a strength and ferocity of purpose that was frightening in its intensity, even leavened as it was by her warmth and humor.

"Father let you move with your mother to the human world to protect you from the nobles who hated you both." Lucie's eyes met Brianna's, avid with curiosity. "But you have enemies of your own who have nothing to do with your mother." She shook her head in exasperation. "Alienating Ulrich was worse than stupid. He's been doing everything he can to turn anyone and everyone against you. Rumor has it that he even contacted mages with human blood to let him through the veil—but got no takers. It's entirely possible he'll call you out for a duel at the state dinner if he thinks he can get away with it."

"He thinks I murdered Viktor."

Lucienne nodded her agreement. Brianna wasn't surprised her sister knew. From what Brianna could tell, it was common knowledge Ulrich suspected her of killing his eldest, most beloved child. Lars, the second son, had been Viktor's shadow. Brianna had always believed he knew exactly what had happened the day of Viktor's disappearance, but she had no proof. Nor could she get any without digging up mud that would sully all concerned. All the same, if it ever came to light that Lars was a party to what happened, he would be in line for a death sentence rather than for all of his father's property. He would be ever so much safer with Brianna dead.

"Did you?" The words popped out of Lucie's mouth, but she waved her hand to stop Brianna before she could answer. "Never mind, I don't want to know."

"I would swear upon the truthstone that the last time I saw Viktor he was hale and whole." He'd been running for his life— but she wasn't going to tell Lucie that. If Brianna could manage it, the story of what happened on her fifteenth birthday would remain untold forever.

"You may have to." The words were deadly serious. "Ulrich has been making serious trouble for father."

At last Brianna understood why Lucie had come to see her. Not out of friendship, or to make an apology, but because their father had sent her. Brianna knew it was foolish to feel disappointed, but she was. Silly of her, but she couldn't seem to help herself. She had this stubbornly sentimental streak that she simply could not seem to get rid of. It was just another reason to get back to the human side of the veil as quick as she could manage it.

"Tell father that if he or Ulrich can talk the Diamond King into letting us use the stone, I'll testify, but I want it to be in private. Ulrich doesn't know it, but he'll want it done privately as well."

Lucie smiled even as she sighed. "I told him you'd figure out he sent me. You may be naive, but you're not stupid."

"Neither are you."

"Please don't spread that around." Lucie gave a wicked grin, flashing deep dimples. "I survive by letting Asara and the others think that I inherited more than my looks from my mother. If any of them had a clue that I have a brain they'd see me dead."

"Your secret is safe with me." And it was. Because deities help her, Brianna liked Lucie. Of all the siblings, nieces, and nephews she was far and away the best.

"Thank you." Lucie's eyes darkened, her expression growing serious. "Are you sure you're willing to use the truthstone? Because there's a good chance father can arrange for it, and once you agree, there's no going back."

"I've done nothing wrong. Embarrassing, but not wrong."

She glared at Brianna, her expression one of distaste. "Only you could honestly say that. You are such a saint."

15

NICK ANTONELLI

That's it. No more anchovy and double-pepperoni pizza before bed. God, what weird dreams. The poisonous monster-bats were bad enough, but jeez, all those naked and half-naked people riding around on horses—I can just imagine what a dream analyst would have to say about that!

Nick knew he should get up and start the day, visit Juan in the hospital. But the bed was soft, warm, and inviting enough that he just couldn't quite make himself do it. Which, come to think on it, was a little weird, because he had been needing to buy a new mattress for a while now. And why was he hearing songbirds instead of traffic noise?

That made him open his eyes, to find himself staring up, and up, and even further up at what had to be twenty-foot ceilings with elaborately gilded floral and leaf designs and a frigging crystal chandelier.

It hadn't been a dream.

"Oh, shit."

"You're awake." David packed more relief into those two words than his brother would've believed possible. Nick turned his head to see David hurrying toward the bed from where he'd been standing next to a set of glass doors that opened up onto an arched porch area that was draped with what looked a lot like the sweet peas that their Grandma Sophie grew back home. With the doors closed the scent was faint, but now that Nick was looking for it, unmistakable.

He started to sit up, stopped in mid-motion, and fell back in pain. He craned his neck to look at himself. His ribs were wrapped in bandages and his abdomen was a mass of emerging bruises. Nick swore roundly. David helped him sit up, propping a bunch of feather pillows behind Nick's back until he was reasonably comfortable.

"Nick, I'm sorry." He gave his brother a helpless look. "I swear, I didn't mean to get you into this."

Part of Nick was seriously pissed. But the truth was, his brother hadn't gotten him into anything. He'd done it to himself. *Me and my big mouth,* Nick growled mentally. He'd volunteered, thinking he was going to protect his baby brother who—truth be told— was perfectly capable of taking care of himself.

"It's not your fault. I insisted on coming."

"Yeah, well . . . bet you're regretting that now, aren't you?" David sounded rueful.

"No bet." Nick managed to find a smile. "So, how the hell did we wind up in a palace?"

"It's not the palace. You missed that. This is prison."

"Whoa." Nick took a long look around. As a cop, he'd been in a few prisons. None of them had looked like this. The bed was a dark-stained carved four-poster that was a work of art . . . and probably larger than his bedroom all by itself. The room it was in was huge, with thick, hand-woven rugs in jewel tones scattered across the white marble floor, their gold fringe bringing out the gold veining in the marble. The furniture was all elegant, and obviously valuable. Nick would have bet his annual salary that any one of the statues decorating the mantel could be sold at Sotheby's for more than his truck.

"Impressive, isn't it?" David's voice echoed a little in all that space. "But I wouldn't want to stay here long. Can't you *feel* it?"

Nick just shook his head, not sure what the heck his little brother was talking about. Other than sore, he didn't feel anything in particular.

"There are prohibitions built into the building and the ground beneath it. No one can work magic here, but it's more than that. It saps your will so you don't want to. You don't want to do anything." He shook his head. It was obvious that he was both admiring and scared. "And it's all individualized. Those sweet peas outside . . ." He gestured in the direction of the porch. Nick nodded. "They first appeared when you started waking up. Now they're fully grown and blooming. Just for you."

Nick wasn't sure what to think about that, or even if he believed it. What he did know was that he was injured, and they were in a strange place—the high-end prison of a foreign land. What happened now? Were they in danger? How were they supposed to get home? What about the language? What about food? He had so many questions racing through his head that he didn't know which to ask first. Still, the one that popped out of his mouth was the one that had him most worried.

"How do we get home?"

David sighed, and took a seat on the chair that the healer had left sitting by the head of the bed. "You're assuming we can," Dave said gloomily. "The Sidhe love humans. They used to kidnap good-looking ones and bring them here."

"And you think your boss will just let them keep us?"

"No. But they may not give her a choice."

"If they don't, how do we get out?"

"I . . . I'm not sure. There's a couple of possibilities, but—"

"But *what*?"

David sighed again and gave his brother a sour look. "But it's a little hard to explain the situation when you don't even believe in magic."

Nick grimaced. "Let's just assume that our little encounter with the bat-monsters . . ."

"Doxies," David corrected.

"Doxies, has made me change my mind. Just start at the beginning, and explain where we are and what's going on. Then we can work out a plan for how to get back."

David leaned forward, his expression avid. "Okay, but this is going to take a while, and you're not going to like it."

"I already don't like it. Now talk."

"Okay, but I don't know everything. Grandma Sophie clued me in on a lot of stuff. She's Sidhe, and was an oracle here under the name of Cephia until she got exiled. I've pieced together some more stuff she didn't tell me since I've been working at Helena's, but some of this is just guesswork."

"Just tell me what you've got."

"Right, Faerie and the human world coexist on different planes with the veil separating them. It used to be that anybody with magic could open a slit in the veil, and drag whoever or whatever back and forth between the two worlds—which is where all those old stories of fairies stealing babies and kidnapping beautiful women came from."

"Right."

"But a while back a human witch got pissed off about that and decided to make it so that only people with human magic could open a slit in the veil and that only willing adults could go back and forth: no kidnappings, no stealing babies."

"Bet that pissed them off," Nick noted.

"You have no idea," David agreed. "Anyway, that witch was Brianna's mom, and a lot of the Sidhe nobles—"

"Sidhe?"

"The ones that look most human, except taller, thinner, with pointy ears. They can use illusion and can use magic like a weapon. They also have this innate ability called the shining or shine and it's dangerous as hell. They use it deliberately to cloud people's minds and overpower their will, so that they do whatever they're told. Your amulet should help you see through it, but you'll still need to be really careful."

"Right. Go on."

"They hate Brianna because of it and they want her dead. They think her mom anchored the spell to her bloodline and that if Brianna dies they'll go back to the good old days."

"They won't?"

"Pug says no, and I believe him. I knew Helena, remember, and she was way sneakier than that."

"So Brianna can take us back."

"Yes. Or we can go back through the portal painting—if the king or Brianna operates it. It's keyed to them."

"Then how'd the doxies hijack it?"

"That's what the king wants to know. I'm guessing here, but I think somebody stole some hair, blood, something with either Brianna or the king's DNA in it and used it to open the portal. But that's just a guess."

"So, Brianna can send us back, the king can send us through the portal, or we can find somebody with human magic and they can send us back. Is that it?"

"Yes and no."

Nick growled in frustration.

David ran his hands through his hair. "I'm sorry. It's just nothing here is that simple. Magic is complicated, and Faerie is complicated, and when you combine the two it gets even worse." He glared at his brother. "And if you keep interrupting me I'm not going to be able to finish this before somebody comes back to check on you again."

"Fine. Talk. I'll shut up."

David gave him a skeptical look. "All right, the king could send us back with the portal painting. Brianna can either use the painting to send us back, or she could take us *outside of the city* to send us back. But it has to be outside of the city, because there are prohibitions built around the city as a precaution to prevent someone just bringing over an army, or a bomb, or something and leveling the place."

"Makes sense."

"Now the king has gathered most of the Fae with human magic into his service and he uses them to move things back and forth. None of them are going to help us without his express permission. I'm pretty sure the dragons—"

"Dragons?"

"Yeah, dragons. Three of them. Last of their kind. Can look perfectly human and are total badasses in any form. Anyway, I'm guessing here, but I'm *pretty sure* that they go back and forth. But I've never actually seen it."

"Dragons." Nick blinked repeatedly.

"Look, it's probably going to be easiest if you just assume that every mythical creature you've ever heard of really does exist—on this side of the veil. And everything and everyone here is dangerous as hell and not to be trusted."

"Not so different from home after all then," Nick joked.

They were interrupted by a light tap on the door.

"Yes?" Nick answered.

"It's Brianna, may I come in?"

"Please do."

When she walked in the door it was all he could do not to goggle at her. Wow, just . . . wow. She'd changed out of her jeans and into the kind of dress that wouldn't be out of place on the red carpet at the Oscars. It was a shade of blue so dark it was nearly black. Sheer as a cobweb it had a halter neckline that left a long swatch of her back bare, while the front of the gown was decorated with a pattern of sparkling crystal beads in a pattern that mimicked the constellations of a night sky. The cloth clung to her in a way that accented every delicious curve.

The front portion of her hair had been pulled back in a complicated basket weave pattern of braids held in place with diamond-headed pins. Her pale skin glowed white against the dark fabric, and there was a lot of skin showing. The gown plunged low in the front, displaying ample cleavage and a faint, faded scar to the skin just above her heart. The dress also had slits that ran from the floor high up on her thighs on both sides. Through those slits he caught a glimpse of other narrow scars, and a matching pair of midnight garters adorned with a pair of very businesslike daggers.

Diamond and sapphire studs decorated each ear, a matching cuff adorned her left wrist. She looked both exquisitely beautiful, and utterly deadly.

David let out a low whistle. "Wow boss, you look . . . amazing."

He was right. Nick had found her attractive in jeans and boots. Dressed like this, it was all he could do to keep from drooling. He didn't want to stare, but he simply couldn't help it.

"Thanks." She smiled, and the ice princess vision melted in the warmth of that expression, a tiny dimple appearing at one corner of her mouth. "I'm to dine with my father, the lesser kings, and selected courtiers in a little while, but I wanted to check in on the two of you, make sure you were okay."

"I'm good," David said.

"I'm hanging in there," Nick said.

"Good. So long as you stay in this building you should be safe. The guards won't let you out—but they won't let enemies in, either.

Saturnino will take care of getting your dinner, and while you should still check everything with your amulets, he won't risk doing anything that would harm you, or keep you here against your will."

"Why not?" David asked.

Her smile became cold, hard, her eyes darkening. "Because he knows what I'll do to him if he does."

Looking into those eyes Nick realized she meant it, and while it made them safer here, it did make him wonder if perhaps the feds weren't onto something back home. Because while she was beautiful enough to take his breath away, she was one tough customer; and, if anything, that made her even more attractive to him. Damn it.

A doorbell chimed, the tone clear and perfect, yet somehow ominous. Brianna turned toward the door. "I have to go. I'll try to get back early. I know we need to talk. But I can't promise anything."

"It's all right," David assured her. "We'll be fine."

"Here's hoping I will be," Brianna said before pulling the door closed behind her.

16

BRIANNA HAI

"Is your grace ready?" Kenneth stood at the door at the front of a group of six guards. Male and female, they were dressed identically. All were in their full dress uniforms of black, white, and silver, leather and metal polished to a high gloss. Their long hair was pulled back in the single, tight regulation braid. They were armed to the teeth, although whether it was to guard her or to protect her was anyone's guess. He, too, wore the traditional uniform, complete with the medals and rank insignia sewn onto the tunic. His cloak was of ebon velvet, its clasp a silver dragon with ruby eyes.

The dark colors were in high contrast to his blond good looks. He looked quite amazing. Even so, she found herself wishing that it would be Nick attending this evening's events with her. Kenneth was her friend, and she trusted him with her life. But he was also gay, and thus a much better romantic prospect for David than for Brianna.

"I am."

Kenneth took the midnight-blue cloak Saturnino had brought

for her from the older man, discreetly checking it for spells and weapons before holding it out for her.

"I am permitted to be armed tonight." Brianna made it a statement, although truthfully, she wasn't nearly as sure as she was trying to sound. Her status in Faerie at this moment was more than a little tenuous.

"You are," Kenneth agreed.

"Good, because I am . . . heavily."

He gave her a winning smile as he slid the cloak onto her shoulders. "Good. So are we." He held open the door for her and the guards fell into position around them, moving in perfect unison, their footfalls falling in perfect rhythm against the paving stones.

"You're looking quite lovely this evening," Kenneth observed.

"Thank you. You're looking pretty spiffy yourself."

He laughed. "I did my best. I was rather hoping that your young human friend might come to the door to see us off." He gave her a saucy wink before gesturing to the guards on gate duty to open it up for them.

"If he'd known you'd show up looking like that he would've," Brianna retorted. "And speaking of my human friends, what are my father's orders regarding them?"

"They are to be kept here and kept safe."

"Good."

The gates swung open, and Brianna's escort led her out into the large courtyard that served the palace complex. There was no dog cart for her, and while she hadn't really expected one the absence drove home again her tenuous status. Still, it was a lovely night for a walk. Her father could have arranged for it to be sleeting, or worse.

"The humans matter to you then?"

"They do."

Kenneth gave her a carefully neutral look. "You realize that could be a problem."

"I know. The nobles will use them against me if they get the chance."

"Which is why I am your escort tonight and not one of them?"

"Among other reasons."

He raised an eyebrow in inquiry.

"You are also quite devastatingly handsome, an excellent dancer— and a man I always want on my side in a fight."

"As long as you've got your priorities in order."

"Of course. I had an excellent tactics teacher."

"Yes, you did."

Several of the guards around them fought to hide their smiles. Kenneth had been teaching tactics at the academy for years— including during Brianna's brief tenure as a guard trainee. He'd built and expanded on the knowledge she'd been given by the private tutors in charge of her education as one of Leu's children. She'd proven an apt pupil. And while he'd never said a word, Brianna had gotten the distinct impression Kenneth had been disappointed when the king had cut her potential career in the guards short.

They had reached the center of the courtyard, and were forced to stop to let a dog cart with Rodan and his date for the evening drive past. Both her brother and Leelee pretended not to see her. To ease the awkwardness of the moment Brianna turned to Kenneth and, sotto voce, said, "That's my brother, excellent breeding, lousy manners." Kenneth, didn't laugh, didn't even smile. He was staring after the dog cart, his expression pensive.

"She's an odd choice for him for a date, don't you think?"

Brianna hadn't thought about it, but he was right. Leelee was half Sidhe and half pixie. She was absolutely lovely, with skin the yellow of a butterfly's wing, and short white hair with faint pink highlights that framed a face with perfect, delicate features dominated by slanted eyes the green of new grass that matched the sparkling crystals of her dragonfly wings. Brianna knew she was quite popular, with a number of powerful suitors, but Rodan had an evil reputation among the lesser Fae, and Brianna knew for a fact that he was prejudiced enough to believe in the superiority of all things Sidhe.

So why would he choose her?

"What are you thinking?" Brianna asked him.

"Your brother is up to something."

"Always. Absolutely always."

They resumed walking, taking their time so that they arrived naturally after the last of the dog carts. Brianna's father waited beneath the portico, and he greeted them both with a smile before drawing Brianna close in a hug. "I see the clothes you left still fit you."

"Barely."

He laughed. "You look marvelous. Everyone else has arrived except Eammon, but he had quite a drive to pick up Ruala. They should be here shortly. There's dancing in the mural room until dinner."

Sliding his arm around Brianna's waist he led them down the hall, his bodyguards falling seamlessly in with hers. At a gesture from the king everyone stopped at the double doors. "I think" Leu turned to the guards—"that two guards apiece will do tonight—and that does include you Kenneth. This is, after all, supposed to be an intimate welcome-home celebration."

No one argued. He was king. With minimal discussion it was determined that Brianna's party would consist of Kenneth and Gwynneth, while the king would be attended by Petros and Warrach.

Petros and Gwynneth each opened one of the double doors. The music stopped, and everyone seated stood, turning with those standing toward the door to acknowledge the arrival of the king.

Standing as she was, just slightly behind and to the left of him Brianna was able to take a good long look at the room and its occupants.

The mural room was well named. It was a large room, but small compared to the other ballrooms in the palace. Each wall was decorated with a mural by a different artist, exquisitely depicting a nature scene from an area of Faerie during one of the four seasons. Wall sconces and chandeliers held old-fashioned candles, with additional light provided by floating globes of magical light that looked a bit like soap bubbles floating through the air. Occasionally as they moved the light would be just right, and rainbows would appear, the effect both fleeting and lovely.

Rodan was obviously there, dressed in a human-style white-tie tux, with Leelee on his left arm. He stood next to his mother. Asara was radiant in white satin, pearls, and diamonds, her long blonde hair in a complicated arrangement that ended in a narrow tail of loose curls that flowed down her back to her knees. Next to her understated beauty Leelee looked a little overdone in her flapper style little black dress.

Brianna's half sister Rihannon stood in the corner beside a Sidhe noble whom Brianna was sure she should recognize, but couldn't quite place. Rihannon was lovely in an ice-blue beaded sheath that flowed like water to the floor. She wore her pale blonde hair loose, with a delicate platinum headband as her only jewelry. She would have been stunning were it not for the vacant look in her eyes—they were glossy, and empty as her smile.

In the far corner the band wore traditional tuxedos.

The band struck up the royal anthem, and the king entered the room to the sound of its refrain. Brianna waited until her father had finished making his entrance before coming through the door on Kenneth's arm. She was greeted immediately by Lucienne, who was stunning in a gown the deep green of pine needles, with emerald and diamond jewels. Her escort for the evening was

Nama'an the Moor, a gorgeous human man who'd lived in Faerie for centuries. The band began playing a waltz. Kenneth turned to Brianna. "Shall we show them how it's done?"

"I'd love to."

Lucienne laughed. "Nama'an?"

"As you wish."

They were soon joined by the other couples, everyone moving gracefully from one dance to another as the band continued playing. They were on their fourth song when King Leu appeared at Brianna's elbow and asked to cut in.

"Of course, your majesty." Kenneth bowed and stepped aside.

Leu was an excellent dancer. The two of them glided across the floor as gracefully as leaves blown across the autumn ground. Brianna relaxed, enjoying just being close to her father. She'd missed him.

"What are you thinking?"

"I've missed you," she answered honestly. "I haven't missed the politics, and the backbiting, or any of the rest of it, but I've missed you."

"Then you don't plan to stay." His voice was calm, but there was a hint of sorrow at the edges, and his beautiful silver eyes had darkened to a smoky gray.

"No. I'm sorry."

"So am I." He gave her a rueful grin. "But I can't say I blame you. You have too many powerful enemies."

"Yes, I do. Did Lucie tell you my offer?"

"She did. I've contacted the Diamond King."

Brianna nodded. As he swept her past the front doors she caught a glimpse of Eammon arriving. He looked dashing, but he was, surprisingly, alone. She might have commented on it, but her father spoke before she could.

"The investigators found out how your enemies used the painting. Somehow they had gotten three of my hairs."

Brianna very deliberately didn't look over to where Asara was dancing with Rodan. "That would explain it."

"I told you that if my carelessness had caused your difficulties I would owe you a debt."

Brianna didn't know what to say to that, so she remained silent.

"I thought I would repay that debt by doing something you hadn't asked for, but which I believe will be quite helpful to you and your guests."

"Oh?"

"For now, time in Faerie is running considerably faster than in your human world. You can spend days here, and only hours will have passed in your absence."

Brianna felt a tension that she hadn't consciously acknowledged ease within her. They could go back to their old lives. She'd been afraid . . . she knew the tales as well as anyone, tales of humans who spent a night in Faerie and returned to find that decades had passed in the human world in their absence.

"Thank you, Father. I appreciate that more than you know." She smiled up at him.

"Good. I wanted to make you smile, and now I have. You don't smile nearly often enough, Brianna. Life is meant to be enjoyed."

"I'll work on that." She kept her face serious, but spoiled the effect by winking at him. It made him laugh. He was laughing when Rodan glided up with Leelee.

"I am surprised you didn't come here with one of your human friends," Rodan observed. "I know that Eammon expected it. He asked Lucie to bring Nama'an so that he could tell them all the advantages to living in Faerie."

"They don't plan on staying." Brianna said it with a smile on her face that she hoped didn't look as forced and fake as it felt.

"But they *must*." Leelee's eyes went wide. "Truly, we need new humans, new blood. If you, of all people, take them away after bringing them here to us—"

The music had stopped, causing her words to ring throughout the room from where they stood in the center of the dance floor.

"We don't plan on staying."

The winged faerie's face contorted with rage. "Such selfishness! I wouldn't have believed a child of our king could ignore the needs of her people the way you do. But I won't allow it. I challenge you to a duel."

And there it was—the real reason Rodan had invited her. And cleverly done, too. "Duels are not allowed within the palace without the express permission of the king."

"Then we will take it outside." Leelee smiled, showing the sharp little teeth she'd inherited from her pixie relatives.

And that was the clever part. If they went outside there would be others waiting: lots of others. If Brianna defeated Leelee, another would challenge, and another, and another, until she wore down and someone managed to kill her.

"Clear the center of the room," King Leu ordered. Servants appeared from where they'd been scattered to do his bidding. "Brianna, deal with this quickly if you would. I detest burnt food and the meal is to start shortly."

"Of course, your majesty." Brianna bowed. As she did she pulled a knife from one of her garters. With quick, deft movements she sliced through the silk panels at the front and back of her dress, shortening it from floor length to where it barely skimmed mid-thigh. She kicked off her shoes as well, for while they were sensible flats, she much preferred fighting barefoot. She kept one bit of the severed cloth, but handed the other to Kenneth, who'd appeared at her side. As the ranking member of the guard present it would be his duty to officiate.

"She'll take to the air soon as she can," he warned.

"I know. I'll be fine."

He gave Brianna a skeptical look. Flying Fae were notoriously difficult to fight. He had taught her that. But it really wasn't a problem. Not anymore. She answered his unspoken question. "I've been practicing with Mei, in her various forms."

Kenneth's smile could have lit the very dungeons. "Good. Then let's get this done. I like my meat rare, too."

He left her side, stepping into the very center of the open space the servants had cleared. All of the guests to the party, the guards, and servants had gathered in a circle to watch. Raising his voice to be clearly heard by all Kenneth said, "Challenge has been given." Leelee gave him the ritual bow of acknowledgment, but her avid eyes never left Brianna.

"And accepted." Brianna bowed in turn.

"Your majesty?"

"Do it."

Kenneth raised the strip of cloth torn from Brianna's dress. "When the cloth hits the floor, you may begin."

As he was speaking Leelee crouched, powerful leg muscles bunching. Brianna gathered her will as she estimated where her enemy's leap would take her.

He dropped the cloth.

17

As Leelee leapt into the air she shouted a single word. A ball of fire the size of a basketball streaked from the tips of her fingers to explode on the ground where Brianna had stood a mere instant before. But Brianna was not there. She, too, had moved, dashing to the right. As she did she spoke a soft word and sent a wave of power into the air surrounding her flying enemy. For a split second it appeared that nothing had happened, that the spell had failed. Leelee's crow of dark glee was cut short, however, when every light globe in her vicinity exploded with a sound like shattering glass and a flare of power so that the air was lit with a rainbow of colors, each as bright as the heart of a magnesium flare. Leelee threw up her arm to shield her streaming eyes, the spell she'd been intending to throw flying wide, to explode against the winter mural on the far wall.

It was exactly the move Brianna had been hoping for. Knowing the purpose of the spell she'd shielded her eyes from the worst of the light, so that now she could see clearly, her target a dark outline against the glare. With careful precision she threw the dagger in her hand, noting with satisfaction the meaty *thunk* of it burying itself to the hilt in Leelee's exposed underarm.

Leelee shrieked in agony. Her wings beat once, twice, trying to remain airborne—each movement opening the wound further, sending a spray of arterial blood flying. She crumpled to the ground, catching herself with her knees and left arm—the right useless, her bright yellow skin dimming and taking on a grayish tone as blood spurted and pooled onto the floor beneath her.

Her eyes widened with shock, then narrowed. Brianna could see that her opponent was gathering her will for one last strike, determined to drag her enemy down with her into death.

Brianna didn't wait for it, didn't give Leelee the chance. She charged across the room in a blur of speed. Leelee tried to move, tried to prepare, but she was too slow, too weak from loss of blood. Brianna was on her in an instant, her fist slamming into the face of the fallen Fae before she could utter a sound.

Seconds later, Leelee was dead.

Brianna stood over the corpse and felt . . . very little. She was tired, certainly, the adrenaline draining from her system now that the battle was over was taking most of her energy with it. And while she would've expected to feel some satisfaction at having won the duel, she didn't, not really. It was such a waste.

God how she hated Faerie politics.

"Well done." Leu congratulated her as a trio of servants came scurrying up. The first carried a pitcher of water, with towels and washing cloths slung over his shoulder. The second held a crystal bowl: the third, soap and a mirror. All three were brownies, their wrinkled dark skin resembling the meat of some exotic nut, wide brown eyes dominating flat faces with only slits for breathing, rather than an actual nose.

"Thank you, Father." Brianna turned to look at her reflection. She was a wreck. Leelee's blood decorated her face and stained her torn dress. With the brownies' help she would be able to clean off the worst of the mess until she was reasonably presentable, for while she would dearly love to go back to Abracham House, shower, and change—or better yet, home—that was not an option.

"Moash of the Doxies has asked to parley with you at your convenience. Perhaps you can meet with him after dinner?"

Brianna scrubbed at her face, careful to avoid smearing the makeup around her eyes. Meeting with Moash was the last thing she wanted to do, but while the king had phrased it as a request, Brianna knew her father well enough to know it wasn't. "Of course, Father. Where is he staying?"

"He's under house arrest in his usual guest quarters."

Brianna dried herself with a towel, then returned it, nodding her thanks to the brownies who bowed in acknowledgment before scurrying away, their leaving perfectly coinciding with the arrival of the butler to announce dinner.

The king himself escorted Brianna to her seat, holding the chair for her and sliding it under her—this despite his rank, and hers. At the table Brianna found herself seated between Kenneth and her oldest brother, Eammon.

She turned to her oldest brother. "I'm surprised to see you here alone."

"Ruala sends her regrets. Ilsa, our youngest, has an ear infection. It will only last a day or so, but she's fussy with it. . . ."

"I understand. A sick child always wants its mother." Brianna forced herself to smile at her half brother. "How old is Ilsa?"

"Only four, Stannis and Willis are seven; and Paria fourteen."

"Four children? I think when I left you only had Paria."

"We did. And while I've had other lovers, Ruala is the only woman who's borne me children." He paused before asking, "Have you had any children?"

"No, not yet."

"Perhaps one of your human companions . . ." Eammon smiled

when he said it, but there was a tension to his posture that told her his comment wasn't as lighthearted as he was pretending it to be.

"As pleasant as that sounds, David exclusively prefers the company of other men." She didn't say anything about Nick. The thought of being intimate with him had undeniable appeal, but she didn't know him well enough yet to want children with him.

"Then you are not deeply attached to them?"

That comment set off all sorts of alarm bells in her mind. Brianna chose her words carefully. "I wouldn't say that. I did, after all, just fight a duel because of them."

"And fought it well." Eammon said it just a tad grudgingly. "But if they are not your intimate companions, surely you would consider having them stay here in Faerie. They'd have a good life here, as well you know."

Brianna sighed, Eammon was Fae to the core, and royal. Nothing she could say would make him understand the deep-seated independence and need for freedom of so many of the humans she knew. Oh, there were plenty who wanted, even needed to be ruled if it came to that. But David was not one of them, and she'd venture that his brother wasn't, either.

"Feel free to ask, but I think you'll find they're not interested."

"You think they should be given the choice?" Eammon was incredulous and didn't bother to hide it.

Brianna chose her words as carefully as if treading through a verbal minefield. This topic, after all, was the one that had led to her mother's act of criminal defiance. Everyone in the room had fallen silent, waiting her response. Was she Fae? Or was she Helena's true child?

"I consider David my vassal, and my friend. I have a duty to him—and by extension to his family. And we both know that not every human thrives in Faerie." It was not a perfect answer, by any means, but it did sidestep the bigger issue.

Eammon gave her a long look over the top of his wineglass, but let the subject drop. Still, that look told her clearly as words that, to his mind, the subject of David and Nick's freedom to leave Faerie was not decided—not in the least.

18

It was late when Brianna reached the apartments of King Moash of the Doxies. Dinner had dragged on interminably. The food had been marvelous, as had the wine, but it was hard to enjoy them when she had to keep checking every morsel and sip for poison. Just as poisonous were some of the honeyed barbs she'd been forced to intercept from Asara and the others.

Thank the deities it was over. Now if she could just get past *this* she could go back to Abracham House and take to her bed. She felt like she could sleep for a week.

Instead, she stood before a heavily guarded oaken door, its surface carved with an elaborate battle scene featuring the room's occupant, the wood's surface polished to a golden sheen.

There were guards on the door. One, Felicia, was familiar to Brianna, the second a man whom she'd met, but could never remember his name. Kenneth would know, but he'd been summoned to a private meeting with the king. Felicia rapped on the door before announcing loudly, "Her grace, Brianna Hai, *Ap Reigh* of High King Leu of the Sidhe, and winner of the battle of Cloverfield."

Brianna kept her features schooled to stillness. It had been a long time since anyone had introduced her with full formality: Hai, the honorific won when she saved the king from assassination; *Ap Reigh*, acknowledged child of the High King, though not in line for the throne; and of course the new part—winner of the battle of Cloverfield. She wasn't sure who had come up with that means of describing her latest adventure, but apparently it was now part of the official version; and wouldn't Moash just hate that.

"By all means, send her in."

The guard opened the door and Brianna stepped through, finding herself in an elegantly appointed living area with both comfortable seating, and a series of sturdy perches scattered throughout the room, with the largest grouping near the windows. The huge doxie stood on the marble tiles before the fireplace, wings furled against his body. The room was lit by an overhead chandelier, but it was set dim, so that parts of the room were in deep shadow.

Standing on the floor Moash stood nearly three feet tall. His black and green mottled scales had an almost oily sheen, his eyes glowing like banked red embers.

Brianna bowed her head in acknowledgment of his rank.

"You bow to me? But you have beaten me child. I have given my unconditional surrender."

"You are still a king."

"You do not claim to be queen? You've won the right."

"Your people wouldn't have me, and who am I to rule the doxies? I can't even fly."

He stared at her for a long moment. "You could be my queen."

Brianna stood silently, considering how best to respond. "While I am greatly flattered by your offer, King Moash, our species are not capable of interbreeding. My father, and king, wishes me to bear children, so I must decline."

He gave her a sincere smile, showing wicked teeth. "Probably wouldn't work anyway."

She returned the smile. "I doubt I'd survive the courtship."

It was meant as a compliment, and he took it as such.

"So, daughter of Leu, what do you want of me?" He gestured toward the couch. When she took her seat, he moved across from her, climbing a bit awkwardly onto a wing-backed chair.

"I would have you swear again your oaths to my father."

"Easily done."

"And I would have you bound to me as an ally—my enemies your enemies, my friends your allies, so long as we both draw breath." She paused. "And the return of the kittens, with a weregild paid to both me and Pug the gargoyle for the loss of the mother cat."

"You would have the doxies allied to you as well as the stone trolls separate from your father's alliance with us."

"Yes."

"You would value a people you so handily defeated?"

"The doxies are respected fighters, and excellent intelligence gatherers. Anyone with sense can appreciate that, and see the benefit of an alliance."

"And you believe you need fighters, and intelligence agents?"

She sighed. "I have come here directly from an intimate family gathering where I was forced to fight a duel to the death. So yes, I do."

He laughed then, and little drops of acid spittle fell onto the fabric of his chair, charring holes in it, so that the scent of burning fabric filled the air between them.

"So an alliance, with my people watching over you, and, I presume, your human guests?"

"Discreetly."

"Agreed. Although when you return to the human side of the

veil it may become problematic. I do not want to risk any of my people fading."

"I'm sure we can work something out."

"You let me off easy."

"Don't be so sure. I have a lot of enemies."

He gave her a long, considering look. "You certainly do."

19

NICK ANTONELLI

There was a light tap on the door to Nick's suite.

"Yes?"

"Your dinner, sirs," a male voice answered politely.

David rose from his seat and went over to open the door. As he did, a group of brown, noseless creatures about four feet tall came in. Three carried wooden chairs, the other pair, a matching table. An older human man wearing black silk trousers and a matching shirt with a mandarin collar and long sleeves carried a bundle of snow white linen. When the table was in place he spread a cloth over it, before deftly folding a trio of napkins into the shape of a swan and setting them at each place setting. As he did, the first group of brown servants left, to be replaced by a new set, one of whom set up one of those trestle things they use in restaurants, another put place settings of china and silver on the table. The third carried a large tray with a bottle of wine and a covered platter that emitted smells that were mouthwateringly wonderful.

Nick's stomach growled. His body might be injured, but it still wanted food, and if his nose wasn't lying to him there was steak under that cover.

The brown creatures scurried out, leaving only the human in attendance. "I am Teo, the king's personal attendant. I hope you don't mind that I join you this evening. His majesty asked me to attend to you and answer any questions you may have. Since I have been back and forth between Faerie and the human world often and recently, he felt I'd be best able to assist."

Nick wasn't sure what to say to that, so he remained silent. Peeling back the covers he moved gingerly into a sitting position. It hurt to move, not as badly as he would've expected, but enough to make things awkward. Equally awkward was the fact that he was naked.

Teo seemed to sense his discomfort. "There is a dressing gown hanging in the restroom." He gestured in the direction of one of the doors before turning his back, ostensibly to pour wine into the glasses set by each of the three plates, but probably also to give Nick at least the illusion of privacy as he slowly limped across the room.

The bathroom was a little disappointing. After all, he was in a completely different world. Shouldn't the bathroom be different? Oh, it was nice, with lots of marble and gold. There were flowering plants, too, that filled the air in the room with a faint fragrance that was light and incredibly fresh. Nick took advantage of the toilet that flushed just like the one he had at home, washed up, then pulled on the housecoat that hung on a hook on the back side of the door to his rooms.

It was long, black, and made of a thick, fluffy fabric that he didn't recognize, but was as pettable as fur and smelled like fresh linen. When he tied the belt, it hung just past his knees. Nick didn't consider himself overly modest, but he had never particularly liked being naked in front of strangers, so he was grateful for the robe.

Hurrying out to join the others, he walked into the middle of a conversation.

". . . understand, why everything seems so much like home,"

David said as he waved his talisman over all of the plates and glasses. "I was expecting everything to be exotic and strange . . . or like something out of those movies they made of the Tolkien books. But everything I've seen here, while it's really nice, is pretty ordinary."

"Ah, well that would be because you're on the palace grounds," Teo explained. "The palace complex is relatively new—most of the old buildings were damaged or destroyed in the coup that forced king Leu to take the throne. Some areas, like the throne room and the tunnels, date from the original construction. Most were rebuilt to the king's specifications—and for whatever reason, he chose to make them in the mold of the human manor houses of the time." Teo took a sip of wine from his glass, then continued, "If you get the chance to go farther out into the city, or to visit other parts of Faerie, you'll see sights that you will no doubt find as strange and wondrous as anything you've imagined." His expression darkened. "But I don't recommend you go exploring without guards. It would be very . . . unwise."

Nick was taking his seat when Teo said it, and he felt a chill run up his spine at the old man's words. So, they were prisoners—or if not, the next best thing. Still, he kept his expression pleasantly neutral, and his hand was steady as he reached for the knife to cut his steak.

"Before King Leu took the throne Faerie was much more different from Earth than like it. He has chosen to change that."

"Why?" David asked.

"I don't know. He hasn't chosen to tell me," Teo admitted. "But it is very deliberate. And the king does nothing without reason. I once heard him tell the dragon, 'If you can't come up with three good reasons to do something, you probably shouldn't do it.'"

Nick chewed a bite of steak, savoring the taste. It was perfect, absolutely perfect. He followed it with a swallow of wine. Gathering his courage he looked the old man straight in the eyes. "Will we be allowed to leave here?"

Teo met his gaze without flinching. "I know that it would make the king most happy should you choose to stay of your own volition."

"That's not an answer," Nick said coldly.

"It is the truth," Teo responded calmly. "Further truth is that, while I do not believe the king intends to hold the two of you here against your will, there are many others who do—if they can get away with it. The *Ap Reigh* Brianna is clever, and skilled, but she is only one woman. If you truly intend to go back you will need to be on your guard every moment. Faerie has always been a dangerous place for humans, and never more so than it is right now."

And those words, while honest, were all it took to ruin an otherwise perfectly good meal.

———

Nick could tell from the sunlight streaming through the east-facing windows that he'd woken early. It was time to do a little exploring. He desperately needed to use the facilities and shower. He stank. The drug the healer had given him had apparently knocked him out cold. At some point in the night his bandages had been removed. Without them he could see that the bruising had faded until his injuries looked days rather than hours old. He was able to move better than he had the previous night, as well. Crossing the room to the bath wasn't painless, but it wasn't the arduous process it had seemed the night before.

He had climbed into the shower and was standing under the spray, letting the pounding of the hot water work on strained and weary muscles, when he heard a light tap on the door.

He turned off the water and called out, "Who is it?"

A male voice replied, "Saturnino, sir. I am the majordomo for the household. The king has asked me to inquire if you are well enough to join him and the lady Brianna downstairs on the patio for breakfast."

The king was inquiring. It wasn't an order, but Nick would wager it was more than a casual invitation.

"I'll dress and come down as quickly as I can."

"I'm sure his majesty will be delighted to hear it."

Nick didn't miss the touch of irony in the words, but the humor disappeared from the man's next comment. "Maybelle will escort you and the others downstairs when you're ready."

"Who's Maybelle?" Nick stepped out onto the bath rug and began toweling himself dry with a plush sheet large enough to serve as a twin bedspread. It smelled pleasantly of herbs and fresh air, as though it had been hung to dry in a garden.

"A winged faerie with green skin—she's part pixie, very easy to recognize."

"Ah." Nick wasn't sure what else to say, so he left it at that.

He was both surprised and pleased to find his clothing—clean, pressed, and neatly folded—sitting on the countertop beside a comb, a toothbrush and, oddly, a tube of his favorite toothpaste. No razor, though, which was unfortunate because his beard needed shaving at *least* once a day. Staring into the ornately framed mirror hanging on the wall, he saw a rough shadow of black stubble on the lower half of his face . . . and Technicolor bruises decorating his chest, stomach, and abdomen.

Nick winced.

Holy shit. A king. He was going to have breakfast with a freaking *king*. Whoa. He had no clue how he was supposed to behave. It wasn't like he'd had any experience with royalty back home. He did know that the first impression he gave would be important.

Checking his reflection in the mirror he winced. He looked like he'd been in a fight . . . which he had . . . and his clothes, though presentable, were casual. But there was nothing he could do about any of that. So he dressed as quickly as he could, ran the comb through his hair one last time, took a deep, steadying breath, and stepped out into the hall.

In keeping with the rest of the palatial surroundings, the hall had tall ceilings with elaborate plasterwork, marble, and gilding, and was decorated with exquisite artwork and antiques. But all that beauty faded to nothing when he saw his guide.

Even with the advance warning it was a bit of a shock. Maybelle was a fairy. Life-size and gorgeous, but still a creature from children's books come to life—and completely naked. She stood five feet tall, her skin a green so pale it was almost white, shimmering in the sunlight streaming through a nearby window. Her hair was green, too, as if every hue from the pale green of new spring grass to the darkest shade of pine needles had been captured in the strands.

Even more phenomenal were her wings. Delicate as lace, they rose from her shoulders in a graceful, iridescent arc. They weren't made of feathers, or scales; instead, they looked as if they were formed of tiny individual crystals. They sparkled like sunlight on snow with each movement she made, scattering rainbows in her wake.

For a long moment Nick was captivated by her unearthly beauty, her nudity and grace. Then the talisman—which he hadn't even taken off in the shower—flared with a heat that made him gasp and close his eyes against the pain. When he reopened them, he was no longer dazzled. Maybelle was still lovely, but looking at her now he could see tiny flaws in her appearance that he hadn't noticed before. Her teeth were a little too sharp, her nose just a little large for her face, her eyes a tiny bit small, the expression in them alarmingly predatory.

She gave a small hiss of displeasure—which was quickly cut off as Pug and David stepped out of a nearby doorway.

At a glance it was obvious the gargoyle didn't like her, and from the malice in her gaze Nick could see the feeling was mutual.

"Shall we go? The king awaits." Maybelle's voice was petulant and sulky, like a child denied a sweet.

"By all means," Pug rumbled. "Lead on."

She led, wings fluttering so that her feet barely skimmed the cool marble floor. Pug went next. David fell into step with Nick.

"Are you wearing the talisman Bri gave you?" David whispered, so low that his brother could barely hear him. Nick nodded.

"Good. You need to use it over everything you eat and drink, just to be sure."

"Huh?" Okay, that little bit of information was not going to make him any less nervous about this whole thing.

Before David could say anything more, Maybelle called impatiently, "Please hurry. It's not good to keep the king waiting."

"We're coming," David responded. "Nick is just moving a bit slowly because of his injuries."

It wasn't entirely a lie. Nick wasn't up to moving the way he normally did. If David didn't want Maybelle knowing what they were talking about, Nick wasn't going to enlighten her. So he played along, exaggerating his discomfort a little bit. It didn't take much. He was better, but it did hurt to move, and this was a big house.

Maybelle gave an exaggerated sigh, and crossed her arms beneath her breasts, one finger tapping impatiently against the flesh of her opposite arm. It was a gesture designed to draw attention to her chest. When Nick chose to ignore it, she hissed again.

When the two humans finally caught up to the gargoyle and the fairy, Maybelle led them down a wide, curving staircase to the first floor, then across the covered walkway of the first-floor loggia into a pleasant, sunny courtyard.

Nick had to fight not to goggle at the sight in front of him. The courtyard was packed with . . . people, but not just people. There were pure Sidhe, looking almost human, but there were also others with hair and skin every color of the rainbow.

They were dressed in human clothing, but oddly. A woman who was probably nine feet tall and built like a centerfold wore tan-and-brown-striped trousers with suspenders and a brown fedora—but without shirt or bra. A short, hairy creature with a thick beard and scraggly hair was clad only in a white man's dress shirt. But his personal favorite was a male winged fairy no more than six inches tall wearing a silver bikini with a black beret.

The same brown noseless creatures that had served dinner last night acted as servers wandering between groups of picnickers with trays of food along with mix of a few stone trolls and doxies, including their king. There were humans, too, though only a very few. Everywhere he looked there was something worth gawking at. But he stiffened his spine and kept his expression neutral. Damn it, he was not going to act like some hick on his first visit to the big city.

Nick walked with the rest of his party. At a rough guess he estimated that nearly a hundred people were there, gathered in groups on what looked like picnic blankets. Clouds of what at first glance looked like brilliantly colored butterflies flitted about. A second look showed him that they had tiny, humanoid bodies—like Tinkerbell in a Disney movie. Sprites, they were sprites.

"Try not to look at anybody directly if you can help it. It'll make it easier to avoid getting shined on." David spoke softly out of the corner of his mouth so that no one would notice.

Right.

A stone picnic table dominated the center of the courtyard. Four people were waiting there, including Brianna and another gorgeous woman, a redhead dressed in shorts and a tank top. Brianna was dressed a bit more formally than the others. She looked great in black jeans and a black bustier over a crimson silk top. Her hair had been pulled into a single long braid with black and crimson cords running through it. Thigh-high boots with crimson laces up the back completed the outfit. She looked dangerous as hell and hot. The last member of the party, a male, stood, tall and proud, his black hair pulled back in a simple ponytail, revealing chiseled features that were a more exotic male version of Brianna's. To Nick's surprise, the king—and there was no mistaking that this was the king, though he wore no crown—was wearing jeans and a T-shirt. The clothes should have been casual, but somehow weren't.

Maybelle stopped approximately ten feet from the table and in a smooth movement no mere human could have duplicated, she lowered herself until she lay face-first on the paving stones, her palms turned upward in supplication.

Behind her, Pug and David both bowed. Nick joined in an instant later, gritting his teeth against the pain caused by bending over.

Maybelle spoke, her voice pitched to carry to the crowd. "I have brought your guests as commanded, your majesty, fulfilling my duty."

"So I see."

Was that a hint of droll humor in his voice? Nick wondered. He knew from David that Brianna had a wickedly mordant sense of humor. She had to have gotten it from somewhere. If it came from her father, Nick might just be able to get through the morning.

"You may go, Maybelle."

She rose and with a little jump was airborne. It startled the hell out of Nick, and he couldn't help jerking from the shock. There were titters from the crowd behind him—until the king glowered at them, creating instant, almost echoing silence.

"Good morrow, gentlemen. I had hoped to have an intimate, casual breakfast with my daughter and her guests." He gave a theatrical sigh. "Unfortunately, as usual, things got a bit out of hand." He cast a meaningful look at a nearby group—the only people dressed perfectly normally in human clothes. Based on their proximity to the king and their attire, Nick guessed they had the highest status.

"Please join me at table and allow me to make introductions." He gestured toward the empty space beside him. David and Pug took seats on either side of Brianna, leaving only one remaining spot . . . next to the king.

Feeling completely overwhelmed, Nick sat, offering a strained smile as King Leu introduced the other woman at the table as his daughter Lucienne.

Lucienne was stunning, with long red curls and ivory skin.

The party on the nearest blanket were, as Nick suspected, the rest of the immediate royal family. The setting might be casual, but Eammon, the king's eldest son, was not. He sat so rigidly he might well have had a steel pole for a spine. The top button of his white dress shirt was unfastened, but the garment had been ironed with enough starch to stand up on its own. His long red hair was pulled back in a tight braid and gleamed in a way that told Nick it was plastered with gel. His features were more square than his father's, and yet there was no mistaking his heritage. Next to him, Rodan looked the part of the family bad boy, with his "rocker chic" image. His dark blond hair was perfectly tousled and he wore a faded Slayer T-shirt and artfully shredded blue jeans. A black opal, bigger than Nick's thumbnail, dangled from his left ear. Rihannon, the daughter, was lovely, but there was a vacantness to her expression. Nick knew that look, he'd seen it often enough. *Drugs: she's on something, I'd bet my life on it.*

"This"—the king gestured to the rest of the gathering—"is the cream of my court . . . at least that portion willing to sully themselves by coming here."

There was a barb in that last, but Nick didn't think it was meant for him, though he wasn't sure who the intended victim was. King Leu might be playing nice, but Nick could tell this was not a man you wanted to cross. He had power: not just the power of position, or even that of magic. No, he had personal power, a force of personality and will that had nothing to do with his position and everything to do with the man.

The king sat and waved his hand. Servants appeared as though from nowhere, some carrying platters heavily laden with food, others pitchers of drink. The food was distributed quickly, but not one person in the courtyard took a single bite or sip until the king had. Only then did they begin to feast.

Nick was given a choice of everything from traditional breakfast foods like bacon and eggs, packaged cereals (who would have guessed they'd have Froot Loops?), to trout almondine and caviar. There was coffee, tea, and juices of every type. It looked like regular food—and smelled wonderful. But the best, overriding smell was of fresh-baked bread. Its delicious aroma filled the courtyard and Nick found his stomach rumbling with hunger in response.

David took a ration of bacon, hashed browns, eggs, and slices of the bread, which he buttered and poured honey onto. Conscious of David's warning, Nick tried to figure out how to discreetly test the food with his amulet, but didn't have a clue how to manage it.

Apparently he wasn't discreet enough. The king noticed and inclined his head to speak directly into Nick's ear.

"Let me guess. She put it on a neck chain?"

Nick blinked stupidly and Leu gave a low chuckle. "I put mine in a ring. Much more subtle." His eyes sparkled with amusement. "May I make a suggestion? When I stand up to make the announcement, drop your napkin. Wrap the chain around your hand so that the stone is on your palm. Then when you use a utensil or pick up a goblet, it'll work without being obvious. I can't tell you how many wineglasses I've 'accidentally' tipped over through the years. My mistress thinks me quite the klutz. She threatened to buy me one of those"— he struggled to find the right words—"mugs you get for babies?"

"A *sippy cup*?"

"Yes." Leu's expression managed to be both amused and angry. "That's the one. Now, before your food cools and becomes inedible, I will make my announcement."

He straightened in his seat, gave Nick a quick nod, then stood. Instant silence. Forks stopped in midair as the nobles came to attention. Nick was not sure that the people with food in their mouths even dared chew. It was impressive enough that he nearly forgot to drop his napkin. He managed, awkwardly, to dump it from his lap and bend down behind the table. He'd no more than reached to pull the talisman from around his throat when he found himself nose to nose with a very suspicious and heavily armed guard. Their eyes met for a long second before the guard's gaze moved to where Nick's hand was touching the chain at his neck. The guard reached a finger out to touch the stone at Nick's throat, the stone heated and flashed in response. Giving a nod of satisfaction, he backed away, but he watched Nick carefully as he wrapped the chain around his hand as King Leu had suggested.

The two men rose almost as one, the guard returning to his stance behind the table, Nick to his seat on the bench. So far as Nick could tell, only two people noticed. Both of them at the "family" blanket. Everyone else seemed mesmerized by what the king was saying.

". . . unconditional surrender. At a meeting last night, terms were reached. The treaty document will be signed at high noon in the palace rose gardens."

"And as most of you already know, the envoy from the oracles arrived this morning bearing the list. It appears Brianna Hai has been elevated to the position of *Ard Reigh*. Alas, there are only so many spots on the list, so her elevation has resulted in Lucienne's demotion to *Ap Reigh*."

Leu leaned forward so that both of his palms rested on the cloth covering the stone table. His features hardened, his eyes grew dark and unfathomable. Still, his words, when he spoke, were calm enough.

"For some time now there has been speculation over the disappearance of Viktor, the elder son of Ulrich." Leu's eyes locked with those of an aging warrior at a blanket in the center of the courtyard. Nick tried to get a good look at him, but it was hard in the crowd. All he could see was a square-jawed, Nordic face with icy gray eyes and a wicked scar that ran from his left cheekbone to the corner of his mouth.

Leu continued, his voice carefully neutral. "As *Ard Reigh* Brianna was the last member of court to see Viktor alive, there have been rumors and accusations spread against her, despite the fact that she was cleared of any wrongdoing."

A slow flush spread up Ulrich's neck, and Nick saw his fists clench and jaw tighten. The older man's eyes blazed, but he managed to remain silent.

Leu continued, voice and expression both grim. "My daughter has suggested, in order to clear up any last vestiges of suspicion, that she meet with Ulrich and two witnesses for each side, in the presence of the truthstone, and give her full statement."

There were gasps of shock, all eyes turned to Brianna where she sat in icy calm.

"The Diamond King has graciously brought the stone and agreed to officiate. Rather than let a cloud of suspicion continue to rest on a woman who is now officially in the line of succession, I have arranged for this meeting to take place immediately after this repast, in my private study."

"Your majesty." Nick looked at the family blanket, where Eammon had risen to one knee and, with bended head, had requested permission to speak.

"Granted."

"Since the accusations against the lady have been made publicly, shouldn't she be allowed to clear her honor publicly as well?"

Brianna made a small movement that caught Leu's eye. Raising an eyebrow, he said, "Yes?"

"May I answer?"

"Feel free." He waved a hand expansively.

She turned to face the man on the blanket, her expression one of bland amusement. "My honor is sturdy enough to withstand a few verbal barbs, Brother." Nick thought he saw a flash of bitter anger in her eyes for a second, but she continued in the same, honeyed tone. "But I thank you for your kind concern."

There was a slight cough behind Nick's shoulder. Turning, he saw the guard covering his mouth to suppress the amusement he couldn't quite keep from his eyes.

"Well said, daughter." Leu gave Brianna a brilliant smile. "Now, if this 'discussion' is finished, I'd like to get back to my meal."

"Excuse me, your majesty." It was Rihannon who spoke up this time, and for a brief moment her features had sharpened, her eyes coming into full focus.

"Yes?" Leu took his seat. One word, but he managed to put both warning and irritation into it. Damn, the man was good.

"Will we be permitted to know who the witnesses shall be?"

His eyes narrowed, but he gestured to Brianna.

"My witnesses shall be King Leu of the Sidhe and Pug the Gargoyle."

Leu turned his attention to the man in the audience. "Ulrich?"

The other man stood, giving Nick a good look at him. Most of the nobles lounging in the courtyard wore very little clothing, and what there was, was mostly flowing and soft. Ulrich was fully clad in trousers and a vest of stiff, dark brown leather. He wore a pair of weapons belts crossed bandolier-style across his massive chest. The throwing stars attached to the leather of the weapons belts gleamed in the bright sunlight.

Controlled rage blazed from his eyes and his voice bore unmistakable malice. "For my witnesses, I choose my son, Lars, and—" he paused. Turning to Nick, he gave a bitter, vicious smile, and continued, "the human, Nick Antonelli."

Nick saw Brianna start to flinch, then catch herself and school her expression to neutrality. There were spots of color on her cheeks, and her eyes, like her accuser's, were filled with anger. If Ulrich's goal had been to upset her, he'd succeeded admirably—and his smile said he knew it.

Shit.

20

BRIANNA HAI

Leu led the small procession to the library, which was much as Brianna remembered it. It was two stories tall and the length of a human football field, with fireplaces at either end of the room and several seating areas placed around the room. Two of the walls were lined with shelves of books and several rolling ladders—the kinds common to old-fashioned human libraries and large bookstores—were scattered about. Glass cases near one of the fireplaces displayed magical artifacts and a few of the valuable gifts that had been presented to the kings and queens of the Sidhe during the past several thousand years. The west wall had a large balcony with a small fireplace and a pair of desks for studying. The portal that looked into Brianna's apartment hung next to the larger desk.

The entire east wall was made up of windows that looked out onto the palace rose gardens. Brianna had no doubt that her father had chosen this location for the meeting with Ulrich so that she could step through the doors for the treaty signing without risking being late and insulting the doxies.

The Diamond King was waiting for them. He had set the covered truthstone in the middle of a circular mahogany table in the center of the first floor. Burgundy leather chairs were arranged in a ring around the table.

The group gathered at the table: the king, Ulrich and Lars, Pug, and then Brianna and Nick. Nick's expression was grim. Brianna doubted he was looking forward to this any more than she was. Damn Ulrich anyway.

Ulrich and the others moved to take seats while Brianna stared at the truthstone in its shroud. Despite the fact that she had no intention of lying and therefore no reason to fear, Brianna felt a cold knot of terror and dread fill her belly. It was bad enough that she had to humiliate herself in front of her father, Ulrich, and the others, but she couldn't imagine what Nick would think of her after this little display. It occurred to her that it shouldn't matter to her what he thought. She barely knew the man. And God knew there were plenty of other, more serious things she should be concerned with. But still, it bothered her. She damned Ulrich again for good measure. Not that it would matter.

The Diamond King came to stand beside her. She could only look at him directly for a moment, the light from the windows hitting his body was blinding enough to make her eyes water. His father had been a stone troll; his mother a gargoyle. His face and build reflected his father, as he stood five-foot-two and was nearly as broad as he was tall. He wore no clothing, so every heavily built inch of him sparkled and shone in the sunlight, casting rainbows and flashes of light around the room.

One day when Brianna had been a child, she had found him in the palace gardens, half starved by his owner. She had given him a name and played with him. He'd sit in the sunlight, moving so that Brianna had to try to catch the rainbows he cast. He'd played along, even to the point of having a Leprechaun pay her a gold coin every time she caught one. But that was before he'd been given speech, before his people had selected him as their king because of his knowledge of the Sidhe court. After her mother gave him speech, he'd continued to visit them.

There was nothing playful about him today. His expression was grim, his heavy jaw with its six-inch tusks set with disapproval. It was obvious that he didn't want her to do this, that he worried about her safety. She wasn't surprised. The truth can be a dangerous thing at the best of times. But this was a necessary risk, and she was prepared to accept the consequences.

The king was sitting in the chair nearest the table. Nick sat on the couch next to Pug. Ulrich perched eagerly on the edge of a chair on the far side of the circle, with Lars fidgeting restlessly in the seat beside him.

"I'm ready."

The Diamond King nodded. With an abrupt jerk of his glittering hand he pulled the cover from the stone.

It didn't look like much, just a large, rust-brown agate with thin bands of cream sitting on a polished wooden stand carved with the words *"Permagnum periculum est, quae veritas tenet."* Loosely translated, "There is great danger in the truth." The relic's simple appearance belied its power. To lie in the presence of the stone was instant, excruciating death. Even the slightest shading of the truth was impossible, for the stone dealt with the intent of deception as well.

The Diamond King stepped back from the table and took a seat a short distance from the central area. He had provided the stone, but his body language said clearly that he disapproved of this endeavor and wanted no part of it. Neither did Brianna really, but she had no choice.

Taking a deep breath to steady herself, she opened her mouth and began the speech she'd prepared. "Memory can be faulty—particularly after a long span of years. Words can be twisted or deliberately misunderstood. To prevent any possible error, I propose to tie the stone to my memories and project them into the room. You will all *see* the events of my fifteenth birthday from my point of view from the moment I met with Viktor until the last I saw him."

Closing her eyes, Brianna muttered the necessary words and felt the cool stone warm beneath her fingertips. There was an audible gasp from the far side of the circle. Opening her eyes, she looked at Ulrich through the misty image projected in the air above the stone. His eyes were avid, blazing with intensity as he stared at his older son on the last day of Viktor's life.

Deities, the man had been handsome in that Nordic, blue-eyed, blond way: slender, but muscular beneath his form-fitting clothing. Fifteen-year-old Brianna had been overwhelmed when he'd shown interest in her. . . . Leu's daughter or not, she was shunned by most of the court nobles.

"You are sure nobody knows where you are?" His eyes were dark, his tone suspicious.

Brianna's voice sounded sulky and very young. "I *told* you. They think I'm sleeping the day away after a late night at the ball. Otherwise we'd never get a minute alone."

Viktor glanced nervously around. At the time, Brianna had thought he was as excited as she was. Now she knew better. But hindsight is ever clear.

"You're sure you want to do this?"

She rested her hand on his arm. "I want to make you happy. If this is what you want, then it's what I want."

Gods, she sounded besotted. It was almost sickening. The image wavered in response to Brianna's emotional reaction, and she forced herself not to think, to just let the memories flow. The vision steadied and moved seamlessly forward, showing the young couple setting up a picnic in a pretty meadow far from the palace. Soon they started necking, then petting. Teenage Brianna was practically panting with need by the time Viktor opened the picnic basket and brought out the restraints: velvet ropes and silver stakes. He asked again if she was sure—and again, idiot that she'd been, she assured him that she loved him and trusted him completely.

And she had. She'd loved him. She'd trusted him enough to let him blindfold her, gag her, and truss her up naked in the middle of the wilderness where no one was likely to find her or hear what little noise she could make. She'd been an idiot. Because as soon as he had her helpless . . .

Because of the blindfold, there was nothing for the others to see, but Brianna's memories continued to unroll through sound alone: the sound of caged animals struggling against their bars; a pair of male voices, speaking softly, as though afraid someone might hear. There was no mistaking Viktor's voice, but the other . . . while it was familiar, Brianna couldn't quite place it.

"Cut her, then loose the gargoyles. They're starving. They won't be able to resist the blood."

"At least let me kill her first," Viktor said.

"You gave your word of honor that you'd do our master's bidding. She needs to be alive and conscious when they attack."

"But—"

"Does your word mean so little to you?"

Viktor let out an incoherent growl of frustrated rage and said, "This is wrong."

"You should have thought of that before you entered into the bargain."

Brianna remembered struggling and heard her soft grunts and whimpers as she fought the bonds that held her. She did her best not to feel, again, the terror, the horror of betrayal, the knowledge that she was going to die. No one would find her for days or weeks, if ever. Brianna had thought of her mother and father and had wondered who could possibly hate her so much that they'd arrange this. She was nothing. She was Leu's daughter, but she was Helena's as well: Helena, a convicted felon. Brianna would never succeed her father. She wasn't powerful or influential, hadn't been smart or talented enough to be a threat. *Why me?* she'd wondered. She still didn't have an answer.

Footsteps approached and the grunts and struggles grew in volume.

"I'm sorry." Viktor's harsh whisper was followed by her muffled scream. He'd slit her thigh with his knife: a long, shallow cut, enough to draw blood, but not nearly enough to nick the artery and risk her bleeding out.

The gargoyles shrieked and growled, seemingly going insane at the scent of blood. There was the sound of stone slamming against metal. Brianna could hear guttural growls and high-pitched whines as the gargoyles struggled to free themselves.

Viktor uttered the harsh syllables that released the magic that bound the cage. The scrape of the metal key in the lock was oddly loud in a sudden, breathless silence. Brianna could see nothing, but she could feel the tension; imagine the gargoyles crouched, readying themselves for escape. Even the birds in the trees grew still.

The silence was broken by the crash of metal on stone.

Things happened so fast—almost in an instant. Brianna shuddered, remembering the sharp scent of urine as she wet herself in pure terror, her body rigid.

Then vision was back, and she saw Viktor, screaming, running away from the clearing, three ravening gargoyles in hot pursuit. A fourth gargoyle loomed over her, all teeth and claws. Even in that first moment, Pug had been oddly quiet, his voice a barely audible rumble.

"You are the daughter of Leu of the Sidhe and the human Helena Washington."

Brianna nodded.

"We are honor bound not to harm you." He leaned forward. Sliding a razor sharp claw between her cheek and the fabric, he cut the gag from her face.

"Why?" she gasped.

He didn't answer. In fact, he seemed almost incapable of more speech. His body trembled, his movements jerky and uncoordinated. Still, he began trying to cut through the velvet restraints binding her arms. It wasn't easy. Apparently they'd been reinforced with magic, and the gargoyle had to stop for long periods of rest between short bouts of sawing.

"Are you all right?" she asked. It was a stupid question. He obviously wasn't.

"I'm dying. They captured me weeks ago, and I haven't had anything to eat or drink since."

And there she was, helpless and bleeding. The perfect meal to save his life, and instead of saving himself he was struggling to free her . . . struggling, and *failing*.

"Would blood help?" Brianna's voice quivered.

"I don't trust myself not to tear your flesh."

Good point. An *excellent* point. But she continued. "You're too weak to work magic or cut the ties without blood. If you die, I'll die right here beside you. I think it's worth the risk." Gods, how hard it had been to say that. She had been so terrified, her heart pounding like a trip-hammer in her chest.

Brianna pulled her hand away from the truthstone, breaking the connection and the spell. What happened next between her and Pug wasn't anyone else's business. The sight of Viktor fleeing his pursuers was the last she'd had of him. To her knowledge, no one had seen either him—or those three gargoyles—again. There were tears in her eyes, but she blinked them back and swallowed hard, then surveyed her audience.

King Leu looked like a statue carved of ice—except for his

eyes, which blazed with a fury she'd never witnessed before. It was bad to see that expression on the face of a king—that look had started wars. Brianna had never thought she would see her father wearing it.

The Diamond King was sitting in the shadows. Without the distraction of light and rainbows reflecting off of the faceted stone she was able to see the troubled expression he wore. Ulrich might well have been carved of stone as well. Lars looked as though it was all he could do to keep from being sick.

Brianna turned her gaze to Nick last. Brianna's stomach was in knots as she met his gaze and saw sorrow and a level of compassion she wouldn't have dreamed possible.

His look strengthened her. She straightened. Taking a deep breath, she addressed the assembled group. "You've seen for yourselves what happened. I have no idea what happened to Viktor or the gargoyles chasing him."

"Are we allowed to ask questions?" Ulrich's voice sounded strained and strange.

"Brianna?" There was no mistaking the rage in that one word uttered by her father. She hoped the anger was not directed at her.

"What do you wish to know?" she asked.

"Do you know who was holding my son's leash? Who was ultimately responsible for this . . . atrocity?"

"No. I couldn't imagine who would want me to die so horribly. During our long walk back to civilization, Pug and I discussed whether it might have been an attempt to start a war between the Sidhe and the stone trolls. That was one of the reasons I didn't investigate or come forward." Brianna gave Lars a long, intense look. "If I had, my first act would have been to question Lars. He and Viktor were so close, I can't imagine he wouldn't have known something about the plot. Capturing and holding one gargoyle is difficult. Four . . . well, that would require a group of Sidhe."

Brianna wouldn't have thought it would be possible for Lars to pale further, but his skin turned a sickly shade of green as he faced his father's silent, accusing, stare.

He swallowed convulsively. "Father," he said, and Brianna knew, instinctively, that he was going to lie.

"Don't . . ." The warning sprang to her lips as she felt the gathering of power in the air around the truthstone.

"I swear I knew nothing about an attempted murder."

The room seemed to darken, as if all light in the space were being sucked into the stone. Brianna felt her ears pop from the sudden drop in air pressure. It was hard to breathe, as if there weren't enough oxygen. Spots formed in her vision, so that she wasn't sure if what she was seeing was really happening. But flickers of light, blinding as miniature stars, formed in the darkness surrounding Lars. They circled him, slowly at first, then gaining speed until they generated a blur of light and color and a sound like the roaring of a tornado. It was hard to see, but Brianna thought she glimpsed the skin flattening against the bones of his face: reddening, burning, blistering, and crisping in the heat. Through watering eyes she saw his shrieking body burn to ash that was sucked into the relentless, tornadic winds.

21

KING LEU OF THE SIDHE

It was a terrible way to die, and a horrible thing to see happen to one's child. Leu couldn't help but feel sympathy for Ulrich, in a very real way he'd lost both of his sons on this morning: Viktor might live, but was not the man his father had believed him to be, and Lars was dead without honor.

And yet, while he had sympathy for Ulrich, he also found himself rightfully proud of his daughter. It had taken courage for her to show them that day and not just because she was in the presence of the truthstone. At only fifteen she'd faced the risk of being torn to shreds by the gargoyle when it was necessary for her escape. It made him proud.

It also made him furious.

It should never have happened. When it did, she should have come to him.

She hadn't.

He'd wager Helena had taken part in that decision.

Leu's fists clenched, and he swore under his breath. Damn the woman. He'd loved her—and hated her with pretty much equal passion. She'd been the only person who ever truly stood up to him, defying him outright with the courage of her convictions.

Their relationship had been an unmitigated disaster in terms of his rule.

But she had given him their daughter.

And what a daughter she was.

Brianna would make a magnificent queen if it came to that. Such a pity the Sidhe nobles couldn't appreciate it. Then again, they couldn't appreciate anyone who wouldn't bow to their influence. The only reason they supported Eammon was the belief that they could manipulate him.

They're wrong in that. He is intelligent, but less clever than I'd wish him. Strong, and stubborn—and he holds a grudge 'til doomsday. Ruala has been good for him, too. She leads him to what he needs to see without trying to push. I could not have picked a better woman for him. He will do what he believes is right, and damn the cost.

Rodan . . . Rodan took after his mother's family. Asara was descended from the Northmen—and Valjeta come to that. Rodan has the cleverness Eammon lacks, along with a streak of ruthless practicality needed in a king. But there is a thread of cruelty that runs through him that's concerning. Rodan would be a strong king, but he might not be a good one.

Leu stood at the library windows, facing the garden, but staring at nothing. The treaty signing was over. He had decided to claim a few minutes of solitude before whatever the next crisis that required his attention raised its ugly head. So he'd come here to think, leaving orders that he was not to be disturbed for the next hour.

It would be one of those three, Leu could feel it. Not Lucie, and not just because she'd dropped off the list. Not Rihannon, whom he loved but would gladly throttle for having been stupid enough to become involved in drugs and unwilling to wean herself of them.

Which one? In times of war the High King could choose his successor. It was imperative that he choose wisely. Because while he hoped to live through the upcoming civil war, there were no guarantees, and the auguries didn't look good.

Years ago he'd raged at Fate in all her aspects, and Cephia for having spared him and none of the others. He had not wanted the crushing responsibility of the throne—and if they could twist the threads of life to save him surely they could have saved his father, mother, *any* of the others.

He'd been so alone. And the curse of the crown was that he still was.

He wouldn't wish that on anyone, least of all one of his children. And yet one of them had to succeed him for Faerie to continue. An acceptable High King or Queen must take the throne.

He had to decide.

A tap on the door interrupted his thoughts. He glanced at the clock, the hour was already gone. So fast, time was moving so very fast. There was no more time to waste.

He needed to choose a worthy successor in case he couldn't manage to snatch victory from the jaws of his enemies. Whoever he chose, the others would hate him for it now. The chosen one would hate him later.

22

LUCIENNE

It was as well-planned and neatly executed a trick as Lucie had seen her siblings pull since their childhood. As breakfast had ended the king had swept Brianna, Pug, and Nick with him toward the library leaving David unattended by all but the guards. Lucie would have gone to him herself if Eammon, Rodan, and Ruala hadn't immediately surrounded her, offering condolences on her having dropped off the list and asking innumerable questions. By the time she managed to extricate herself without mortally insulting any of them all she could see of Brianna's human vassal was a glimpse of his back ducking through one of the servant doors with Rihannon and a gorgeous male toady by the name of Brendan—as notorious a drug user as anyone in the kingdom.

Oh, that was not good. And it left Lucie with a choice. She could pretend she hadn't noticed, making Eammon and the others happy. Or she could try to intervene—which would piss them off, but put her solidly in Brianna's good books.

Damn it anyway. The human really should know better.

But either he didn't, or he couldn't help himself.

She really should mind her own business, in the interests of her own continued health and well-being.

And still she found herself hurrying down the path toward that doorway, without so much as a clue as to what she'd do if she actually did catch up with the pair of them, just the absolute certainty of her other sense screaming that if she didn't there would be real, serious trouble.

The door was unlocked when she tried it. The hall it opened into empty. Still, she could hear Rihannon's clear soprano chattering cheerfully on about showing David the amazing artworks in her father's gallery in the main palace.

The only thing was, their father didn't *have* a gallery. The whole blasted place was used to display his collection. It was a lie, and while among the Fae lying was for weaklings, David wouldn't know that and Rihannon obviously didn't care what he thought of her anyway.

Think Lucie   if she's taking him to the palace she'll need to go through the front gate. It's the only way out.

Dignity be damned, she slipped the strappy sandals from her feet and bolted back out the door and through the garden and past the greenhouse ignoring the stares of everyone she passed.

There, in front of the gate, a dog cart waited, it's carriage covered, despite the beautiful morning. She skidded to a somewhat breathless stop in front of the carriage. "Who are you here for?" she asked the gnome who was driving.

"I am commanded to wait for the *Ard Reigh* Rihannon and none other. I am sorry *Ap Reigh*, for I see you are in a hurry."

Lucie thought furiously. She only had a minute, maybe two before Rihannon arrived—Rihannon, who now outranked her, damn the lists anyway.

"Fine, now here are my orders. Disable the carriage so that it cannot be used until after repairs."

"Ap Reigh?"

She gave him the glare she'd practiced before the mirror, petulant and stupid, but mean. "Do it now! She's insulted me. I can't
challenge her, but I *can* make her walk." Lucie smirked.

It worked, he set to it without further argument, the prank
definitely in character with the person he believed her to be.

Lucie thanked the deities. It might be useless, and a waste of
time, but if she was unable to find a way to stop Rihannon from
taking David, at least having the carriage disabled would slow
them down, leaving them on foot or waiting for another dog cart.

She'd barely had time for three breaths when Rihannon and
Brendan appeared with one of her favorite male toadies, the two
of them half carrying David.

Lucie hurried toward them hoping to buy a minute or two for
the gnome to do as she'd bid. "Rihannon, what in deities name do
you think you're doing with that human?" Her greeting wasn't at
all diplomatic, but direct enough that her sister would feel com-
pelled to stop and address her rather than just brushing past.

"He's unwell. Morguenna is at the palace." She gave Lucie a
positively poisonous smile. Brendan, meanwhile, seemed to think
better of the whole business, taking the opportunity of the confrontation between the sisters offered to slip quickly away.

Lucie let him go. Rihannon was the bigger danger. Besides,
her sister hadn't lied. Both the infirmary and Morguenna's permanent quarters were in the palace, and David looked like death.
His skin was gray and clammy, his eyes glassy and unfocused—
nothing like the handsome and animated companion Lucie had
sitting beside her just a few moments ago at breakfast.

"Morguenna can come here," Lucie countered, and before Rihannon could argue or even say another word Lucie shouted to the
guard at the gate. "Summon Morguenna, at once. Tell her the
human, David Antonelli is gravely ill."

The guard nodded. Stepping outside the ring of protections

surrounding the property he made a series of gestures. The air in front of him took on a glassy sheen, and Lucie saw the image of Morguenna's face reflected there.

Rihannon hissed in displeasure. "That was poorly done sister. You will regret it."

Lucie's temper snapped, "*Look* at him Rihannon! I don't know what you gave him, and don't much care, but he'll be no use to anyone dead, and that's what will happen if we don't get him help, and now."

Rihannon scowled down at him. "It wasn't supposed to happen like this. I tried to talk to him, but he wouldn't cooperate—even when I used the shine on him and took his talisman. Brendan said we'd have to drug him. I just gave him a little bit."

David's breathing was barely audible, his body totally limp.

"A little bit of *what*?" Morguenna had jumped down from a dog cart and rushed up and through the gates while Rihannon was speaking. Her voice cracked like a whip.

"You do not speak to an *Ard Rxigh* in that tone, healer." Rihannon whirled on the older woman, her eyes narrowing with hatred.

"Just tell her Ri," Lucie said. "She needs to know to fix this. You don't want him to die."

"Are you so sure?"

Lucie counted to twenty internally before answering. Getting Rihannon more upset would be counterproductive—never mind how much she really *really* wanted to throttle the little bitch.

"Think how disappointed Rodan and the nobles would be," Lucie suggested, "and how furious it will make Brianna. She may not be able to duel or kill you, you're on the list after all. But she can make you wish you were dead."

Rihannon visibly winced at their brother's name. At Brianna's she scowled. "She'd do it, too."

In a heartbeat, and without a qualm. Lucienne didn't even blame her.

"Fine, it was Demon's Blood."

Lucie saw Morguenna's expression darken, a fine rage began burning in her eyes. Turning to Lucie she said, "Quick, we need to get him to the infirmary at the palace if he's to have any hope at all."

23

NICK ANTONELLI

"Deities, what a queen she would make. I just pray her father doesn't choose her to rule."

"Why?" Nick asked the Diamond King. They were standing in front of the French doors, watching King Leu escort Brianna down the path through the formal gardens and out of sight. Behind them, Leu's assistant was barking orders to scurrying servants trying to clean up the mess created by Lars's death.

"Because I like her. I always have. I would see her happy. And while she would be a great queen, ruling is not a happy business."

Based on what Nick had seen of her today, he believed it. It was a side of royalty that most people don't think about, the price they paid for all the fame and riches. Brianna had been forced to endure an emotionally brutal morning, including witnessing a horrific death from inches away. In fact, she'd been standing close enough that there were burn marks and smudges of soot that was all that was left of Lars on her clothes. But after just a few minutes rest she'd insisted on going forward with the treaty signing rather than risk offending the doxies. It made sense politically. Nick understood that. But a part of him was pissed that she had to do it, and that they'd not only let her, they'd encouraged it.

"I've been meaning to ask, how are you doing?"

"The injuries are healing."

"Good. But that's not what I meant." The stone troll gave Nick a very direct look. "You've been through a great deal of trauma over the past couple of days. There's been a lot to absorb—"

Talk about your understatement. These past two days had been hell, both here and at home. He thought about Juan, wondered how he was doing, and realized that he hadn't thought or worried about his best friend . . . really since he arrived in Faerie. A wave of guilt hit him. Juan was injured, maybe dying . . . and—

The Diamond King noticed his distress. Placing his hand on Nick's shoulder he said, "I'm sorry. I did not mean to make it worse."

"It's not your fault. It's just . . . I've been running from one crisis to the next so fast I haven't had time to think. This is the first time I've slowed down enough for it to really hit me. I really am in another world."

"You really are. And if the Sidhe nobles have anything to say about it, you'll be staying here."

Nick's head jerked back as if he'd been slapped.

"Brianna's already had to fight one duel so you could go home. The nobles see you and your brother as a symbol. How Leu handles your staying or leaving will have huge repercussions. But it has occurred to me that its possible nobody has bothered to ask you what you want. Given a choice, do you want to go home? Or would you stay here?"

"Home. Definitely home."

Nick thought about his life in the normal world, where the worst that was likely to happen was he'd get shot, lose his job, or both. Amazing what a difference a day could make in a man's attitude.

The Diamond King gave him a long look. "We should probably leave. They don't dare tell me to go, but they need the room." He sounded amused. "Would you mind accompanying me to my quarters? I would like to speak with you for a few minutes, and I need to put this"—he patted the pouch with the stone—"behind wards before some idiot tries to steal it."

Nick hesitated. He didn't know this guy. Yes, Brianna considered him a friend—but he didn't know her that well come to think of it. God he hated feeling so out of his depth. What was he supposed to do? Was there anybody here besides his brother he dared trust?

Nick took his time making the decision, with Adam watching him patiently. Finally, the stone troll reached down to loosen the drawstrings of the pouch. "If it will help, I swear to you by this stone and on my honor that I mean you no harm and will do nothing deliberately that would affect your ability to choose your own path."

The rock flashed in response to the words—but otherwise was quiescent.

Nick looked into the creature's eyes. They were filled with compassion. And hey, as oaths go, that was a good one. Nick had seen firsthand what that stone could do.

"Okay, good enough I guess." He did want to get out of here. He'd been trying to put a good face on things, pretend he was fine ("fake it 'til you make it" as Juan always said). But the truth was he was still a little in shock from everything that was going on, particularly at how Lars's death was being handled. He was not sure what he had expected, but everyone was being so damned matter-of-fact. A man had just died a horrible death, and the only people who seemed affected were Brianna, Nick, and Ulrich. Granted, Lars had conspired to murder Brianna, but it just seemed wrong that life was taken so cheaply here. He hadn't loved all the hoopla about the gangbanger's death back home, but damn it, at least there *was* hoopla.

Nick shook his head, trying to get his mind to focus. "Right. Let's go."

The stone troll lifted his cloak from a chair and settled the hooded garment over his shoulders. Immediately the light in the room dimmed as the sparkles and rainbows that poured from each facet of his body were cut off.

As the two men left the library, the Diamond King paused to address one of the bustling servants. "Please have someone find the gargoyle, Pug. He was last seen giving his statement to Ulrich and the Duty Captain of the Guards. Tell him we will meet him at Abracham House."

"Of course, your majesty." The servant bowed low. "It would be my pleasure."

"Thank you." He swept down the hall with Nick a step behind him, feeling out of place. Everywhere they went servants and nobles alike stopped what they were doing to clear a path for them and bow in respect. At first it surprised Nick that the troll didn't have bodyguards, but then it occurred to him: what exactly could damage a five-foot-four, mobile, intelligent piece of solid diamond? Nick couldn't think of a thing. The troll was practically assassin-proof.

"You should call me Adam." The stone troll glanced over his shoulder to make sure Nick was keeping up with his brisk pace.

"Your majesty . . ." Nick protested, "I'm not sure—"

"I am." He gave Nick a long look. Nick wished he could read his expression, but concealed in the shadows of the hood, his face was, for all practical purposes, invisible. It would make him one hell of a negotiator, or poker player for that matter.

"My proper name is Adamante. I prefer that my friends call me

Adam. Being king is a relatively new thing for me. For the most part I dislike the trappings." Nick heard a smile in the creature's voice.

They passed into a secondary corridor that branched off of the main hall. The place was a gorgeous, well-decorated maze of marble and columns, a museum run amok. It occurred to Nick—belatedly—that he was following a relative stranger and that without a guide, he'd be lost in an instant. Still, oddly, Nick trusted the Diamond King.

"Here we are." Adam stopped in front of a set of elaborately carved wooden doors and whispered a few words under his breath. Nick suddenly saw a web of blue and red lines overlaying the entrance; the lines shimmered, then seemed to withdraw to the edges of the door frame.

Adam pushed the door open and passed through. Nick followed, but couldn't resist looking behind him. Sure enough, the web moved back in place the minute they were through, before the door closed.

"Wards," Adam explained. "I'm not surprised you can see them, based on your bloodlines. Cephia was a remarkable woman. A shame that she had to leave, but that's politics."

"You knew my grandmother?"

"Knew and liked her. I'm not surprised she didn't fade in the human world. She's always had quite a strong will."

That was the truth. No doubt about it.

"Grandma Sophie was a Faerie." Nick shook his head, bemused.

"I wouldn't use that term with any of the Sidhe if I were you. Most would take mortal insult. They put themselves far above the rest of us."

"Why?"

"An excellent question, and not one I can answer. Still, Pug tells me there is plenty of prejudice in the human world, so you shouldn't be surprised to find it here."

Nick had no good answer to that, so he remained silent, taking time to look around the room as he gathered his thoughts. So much had happened his mind was reeling.

While his own rooms at Abracham House were nice, the king's suite was magnificent. Thanks to time spent with his brother, David, Nick had picked up a fair amount of art knowledge. He was pretty sure that the sculpture in the corner was by Michelangelo, and he'd bet that at least two of the paintings on the walls were original Monets. He wished David were here. His brother would truly appreciate the beauty of each piece.

"It's funny," Nick said, "I've known my grandmother all my life, but now I feel like I've never really known her at all."

"She is a remarkable and complex woman. Very willful, very determined. It took great courage to do what she did, knowing the kind of enemies she would make. But she had the courage of her convictions. I don't think it even occurred to her to hesitate."

"You sound like you admire her."

"I do." Adam smiled. "In truth, I've liked all of Leu's mistresses but one."

Nick blinked at the thought of his grandmother with the king. But in a weird way, it wasn't as shocking as it should have been. Grandma Sophie was unique. He could almost picture the two of them together.

"Which one do you dislike?"

"Asara," Adam said. "I'm very old. Before I was royal, I spent generations enslaved by one of the noble families. My most recent owner was the Lady Asara."

"Oh." Nick wasn't sure what to say to that. From the little he'd seen of Asara at breakfast, he was betting condolences were in order, but he couldn't be sure. He'd learned long ago that when in doubt, make neutral noises. There were times when it was good to stir the pot, make things happen. At other times it was better to let a witness tell his story in his own way—to shut up and listen without passing judgment.

"Asara is wicked, but she is *nothing* compared to some of her predecessors." Adam gave Nick a long look. "I would say the worst, the one truly evil person I was owned by, was her grandmother Valjeta. Oddly enough, she's the one responsible for your grandmother's exile."

Adam dropped the leather pouch containing the truthstone into a carved wooden casket sitting on a table. With a sigh that sounded to Nick like relief, he closed the lid and tripped the lock. Going down on one knee he moved a thick oriental rug aside to reveal a floor safe. He muttered something—presumably a spell— then worked the dial and opened the safe. He set the box with the truthstone in it with exquisite care. Once it was safely inside he slammed the safe closed, twisted the dial, and muttered another batch of words.

"Thank the deities that's done. I hate that damned rock." Adam smoothed the rug back into place and rose to his feet, then crossed the room and opened a cabinet to reveal an array of liquor bottles. "After everything that's happened this morning, I need a drink. You?"

Nick hesitated. He could definitely use one, but he remembered David's warning.

Adam smiled. "Smart of you to be careful. But I did already give you my oath." He reached into the cabinet, choosing a stoppered crystal bottle of amber liquor. With practiced movements he poured a generous portion into a cut crystal glass.

"In that case, I'd love one. It's been a long morning." After a moment's inner debate he decided to ask the king . . . Adam a question that had been bugging him. "David has me checking everything I eat and drink, and so is he. The king does, too. But I don't see Brianna or any of the others doing that. Why?"

"It may be that they're just being subtle about it," Adam suggested, "or it's simply that they don't need to. You and David need to be protected from enchantments in the food or drink that would trap you here in Faerie forever. Leu is always on the lookout for assassination attempts." He shrugged. "Ultimately, it's in your best interests to do it if you want your life to remain in your own control." Adam poured a second helping for Nick and handed him the glass. "Have a seat. Make yourself comfortable."

Nick settled onto the couch. As discreetly as he could he checked the drink, using his amulet. Once he had the all clear, he took a drink. It was scotch, aged to a smooth perfection. Then again, what else would you expect between kings?

Adam took a seat in the chair across from Nick and took a long pull from his glass. The liquor, Nick noted, just disappeared. He'd wondered, since the Diamond King was made of clear crystal, if he'd see it pass down, and was glad that he hadn't. That would just be too weird.

"I'm sorry you had to be there today. It was a cruel trick by Ulrich, but he's certainly paid for it."

Cold, but true. And while he'd barely met the man, Nick found he felt sorry for Ulrich—he couldn't imagine how horrible it would be to watch your son die like that. He shuddered at the memory, and took a long pull of alcohol in an attempt to warm the chill that seemed to creep into his bones at the memory.

Adam was about to say something further, when they were interrupted by a knock on the door.

"Yes?"

A brownie appeared in the doorway, looking anxious. "Your majesty, I apologize for the interruption, but I was told the human Nick was with you here."

"I am."

"Sir, I've word from the guards that you're needed at the palace infirmary right away. Your brother has fallen ill."

Nick leaped to his feet, spilling his drink as he did. Adam too, stood, and it was he who spoke. "I'll take you there."

Nick set the glass down without really seeing where he put it. He rushed toward the door, but found Adam blocking the way.

"Get out of my way." Nick's voice was a low, threatening growl.

"Are you armed?"

Nick glared at Adam. "No."

"Well, you need to be. And I'm coming with you. It could be the truth, but it could also be a trap."

24

BRIANNA HAI

Thank the deities that was done. The confrontation with Ulrich was over, for good or for ill. The treaty with the doxies was signed and in full force. She, David, and Nick were now officially guests, free to move about as they willed. Well, her will was to get the hell out of here just as soon as tonight's banquet was over. Every minute, every *second* they spent here was a danger. Even standing here waiting at the head of the line for the dog carts her shoulders were tense, all her senses alert for a possible attack.

I cannot believe I was actually homesick for this place.

Not anymore. And yet, it had been good to see her father, and Lucie, Adam, and even Eammon. She smiled at the thought of his growing brood with Ruala and determined that it would do no harm at all for her to send presents to the children—they'd consider anything from the other side of the veil an exotic treat.

There were one or two others she had not seen yet that she'd like to. A visit to Elena would not be amiss before she went home. Frankly, it seemed odd that her old friend hadn't already visited.

Abracham House was not so far from her tree. The dryad had often stopped by when Helena and Brianna had been in residence. But there'd been no sign of her thus far, which seemed . . . odd.

"*Ard Reigh*," the brownie Jinna pushed through the crowd, many of whom grumbled against her temerity in doing so. "You are needed at the palace infirmary. The human David Antonelli is gravely ill."

There was a second of silence, followed by the rush of voices. Brianna ignored them all. Turning, she sprinted back into the palace, not caring who saw or what they thought. *Gravely* ill meant dying. If David died, here in Faerie, it would be her fault for having brought him, and she would never forgive herself for it.

The palace infirmary took up the basement portion of the west wing of the palace. It wasn't as large as a human hospital—most Sidhe, particularly the nobles who would be on the palace grounds, had enough personal magic to heal minor injuries without assistance, and most of the nobility kept a family healer on staff for major problems. Still, there were enough humans, part humans, and lesser Fae on the palace staff to warrant having two full healers and four assistants at any given time.

The patient care rooms were downstairs, as were all of the supplies and sundry, but to reach those rooms required passing through a lobby on the main level of the west wing with a small waiting area for friends and family of patients and a single large desk that barred access to both the stairs and elevator leading down. This desk was always manned by a clerk chosen for the ability to be both polite and formidable.

That august individual took one look at Brianna, bowed, and got out of her way.

Unwilling to wait for an elevator, Brianna thundered down the stairs. She'd lost Jinna somewhere along the way, the brownie being unable to keep up with the larger woman's speed.

Brianna was met at the base of the stairs by a large male healer whose name she didn't know and a pair of red-robed assistants. All three gave her courteous bows, but barred her entrance.

"*Ard Reigh,* perhaps it would be better if you waited upstairs," the healer suggested.

"You might as well let her in, everybody else is here." Morguenna's voice was clearly audible, coming from the treatment room at the end of the hallway. She sounded frustrated, disgusted, and more than a little angry.

The men stepped aside, letting her pass, and Brianna rushed to join her friend and the healer.

The treatment room was large, well lit, well stocked, and, like a human hospital, smelled faintly of antiseptic. But the shelves mounted on the white walls held more than traditional human implements of healing. There were spell components, potions, well-thumbed grimoires, and more.

David lay stretched out on a hospital bed with Nick standing on the left side of David, and Morguenna and a red-robed assistant worked magic and medicine on him with quiet intensity on the right. Lucienne perched on a chair nearby, her face pinched and drawn with worry, but with a flash of anger in her eyes. Beside her, Adam stood still and silent, his expressions unreadable.

The moment Brianna stepped through the door Nick rounded on her. Eyes flashing, fists clenched, he stormed across the room until they stood toe-to-toe.

"This is all your fault. You tricked us into coming here."

"Bullshit." Lucie's voice was crisp.

He whirled, furious, but she continued relentlessly. "You are both adults, with free will. If you hadn't actively chosen to come she wouldn't have been *able* to bring you."

"We didn't know . . ."

"Again, bullshit. You were following a doxie raiding party.

Don't tell me you couldn't see it was dangerous. You're not that stupid. No, you don't get to blame Brianna for this. She's done everything in her power to keep you safe." Lucie stood, and while she was not as tall as Nick, she was obviously not intimidated by him. "But Faerie isn't safe for humans, never has been. The only reason your brother is alive at all right now is that there is also Sidhe blood in his veins."

"He's part Sidhe?" Morguenna's tone was avid.

"He told me so. His grandmother Sophie is an exile."

Morguenna looked from Lucie to Nick. Her eyes were alight, her expression eager. "Is this true?"

"Yes."

"What are you thinking, Morguenna?" Brianna asked.

"There is an antidote—combined with magic, it might be enough. I wouldn't dare try it on a regular human. It's too dangerous."

"If it will save him, do it." There was no hesitation in Nick's voice—it was the exact same lack of hesitation, the determination to protect his brother without regard to the cost, that had brought him through the veil with her in the first place. Obviously he hadn't learned caution from that mistake. But she had.

"What will it involve?" Brianna addressed Morguenna directly, ignoring Nick's scowl.

"David has been given an overdose of Demon's Blood. We've been trying to counter it with magic and the cures I use on humans, but it's simply too powerful and he's got too much in his system. The antidote is meant for the Sidhe, and works with their innate magic to help counter the Demon's Blood, but he has to *have* magic, and anything latent will be permanently enhanced."

"Do it," Nick ordered.

Morguenna looked to Brianna for confirmation, which obviously infuriated Nick, but he kept his mouth shut.

"How will we know if it works?"

"If it works, David's condition should improve immediately. It will be obvious. This really is his best hope, *Ard Reigh*."

Brianna looked down at David's still form on the bed. It was obvious something needed to be done, and now, or he wasn't going to make it.

She turned to Nick, looking so angry, frustrated . . . helpless in the face of his brother's illness. He'd had no control over anything in his life since he'd been on this side of the veil, but he'd kept himself together admirably. But this, this was the one thing that was proving to be too much.

He didn't beg, didn't say the words, but the plea was there in his eyes as he looked at her.

"Do it."

As she said it, Lucienne was moving toward the door, intending to use the confusion caused by the spell preparations to cover her exit.

"Stop right there." Brianna's command was just that. Lucie flinched, but stopped.

"Was it you who did this to him?"

Lucie turned, but before she could answer, Morguenna spoke up. "No, *Ard Reigh*, it was not the *Ap Reigh*."

"Then who?" Brianna's voice was cold as midwinter, harsh and cruel. Brianna saw Lucie flinch again in response to the words, but it didn't matter to her.

"The *Ard Reigh* Rihannon and Brendan," was Morguenna's prompt reply.

Brianna was filled with an instant, cold fury. She felt her power build, saw the light in the room brighten as her magic brought with it the shine she usually lacked.

"Brianna . . . *Ard Reigh*." Lucie's tone was urgent. "You mustn't, you *can't*. She's on the list. It would be treason."

Lucie was right. She couldn't kill her sister, couldn't call her out for a duel—unless she wanted the totally unsatisfying spectacle of watching her chosen champion fight her sister's. *And isn't that just handy for Rihannon,* Brianna thought bitterly, and stopped, a slow suspicion dawning on the very edge of her consciousness.

"The list—" Brianna's voice grew thoughtful. She was still glowing like a star, still angry, but now she was controlling it, not it her. She turned from Lucie to Morguenna, who with her assistant was busily working magic over a small stone bowl filled with blood from her patient.

"Morguenna, may I use your office?"

The healer nodded, not breaking her chant or giving any other indication she'd heard. Already David's coloring was looking better.

"Come with me, Lucie." Brianna paused, realizing how brusque she'd sounded. "Please."

She led her sister a short distance down the hall to where she remembered Morguenna's office to be. The door wasn't locked, so the two women walked in.

Brianna had been in the office years before, after she'd been healed from the injuries incurred saving her father. The place hadn't changed much. It was still a small, starkly functional place, the walls filled with bookshelves. The furnishings were an old wooden desk, modern office chair, a single leather desk chair, and an apothecary's cabinet. All were pristinely neat and well cared for, with no dust or clutter to be found anywhere.

Brianna took a seat on the edge of the desk. Lucie took the guest chair.

Brianna spoke quickly. "We probably only have a few minutes. Once the nobles realize David and Nick are here they'll descend in droves—demanding to be healed of whatever minor injuries they can inflict on themselves to get here, so I don't have time to waste on being polite."

"So don't."

A quick grin flashed across Brianna's face. "Thanks. And thanks for saving David."

"If we don't have time to be polite, there's no time for thanks, either. What do you need?"

"I'm trying to remember, does the *Ard Reigh* position come with guards?"

"Yes."

"How many?"

"Teams of six. But nobody ever uses them."

Brianna's smile was positively vicious. "That is about to change." She slid off of the desk and opened the office door. Not seeing anyone handy, she called out. "I need a pair of messengers, *now*."

A brownie poked her nose out of a door down the hall. Seeing who'd made the demand she bowed low, and nodded. By the time Brianna had stepped back into the office and resumed her seat on the desk a pair of sprites had appeared, each bearing the pink and red knotted ribbons that marked them as messengers for the healers.

Brianna turned to the first, a red-winged male with swallow-tail wings. "Find Kenneth the guard captain and bring him here as soon as he may come. Tell him the *Ard Reigh* Brianna has urgently requested his presence." The sprite zipped off in a blur of light.

To the second, smaller female sprite Brianna said, "Go to whoever is in charge at the guard barracks. Tell them the *Ard Reigh* Brianna requires her coterie of guards all report *immediately* to duty at the palace infirmary, and that I want them to clank when they walk." The sprite bowed and was gone in an instant.

Brianna slid off of the desk again, pacing in the small space. "Is it just me, or does it seem odd that now, of all times, I'm finally put on the list? And rather than bumping off Rihannon, who is obviously unsuitable, or Rodan, who is just terrifying, you are the one demoted?"

Brianna watched her sister's face grow pensive. "You think someone has bribed the oracles?"

"I think they wouldn't have to. The oracles are in exile. Nobody sees them. Our only contact is with a messenger in uniform *claiming* to have the list they've given him."

"So, they could corrupt the messenger."

"Or kill him and replace him with someone else. Who'd know the difference at this end, and what could the oracles do about it at theirs? They are *only* allowed to send the one messenger. They'd have to wait until the next release date and send an additional message—and hope it got through."

"It could work," Lucie admitted. "But why?"

"That is an excellent question, and one I'll get to the bottom of eventually. But for the moment we have other priorities."

Brianna poked her head out of the office door. Catching a glimpse of Adam she called, "Your majesty, how's it going in there?"

He stepped out into the hall. "Well, very well. Morguenna says that David is going to make it with minimal permanent damage."

"Excellent!" Brianna turned to face the opposite end of the hallway, where Pug and Kenneth were arriving at the head of a group of guards in full uniform and obviously and excessively armed.

"*Ard Reigh?*" Kenneth bowed low, but used her title as a question.

"Kenneth, Pug, and Adam, could you please come into the office?" Stepping out into the hall, she addressed the guards as her friends moved past her. "Ladies and gentlemen of the guard, here are your orders.

"Four of you are to station yourselves guarding that room at the end of the hallway. I want you to be very conspicuous about it, and feel free to tell any nobles who arrive who you're working for and what you're doing." Four of the guards immediately moved into position as ordered. The two remaining faced her expectantly.

"The two of you are working on an investigation for me. I will need your absolute discretion. You will report what you find *only* to me or to High King Leu, and no other." When they nodded their understanding she continued, "I want you to track back the courier that arrived with the list. I want to know everywhere he went on his route, everywhere he stayed. I want to know, for a fact, that the man who arrived here was the man who was sent by the oracles, and that the list he brought is the list that they sent. There are two of you so that you can watch each other's back, and act as each other's witness should anyone question what you find. Again, this is for my and the king's eyes and ears *only*. Now go."

The guards gave her deep bows before leaving.

That done, Brianna hurried inside the now extremely crowded office. Adam had taken the chair behind the desk. Pug and Kenneth leaned against the wall near Lucienne. Brianna was left with a small amount of room to stand in just inside the office door. But that was fine. This wasn't going to take long.

"What happened to David this morning makes it clear how vital it is that I get the Antonellis away from Faerie immediately."

Nobody argued. In fact, no one said a word.

"I don't think it is in their best interests for them to even stay here in the infirmary any longer. I was in public when I was told he was here. I've no doubt word has already gotten out of their location."

Kenneth gave a nod confirming her suspicions. "There were nobles right behind us. Only the admissions clerk stands between them and the infirmary, and he won't be able hold them off for long," Kenneth announced.

Brianna didn't swear, but she wanted to. Turning to the stone trolls she asked, "Adam, Pug, where's the nearest entrance to the tunnels?"

The Diamond King answered, "The linen closet in the examination room next to the one they're using for David."

"Good. We need to move them, now." She opened the door,

leading the others into the hall. In the distance she could hear strident voices raised in argument. The male assistants who had blocked Brianna's passage earlier brushed past, heading for the stairwell. The male healer turned a key in the elevator controls, locking it off from use before joining them.

"So the guards are a distraction?" Lucie whispered.

"Yes. And a delaying tactic."

Their group dashed down the hall. "Kenneth, can you help Nick carry David?" Brianna asked. He nodded his assent, rushing over to the young man's bedside.

"What do you think you're doing, *Ard Reigh*?" It was worded as a question, but Morguenna's voice had a tone of command. She might not be royal, but this was her hospital and her patient.

"The nobles are on their way. We have to get them out of here. You can come with us if you want, but we're leaving, *now*." Brianna had moved beside the door, listening hard to hear any sign of the nobles' approach.

Kenneth held David's shoulders while Nick took his feet. David was looking much better, but still unconscious, completely unresisting as the two of them lugged him behind Pug and Adam into the next room.

"This is preposterous!" Morguenna protested—but she didn't get in the way. Instead, she began hurriedly grabbing spell implements from off of nearby shelves.

Lucie followed the men with Brianna taking up the rear. As she did she heard the commotion at the top of the stairs escalating, with her brother Eammon's bellow clearly audible. "I am *Ard Reigh* and I say you will let me and my companions through *now*."

"Shit!" Lucie swore. Brianna couldn't have agreed more. She hadn't expected either of her brothers to come—they had enough rank that the charade she'd set up might well fall through at a single order.

They hurried, rushing through the door past an open-mouthed

woman in assistant healer's robes and into the door to the tunnels with a laden Morguenna at their heels.

"For deities' sake don't tell them where we've gone!" Morguenna ordered in the instant before Pug pulled the lever that slid the passage door closed and activated its concealing magics.

25

KING LEU OF THE SIDHE

The cavernous throne room was coldly beautiful. Walls of white marble had been carved both with magic and by hand to depict every living thing. A checkerboard pattern of black-and-white tiles lead from the golden doors of the main entrance to the thirty-two steps up to the royal dais and the massive throne of silver-veined black marble. Sixty four pillars of the same black marble marched in pairs on two levels from one end of the room to the other. The vaulted dome of the ceiling was painted to depict the sky, from the sun rising at the point of due east, to the darkest midnight, with a brilliant dusting of diamond stars. The faceted crystal at the apex of the dome captured even the faintest light from outdoors, reflecting and refracting the beams so that only on the night of the new moon was it necessary for the chandeliers to be lit.

The throne itself hummed with contained power and while Leu sat in it when occasion called for it, he often said it was not a comfortable seat. Nor was it meant to be. The magic in the throne acknowledged him as the *Seelie Reigh*—the rightful ruler of his people—but he did not believe for a moment that it *liked* him.

He was not thrilled to have this meeting here, but it was the only space that was both secure and large enough to hold Ju-Long in his dragon form.

The dragon, a vast bulk of scale and muscle, lay comfortably stretched out in the center of the floor. His body lay in looping ebon coils on the floor, his tail curled slightly so that its spiked tip rested mere inches from the doors. Razor-sharp spikes formed a ridge along his spine. The tips were a deep, angry red that shaded into black where they joined his body, some longer than Leu's outstretched arms. Similar spikes formed a mane around a squarish head dominated by golden eyes with the slit pupil of a reptile. Lazy wisps of smoke drifted up from the nostrils at the end of his snout with each breath. His presence in dragon form raised the temperature in a room that was normally chilly until it was quite comfortable.

Leu had known Ju-Long since childhood and had gladly accepted the beast's oath of fealty when he'd taken the throne after his father's murder. Much better that the greatest of the last few remaining dragons and drakes be with rather than against him. Leu had seen Ju-Long in action once—a sight never to be forgotten.

A booming knock echoed through the chamber, disturbing the king's musings. "Enter." Leu's voice carried easily through the room and outside the doors, the throne's magic amplifying it without the slightest distortion.

The brass doors swung open, revealing Gwynneth, in full uniform. Behind her stood Asara.

Gwynneth bowed low, placing her right fist over her heart in the traditional salute. Only when Leu acknowledged the action did he speak. "The Lady Asara, your majesty."

Leu didn't rise. "Send her in. Then leave us."

Gwynneth gave a curt nod, then backed from the room. Asara walked in past her. The vast brass doors closed behind her with an ominous boom.

As was proper, Asara had sunk into an obeisance upon entering the throne room.

"You may approach the throne."

Asara rose. Moving with exquisite grace, she swept up the aisle. She glided past the dragon's deadly spikes, then yard after yard of coiled dragon, but gave no sign of fear, showing nothing but seeming confidence.

Deities but she was lovely. She'd borne him children, but there was no sign of it on that body, slender, yet sweetly curved beneath the ice-blue satin she wore. The strapless dress revealed her smooth, milk-white shoulders and clung to her like a second skin as it skimmed over her torso. It was cut high, to show the tops of her perfect thighs, then came to a point, modestly covering pubis and ass. Flowing over her thighs and down to the floor was a filmy layer of sheer, shining fabric as delicate as mist, lightly embroidered with beaded flowers that shaded from pure white to deepest midnight.

Her hair hung in silver-blonde waves to her knees, the front sections pulled back with a sapphire clip to bare a face as unlined and perfect as the first day he'd set eyes on her.

Asara stopped just short of the dais: twelve sets of three steps each separated by a small landing. She dropped into a low curtsy, head bowed and eyes lowered. Her movements were perfectly proper, but there was steel in her spine. Part of him admired her spirit. But only part.

"Your majesty."

Leu rose from his seat and strode down the stairs to stand directly in front of her.

She held the curtsy, and though he knew it would quickly become painful, he let her. In this case a little pain was no bad thing. He only hoped that it would *only* be a little pain. He might not love this woman, but he valued her. He did not want to see such beauty and strength laid waste—did not want to believe her a traitor.

"As you made your long return from the hunt, you met with the prince of the doxies. The same prince who hours thereafter used a sample of my hair to activate the portal to the lady Brianna Hai's apartments and execute a raid that could have led to war."

She didn't flinch; didn't react at all, merely held the curtsy. Studying her, Lcu could see her thigh muscles beginning to quiver with the strain.

Leu reached forward, displaying the king's ring on his finger. It was a simple band of gold, set with the seal of his office, an actual seal that he pressed in wax to prove the verity of documents going out under his name. But it was much more than that.

"This ring is a most useful tool, milady. Did you know that it has been spelled to protect the wearer from treason? Should it so much as brush a traitor's flesh, it will sear and scorch to, even through, the bone. Shall I touch you with it?"

"I am no traitor." Asara looked up, her gaze locking with his. "Yes, I met with the doxie. I was angry, humiliated. I wanted to hurt you. The best and easiest path was to hurt *her*."

"It could have led to war." Leu's silver gaze locked with her blazing blue eyes.

"No." Asara's voice was firm. "It wouldn't. The girl is young, but she's no fool. She was a member of the guard, even if only briefly, and she retired to earth with high honor after saving her king. Brianna would never do anything that might risk war—even if it cost her her life."

Leu reached forward, cupping Asara's cheek in his hand. The ring on his finger remained quiescent. His eyebrow rose, but showed no other physical reaction.

"You wanted her dead. You tried to arrange for it to happen."

"She was not on the list. It was not treason."

"You tried to kill my daughter!"

"You know as well as I that if she is to survive in Faerie she needs to be able to take care of herself. Which she did. Admirably." Asara's voice was a trifle sour as she spoke the words. "I want," Asara said coldly, "one of our children to succeed you." Her mouth twisted in what amounted to a wry grimace. "I am *not*, however, in any hurry to see it happen. I have counseled all of them to patience. You never wanted the throne. I believe you will eventually tire of ruling and will step down voluntarily."

Leu stepped back. "I *tired* of ruling less than an hour after they put the crown on my head and this ring on my hand." With a gesture he signaled permission for Asara to take a seat on a small stool that sat on the third landing, a dozen feet from the throne where he, once again, took his seat.

She sank gratefully, and less than gracefully, onto the proffered seat.

Leu looked down on her, a debate raging within him. She wasn't completely trustworthy. He knew that. But she was brilliant and cunning, and the ring had shown her to be no traitor. In the end he decided to take a chance.

"Unless I take drastic action, I am fated to die at the hand of a traitor, and soon."

Asara's eyes widened. It was a full minute before she spoke. "Not by my hand. I swear it."

"One of the children?"

She considered that. "I don't like to think it."

"Nor do I." The words were dry.

They sat in silence for long moments. It was Asara who finally broke it.

"May I ask a question?"

"You may," Leu answered.

"Why is the dragon here?"

"Should you have failed the ring's test, he would have gotten rid of the evidence." He saw her give a slight shudder. "Since you passed, he will perform another service."

"Please, your majesty." Asara's voice was soft. "I do not wish to have my mind and memories altered. I can hold my tongue."

"I am sorry, Asara. I don't think you would talk. But even as fine an actress as you would not be able to fool our children. You would look at them differently, without even meaning to. We cannot afford to take that risk." He used the royal we deliberately, and saw her take note of it. He watched her give a hard swallow followed by a tiny nod. When he stood, she stood with him.

The dragon stirred, turning its head so that its great eyes stared directly at her.

"I understand," Asara answered.

Leu watched as she steeled herself. Standing tall and proud, she stared unflinching into the slitted golden eye. Her next words were addressed to Ju-Long. "Do it."

When the deed was done, Leu ordered a pair of guards carry the unconscious woman to her private apartments and sent Morguenna to tend to her. It was the least he could do, and not much at that.

When the doors closed and he was alone again with Ju-Long, Leu settled onto the throne, his expression pensive.

"A word your majesty?" the dragon rumbled.

"Go ahead."

"Have you chosen Brianna your successor then? Admittedly, she'd be a good queen. She is both honorable and strong. But she has little, if any support among any Sidhe other than the guard. The lesser Fae like her, and she does have alliances with the stone trolls and now the doxies, but her mother was a convicted criminal. Ulrich may not be her enemy any longer, but he is not her friend. Your other children—"

Times were desperate. Leu was not willing to mislead Ju-

Long, or lie to himself any longer. "If neither Ulrich nor Asara is the traitor, it must be one of my children." Leu's words were bitter acid in his mouth. "Who would you have me choose as a successor?"

"What of Eammon and Rodan?"

"I've not completely discounted Eammon. Fatherhood and the right woman have been good for him." Leu met the dragon's gaze, his expression dark and troubled. "But there have always been whispers . . . rumors . . . about Rodan. I did not wish to give them credence . . . but if he is truly likely to ascend to the throne, I need to know. I must be sure."

"I can have Chang look into it."

"He will need to be discreet."

"He always is."

26

NICK ANTONELLI

There were twists and turns and stairs leading downward. Without Adam to guide them he'd have been hopelessly lost. As it was his stomach was in tight knots knowing that he was trusting his life and his brother's to relative strangers. He wanted to believe that Adam, Pug, and Kenneth the guardsman were acting in his best interest. Intellectually he knew that they were his best chance of getting back to home and sanity. But he didn't like feeling helpless. He was used to being in charge—and armed. Now he was neither. The healers had taken the weapons Adam had given him, which upset him more than he could say. And while he wasn't precisely claustrophobic, being stuck underground with only the light of Adam's lantern to guide him was making him jumpy.

David had to be feeling like hell. He'd been at death's door less than seven hours ago. They were both upright, and technically healed—if not precisely well, and while it was miserable to be going through this, he'd do worse to get them the hell back home.

After fleeing the hospital ward they'd taken a short, but twisting, climbing route through the tunnels before exiting in a large room filled with catering supplies. One long wall was filled with crystal and china, the opposite with stacks and stacks of linen. Two large tables had rows of narrow drawers that he suspected were labeled as storing silver and cutlery, and each had rags and large tubs of silver polish resting on top.

Lucie had been the first to leave—taking off before their escape plan was hatched with a terse "What I don't know I can't tell them." Brianna left once the plan was in place. Morguenna, the healer, stayed the full five hours until they left, determinedly making sure her patient was capable of the long hike required for their flight.

The plan was simple. Adam and Pug would guide Nick and David through the tunnels. They'd come up at a guard's pub at the edge of the northwest side of the city, then go overland until they were clear of the ring that marked the edge of the area around the city where it was illegal to create an opening in the veil. Once they were in the clear, Kenneth would use his human magic to send Nick and David back home.

It was a good enough plan, as far as it went; although he would have preferred to have Brianna here. But she had to appear at the ball tonight celebrating her treaty with the doxies. And, as Kenneth had pointed out, it was good tactics. The nobles wouldn't believe that Nick and David could, or would, leave without her. Her very public presence might be exactly the cover they needed to escape. Maybe.

Nick shook his head. *Stop it. The decision's made. This is our best chance of getting out of here alive.*

He knew it was the truth. But he hated it passionately.

The first tunnel had been ten feet tall and wide enough to walk with arms extended and not touch either side. The next had been so cramped and narrow that Nick was forced to crawl and feared he might get stuck. He'd come out of it with deep scrapes on his hands and the injuries he'd sustained during the battle with the doxies giving him hell.

Their passage was stirring up the dust that lay, inches thick, on the floor. Cobwebs hung everywhere. Behind Nick, Kenneth stifled a sneeze; Nick had felt the same urge more than once. While he didn't see any spiders, he glimpsed evidence of them in the drained husks of insects and skeletons of tiny sprites trapped in the hanging webs.

Adam stopped so abruptly that David tripped trying to come to a halt, running into Pug, and Nick into him. Nick opened his mouth to protest, but Kenneth's grip on his arm urged him to silence.

"Is everything in place?" A man's voice, and one Nick had heard before but couldn't place without a face to pin it to.

"He suspects something." A woman. Nick didn't know her, and from the sound of her waspish, angry voice, didn't want to.

"Of course he suspects. He's king, and nobody's fool."

"If he finds proof . . ." Her voice shook slightly.

"He won't." The man's confidence bordered on arrogance until, quickly as a thought, his voice took on a dangerous edge. "Unless you intend to give it to him. Do you, Elena?"

"Of course not." She tried to scoff, but Nick could hear a hint of real fear in her voice. "I want the larger male. You promised him to me."

"Only if you carry out your part of the plan."

"It's done. Maybelle and the others are in place outside the king's study and in the tunnels, in case they try to escape through the king's portal. Spells have been laid on the ring surrounding the city. If either of the humans so much as touch the stones of the circle, we will be alerted to their location.

"And immediately after the command performances, before dinner is served, Alaric will challenge Brianna to a duel."

Kenneth's hand tightened so painfully on Nick's arm that he knew he would have finger-shaped bruises by tomorrow.

"Alaric was an excellent choice," the man said. "He's the best fighter of the Sidhe. She will not be able to find a champion who can best him unless she chooses one of the dragons—and even then he'll have dipped his blades in dragonsbane. Still, I'm surprised he agreed. He has no quarrel with my father." The words hit Nick and the others of his party like a blow, but they remained silent and still, listening hard for any details they could learn.

"Like the rest of us, Alaric wants the veil opened. We need new blood and new humans for mating and as servants. The king is putting his love for Brianna above the good of the kingdom," Elena responded.

"True. But it is still a surprise." The man paused. "What of the doxies?"

"Moash has refused to aid us. He will not move against Brianna or the wishes of King Leu."

"Really? How annoying. What of his son? The prince has always been more amenable to our plans."

"The doxie prince has been imprisoned," Elena answered.

"On what charge?"

"General idiocy," was the prompt reply.

The man laughed merrily. "Seriously?"

"That's what the card on the cage reads."

"He's in a *cage*?"

"The bespelled carrier cage that Brianna brought with her from the other side of the veil."

"Oh, my."

At a gesture from Adam, Nick and the others backed carefully away, retreating a good distance down the passage. Finally Adam signaled them to halt.

"We won't be overheard here," he said. "We'll have to change our plans. Pug, you know these tunnels well, can you get them from here to the Guardsman Tavern detouring around the paths under the city gates? The tunnels are very near the surface there, and we can't risk our enemies hearing your passage."

Pug nodded curtly.

"Good. I'll go back to warn Leu."

"Not Brianna?" David asked.

"No. She's not actress enough to pretend ignorance. Her temper would get the best of her. And Leu needs to know just how high the plot has risen in his court." He paused. "I don't look forward to telling him. He'll not be happy."

That'd be putting it mildly. Nick suspected the king would be utterly furious. He shuddered, remembering the look on the man's face after Brianna's ordeal with the truthstone. *Better Adam than me.*

"Will she be all right?" David asked.

"Leu may not have as much control over his court as he wishes, but he's certainly capable of seeing to his daughter's safety," Adam said reassuringly. "Now I must go. And so should you. Deities protect you. You'll need it."

Nick and the others watched Adam until a turning took him out of sight—and with that, the light from his lantern vanished. A faint shaft of light coming through a ventilation slot far above was their only illumination.

"All right then." Pug's voice was a rumbling growl. "This is going to be a much longer and more difficult trip than originally planned. We'd best get moving."

He led them through a short passage before pressing a stone on what appeared to be a blank wall. Nick felt the faint stirring of air moving against his skin as the wall wavered, like a curtain caught in a heavy breeze, then vanished altogether, revealing a narrow staircase that descended steeply into cold and stygian darkness. At the top of the stairs a narrow niche held a bowl full of chunks of crystal. Pug grabbed one, muttered a quick spell, and blew on the stone, which began to give off a wan, reddish glow. It was barely enough to see by, and Nick knew without being told that this dim light would be less likely to be noticed as the group passed ventilation shafts and other openings where their enemies might be looking for them.

They traveled underground for hours without food, drink, and little rest. The silence all about them was broken only occasionally by snatches of conversation echoing from far away or by the distant sounds of a fierce thunderstorm that sent water streaming down the wall and along the floor. Footing grew treacherous.

Nick's bladder began bothering him around dinnertime, its demands more urgent even than the hunger that was chewing at his belly. But he knew that this was not the time or place to relieve himself. In the darkest corridors he sometimes heard the faint scraping of claws on stone. They were not alone in these tunnels. Better not to leave a scent trail that would draw whatever hunted there to them.

Eventually, tired and miserable, they came to another staircase, one that wound upward. At a muttered word from Pug, the light vanished. The darkness was complete—Nick placed a hand on the wall for guidance and tried to extend his other senses. He could hear the ragged breathing of his companions, and beyond that, behind the wall, muffled movement; he smelled animals, and . . . manure.

There was no sound, no warning, when Pug opened the passage. Nick suddenly was blinded by light. His eyes immediately began to water.

When his vision cleared, he saw that they were in the tack room of a stable. Nick didn't know much about horses, but he was able to recognize the bits, bridles, and some of the various implements hanging from nails driven into the wood plank walls. The lone window looked out on a pair of corrals, one holding horses, the other, dogs big enough to pass for ponies. They all were acting nervous. Nick didn't blame them. The storm he'd heard faintly in the tunnels was roiling on the horizon. The clouds were thick, black and ugly, with the trace of green that usually means hail and strong winds. Nick had seen a tornado up close once. He didn't want to see another.

"I don't suppose there's a bathroom handy?" David's whisper was a little strained. Kenneth opened the tack room door, leading them quietly into the main stables. He gestured to a door. David hurried toward it with Nick right at his heels. As they pulled the door closed behind them, Nick did a quick inspection.

The room was a little bigger than your average gas station toilet with a toilet and a small sink, both linked to a single water tank overhead. A small square of chipped mirror hung above the sink; beside it, a strip of blue toweling hung from a nail. Through the door, Nick could hear Kenneth talking to Pug.

"Keep an eye on them. I need to talk to my uncle."

"Your uncle?" Pug asked, his voice easily heard even over the sound of David using the facilities.

"He owns the tavern," Kenneth answered.

"Won't they be expecting us to come here then? Seems like the perfect place to lay a trap."

David stepped aside, gesturing for Nick to take his turn, which he did with considerable relief. That done, he dropped the lid, sinking gratefully onto the toilet seat to just rest. David, meanwhile, sank into a sitting position in the small piece of floor between the toilet and sink. Leaning wearily against the wall he closed his eyes with a groan.

"You look like hell," Nick observed. David was filthy, covered in dust, but more than that, his skin had an unhealthy pallor.

"I feel it. I can't wait to get back home and into my own bed. Swear to God I may sleep for a week."

"I can't believe you're sitting on the floor. This *is* a stable."

"I can't exactly get any more dirty," David retorted, "and I'm too damned tired to care. Besides, you took the only seat in the place."

"Guess I did," Nick admitted.

There was a tap on the door. Pug inquired, "Are you two done in there? Kenneth has gone to get food, and I thought you might want to shower before you ate."

"There's a shower?" Nick perked up a little, and saw that David did the same. Rising, he extended a hand to his brother, and helped him to his feet. David opened the door revealing the gargoyle standing patiently, towels draped over his shoulder.

"Yes."

"Where?" David asked.

Pug pointed a claw to a door just next to the one where they stood. Nick wondered why anyone would design the facilities in such a way, and got his answer when Kenneth strode in. "The shower was added after my aunt complained one too many times about her sons' condition coming back into the inn after cleaning the stables."

"Makes sense to me," David said. "I get first dibs."

"Yeah," Nick grumbled, "just don't take all the hot water."

———

They ate at a small wooden table in the corner of the stables. It was battered, but clean. David took the only chair, Kenneth a milking stool, which left Nick an overturned bucket. Pug stood as he ate.

The meal was bread and honey, with a hearty beef stew that was both filling and tasty. Being clean, rested, and fed helped them all both physically and mentally. Nick was relieved to see that David's coloring was nearly back to normal.

"Wait here. I need to go tell our escort we're ready to go."

"Escort?" Nick couldn't quite manage to keep the suspicion from his voice—but David put a hand on his arm. His little brother had an odd smile on his face. "It's okay, Nick. This is our best chance. Really."

"David . . ."

Kenneth gave the younger Antonelli a long, appraising look. "You have your grandmother's gift, don't you." It was almost an accusation.

David nodded; his eyes were unfocused, as if he was looking into the distance or at something that wasn't in the room with them.

"What do you see, human?" Kenneth's voice was harsh. "Do we die tonight?"

Lightning flashed across the sky, followed by the boom of distant thunder. David answered, "I'm not sure. I don't think so. But someone will."

27

KING LEU OF THE SIDHE

Leu stood in the turret, the wind whipping his hair and clothing. A lightning bolt blasted, connecting earth to sky by way of the ancient oak that stood between the palace and Abracham House. The tree exploded, chunks of wood flying, deafening thunder simultaneous with a pillar of blinding blue-white light.

Leu fought down a wave of fury. He must control himself tonight. He *must*. His plans depended on it—plans that had to succeed, for the sake of his kingdom. But the news from the Diamond King had ignited a rage within Leu that only barely covered the pain beneath it.

One of his sons was a traitor. All evidence pointed to that conclusion. But *which* son? The Diamond King had not recognized the voice—hadn't even been certain that the speaker was one of the princes until he'd used the words "my father."

He needed Chang's report *now*. He needed to *know*.

His people were on the brink of civil war. His own death might well be imminent. He had to know that his people would survive.

He'd done all that he could for them. But it would all be for naught if he chose the wrong successor.

So many mistakes: So much undone and unsaid. Tonight might well be the last time he saw Brianna. And tonight, to save her and his people, he would have to publicly humiliate and hurt her, to wound her, knowing there would be no chance for forgiveness.

He would do it.

He had to. He was king.

28

BRIANNA HAI

Don't worry. They'll be fine, Brianna told herself. She didn't believe it. Not really. She wished desperately that she could be the one escorting David and Nick to safety. But it wasn't practical. They were much, much safer going without her. Too, by now her message would have been given to her father.

She'd tried to see him in person, but he'd been locked in the throne room with orders that he was not to be disturbed for any reason. So she'd left a note with his secretary. It was the best she could do, under the circumstances. But she still didn't feel good about it.

Her father had to have gotten her note by now. As king, Leu had access to resources Brianna couldn't even dream of. If it was possible to get to the Antonelli's home safely, her father was the best bet to do it.

And even if he didn't . . . Adam, Pug, Kenneth . . . she couldn't think of any group of people more trustworthy and skilled—

Don't think about it, she told herself sternly. *You've got enough on your plate just getting through tonight.*

She always gave herself such great advice. Why was it so hard to follow?

In this case the reason was simple. Worry. David was one of her best friends, and Nick . . . was undeniably attractive. She didn't really know him yet, but she wanted to. It wasn't just physical attraction, either. He'd impressed her with his courage, his loyalty to his brother, and the fact that he hadn't cracked under the stress of learning about magic and the world of the Fae. Assuming they both got through the next twenty-four hours alive she was definitely going to see what she could do about seeing where the potential she sensed between them led.

If they survived.

He'd impressed her—but she wasn't sure the reverse was true. She couldn't completely discount the angry words he'd used against her in the infirmary. Yes, he and David had come willingly, but not with full knowledge. It had been her responsibility to see to their safety, and she'd failed at that at every turn.

Still, it was a shame he couldn't see her right now. She looked *good.* Rather than risk being completely out of fashion she'd chosen a classic dress that had "old Hollywood" style. Long-sleeved, with a scooped neck, it was heavily beaded with crystals shading from silver at the neckline to jet black where the hem skimmed the floor. A slit ran from that hem all the way up to her upper thigh, allowing her mobility and making her legs look sexy as hell in the process. She wore simple onyx and diamond jewelry.

She would not be allowed to duel, she was on the list now, after all. Still, she wasn't foolish enough to believe that a place on the list would guarantee her safety. Vanity aside, if push came to shove she wanted to be able to defend herself both magically and physically. To that end she'd armed herself. Her up-lifted hair was held in place by a pair of silver chopsticks with dagger-sharp points. A dagger was strapped to her upper thigh, and there was a Derringer tucked with a comb in her little black purse.

She'd worked hard on her makeup as well, keeping it subtle but enhancing her eyes and the shape of her face.

She looked lovely and lethal: a true Sidhe princess. She forced herself to smile at her reflection, feeling uneasy. For all her preparations, Brianna had overlooked something. She just didn't know what. But whatever it was, it lurked in the background, waiting to bite her in the ever-so-elegantly-clad ass.

Closing her eyes she wished fervently she was back in her own apartment getting ready for bed—or, really, anywhere but here, getting ready to play politics.

But as her mother used to say, "If wishes were horses, we'd be up to our armpits in shit."

The memory made her smile. Opening her eyes, she stiffened her spine, and went out to the front courtyard and the waiting dog cart.

The gnome that was driving was the same one who had been stuck there earlier with a damaged vehicle, but the repairs had apparently been made, and he was dressed in his evening finery. His red peaked cap exactly matched his red trousers, his bright blue jacket with its gold braiding and brass buttons was neatly pressed and belted with a wide black patent leather belt that matched his glossy black boots. His snow white beard and hair had been combed and trimmed, and bright gold rings graced the tips of his pointed ears. He looked dashing, and Brianna told him so.

"Thank you your grace. And may I say you are looking especially lovely tonight?"

"You may. I just hope we arrive before the weather worsens, or I won't be staying that way."

It wasn't raining . . . yet. But green-black storm clouds had massed overhead, lit by frequent lightning. Thunder boomed repeatedly. Brianna forced herself not to flinch. Often as not, the weather in Faerie reflected the mood of the ruler. If that was the case tonight, her father was in a fine fury.

Deities please, don't let it be at me, was her silent, fervent prayer.

"Allow me, your grace." Saturnino bowed almost double before opening the door to the open carriage with its gleaming black paint and silver accents. Brianna acknowledged the bow and used the little silver steps he'd unfolded from the carriage to climb in, lowering herself carefully onto the thick velvet seat. When Saturnino closed the door, the gnome called a sharp order to the matched pair of dappled gray mastiffs harnessed in front. The cart pulled smoothly forward and through the gates of Abracham House. As they neared the huge oak where Elena lived, a huge bolt of lightning smashed into the tree. Brianna threw out a magical shield on pure instinct as the tree exploded with a roar.

"Sweet God and Goddess . . . Elena." Brianna rose, intending to rush to check on her old friend, the dryad who lived in the oak, then stopped. The tree was destroyed, which meant the dryad was dead. Only one man could control the weather in Faerie, the king. That he would choose to personally and publically execute one of his subjects thus couldn't possibly mean anything good.

"Deities, Elena, what did you do?" Brianna's words came out in a hoarse whisper. She hadn't meant the gnome to hear, but he had, and he answered.

"Nothing good, you can be betting on that." There was a hint of a growl in his voice. Brianna wanted to ask him what he knew but he'd already turned back to the dogs and starting them forward with a crack of the reins. Brianna was practically thrown backward onto the carriage seat. It began to rain; the gnome muttered something Brianna couldn't make out and pressed the button to raise the carriage's mechanical roof. Brianna was protected from the elements but completely cut off from any hope of conversation with the driver.

Brianna drummed her fingers against the seat. She couldn't

ask after her friend, not without risking infuriating her father—
who was apparently already in a dangerous mood. But why?

The cart stopped; Brianna looked out the window to see that they
were at the end of a line of carts heading up to the portico at the
side entrance to the palace. Again, she had a sense of misgiving.
Surely there should be more carts than this?

Finally they reached the portico. The footman stepped up, and
placed the stairs by the carriage door, then opened it. "Your grace."

"Thank you." Brianna smiled at him, taking his hand and allowing herself to be stepped down to solid ground. Once there,
she turned to the driver, "What is your name?"

"Grum, your grace."

"Well, Grum, I am glad that you were able to get your cart
repaired in time for this evening's event. Please be sure to present
the bill to the seneschal for payment from my personal account.
The damages were incurred in my service after all."

"Thank you, *Ard Reigh*." A warm smile lit up his face, but faded
quickly. "Be watching your step tonight, your grace. Something's
afoot, and there's plenty'd do you harm if they could."

Brianna felt her eyebrows rise in surprise. Though she would
swear she'd never met this gnome before, there seemed to be gen-
uine concern in his voice.

He noticed her surprise and answered the question she'd left
unvoiced. "The Sidhe aint t' only Fae, an' not een the only ones t'
choose the ruler. Which is why you've found your place on the list
at last." With that, the gnome bowed low. For a long second Brianna simply stared. She'd done nothing to earn the lesser Fae's
support. Of course, she supposed, she could have won it by default.
Just what had the others been doing in the years of her absence?

Shaking herself like a dog shedding water, she strode down the
steps.

Brianna made it into the foyer without getting wet, despite the
sheets of rain that were slashing down. Stepping into a small

anteroom, she straightened her hair with the small comb she'd stowed along with a Derringer in the small clutch she carried.

The Sidhe aint t' only Fae. She shivered. Her father was not old by Fae standards, but it was no secret that he'd never wanted the crown, so virtually from the moment he'd taken the throne, people had been jockeying for position as potential heirs. The thought terrified Brianna. She hadn't lied to Lucienne—she didn't want to rule. But she didn't want to see almost any of her siblings in charge, either. Lucie wouldn't be too bad, but the thought of any of Asara's brood on the throne filled Brianna with dread. The second any of them took power, she could start counting the days left to her. They simply would not tolerate letting a possible rival live.

The best of the batch was Eammon, and he could be a pompous and overbearing ass. The others were all smarter, but had fewer scruples. Of course, there was a bigger question: were any of them strong enough to stand up to their mother, or would she finally rule through them the way she'd hoped to rule through Brianna's father?

Not that I'd live long enough to see what happened one way or the other.

It was almost enough to make her throw her hat in the ring . . . almost. Still, were Brianna to have the vote of every lesser Fae, she still couldn't rule—not without bloodshed. The Sidhe were the most populous, and the election was sacred. Only in time of war was the king permitted to choose his own successor. But assassins had struck before, and there were always duels of honor. Brianna was an excellent fighter thanks to years of training with both private tutors and friends in and out of the guard, but while on the list she wasn't allowed to defend herself, and would have to choose a champion instead. Some members of her father's court had spent hundreds of years perfecting their skills, but most wouldn't willingly champion the daughter of Helena Washington.

If one of Asara's children didn't kill her, one of the nobles would, if only because it was widely believed that her death would put an end to the barrier between Faerie and the human world.

"Here you are!" Teo poked his head in the door. He, too, was in his full dress uniform, and while Brianna had never considered him a handsome man, he was striking, charming, and very intelligent. For the most part Brianna liked him, and he had always been unfailingly polite to her.

"I saw your cart, but couldn't find you," he said. "We must hurry. Your father awaits!"

"Of course." Squaring her shoulders, Brianna took the arm he extended to her, and with as much grace and dignity as she could muster they made their way to the ballroom doors to make her grand entrance.

———

As the child of a ruling monarch Brianna had been either allowed or forced to attend many formal functions—though never before as one of the guests of honor. Her previous experience of state dinners was that they were boring and tedious. Well, aside from making sure her food wasn't being poisoned or cursed, and that she didn't say or do anything that could be construed as offensive enough to cause an incident, a duel, or both. So far, tonight's event had held true to form. Thus far she had been listening to speeches and command performances. The food would arrive . . . eventually . . . hopefully before she expired from hunger.

She longed to be somewhere, anywhere, else. Her favorite possibility was at home, in bed, and preferably not alone.

Just thinking about it made her smile, then frown when the worry set in. Had Nick and David crossed the veil? If Pug was here, she'd know they were all right. But there was no sign of the little gargoyle, and the Diamond King was seated three places down from Brianna at the head table—too far away for conversation. Whether Adam looked grim because something had gone wrong or because he had been seated between Moash and Asara, Brianna had no clue.

Brianna wondered if her father was trying to use the gargoyle to start a diplomatic incident. The doxies' actions had insulted the stone trolls at least as much as they had Brianna, and Asara and Adam loathed each other from personal history. Brianna forced herself not to stare, to keep her expression pleasantly bland, and to respond appropriately to the inane chitchat of the woman to her left, whose name she couldn't have remembered to save her life.

"What are you thinking, daughter dear?" King Leu's voice was cold.

"The musicians are quite good." Brianna looked over at him and smiled.

He snorted and took a drink from his wineglass. Brianna saw the tiny pause in his movement as he used his ring to check it for poison or a spell first, as always.

"Have you noticed anything peculiar this evening?" he asked as he set down his glass, meeting Brianna's eyes, his expression serious.

She thought for a moment. "The crowd seems a bit thin. And there are more men than women." That was unusual. Most Fae women, and the Sidhe in particular, were viciously competitive. It was practically unheard of for them to miss a banquet or ball when there might be a chance to upstage their enemies.

"Yes, there are. Do you know why?"

"I have a suspicion."

Leu stared at Brianna for a long, silent moment. She had no idea what thoughts might be going through his head. He loved her. She knew that. But the love of a Fae and a king was not the same as the love of a human parent.

"Do you know I am nearly as angry as I am jealous of your friend the gargoyle?" King Leu's expression was bland, the words spoken so softly and lightly that the woman seated next to Brianna, who had turned away to flirt with Rodan, did not hear. But Leu's eyes were dark as storm clouds outside, and Brianna could feel the power of his magic, kept in check by force of will alone.

She blinked rapidly. If she had been standing she would have dropped to a full obeisance. But they were at the head table and the king was deliberately being subtle. So she dropped her gaze. Keeping her voice and posture very carefully submissive, she answered, "I don't understand."

"You did not come to me as your father when an attempt was made on your life. You did not come to me as your king, though you must have known that the attempt was most likely a political machination against me. You did not come to me for assistance when your home was invaded, though the invasion was by members of a race of lesser Fae with whom I have standing treaties. And while technically staying as a guest, but under guard, you did not come to me when you heard of a threat against those to whom I've offered my protection. Instead, you asked a foreign monarch for aid. Do you believe me weak—or do you doubt my word?"

Brianna was speechless and horrified. But he hadn't offered David and Nick protection—not officially. And she'd tried to contact him—he'd been unavailable. As a result it hadn't occurred to her that her actions could give him offense—but they very obviously had. When Viktor had tried to kill her, she'd gone to her mother, too embarrassed by her own stupidity to talk to her father and king. She had assumed Helena would tell him what had happened; after all, at fifteen, she'd been little more than a child as the Fae reckon time.

But there was no excuse for the rest. She'd been thinking like a human, trying to solve her own problems when she should have been thinking like a Sidhe, and her father's subject. She'd pricked his pride, publicly humiliated him, and made him look weak. It was unforgivable, and stupid. Brianna tried to think what she could say to make it better, but nothing came to mind.

The king waited as the silence between them grew long and leaden. Brianna kept her head lowered. When she finally spoke, it was in a bare whisper, and she tried to put honest contrition in every word. "I am sorry, your majesty. I meant no offense. I've been among the humans too long, and forgot the proper way to think and act on this side of the veil."

She became aware that the room was growing quiet, that people were realizing something important was going on at the head table.

"Your words, and your presence offend me." Her father's words were like ice. The king rose. "Guards, escort the lady Brianna to the veil portal in my office. When she is through, close it against her."

The head guard stepped forward, clicking his heels and bowing in acknowledgment. He selected half a dozen of his compatriots from throughout the room, and they gathered at attention before the high table.

Brianna rose at the king's gesture, her vision blurred with unshed tears.

King Leu's voice rang harsh, yet clear, through the now-silent room. "Brianna *Ard Reigh,* you are hereby banished from this realm under pain of death unless said ban shall be lifted by the high ruler of the Sidhe."

There were gasps throughout the hall.

"Be thou gone from my sight."

29

NICK ANTONELLI

"I'm not sure we want to go out in that," David observed.

Nick glanced out through the open stable doors and saw that his brother was right—the weather looked even worse than it had earlier, and he wouldn't have thought that was even marginally possible. The sky was filled with dark clouds that had the greenish tinge to them that hinted at hail or even a tornado. Fierce winds howled through the trees. Thunder rumbled ominously in the distance.

"Not good traveling weather," David continued with a sigh. "And I don't know about you, but my feet are killing me. I don't want to take another step for at least a week. Maybe two."

"Then you'll be glad to hear I've found us another means of travel." Kenneth entered the stable, followed by a woman in what looked to Nick like a dress uniform. Both were carrying armfuls of black clothing.

"You have?" David didn't bother trying to hide his eagerness.

"What did you have in mind?" Nick asked a bit more cautiously.

"It's simple, really," Kenneth answered. "I'll explain while you change." The two guards passed over stacks of clothing to each of the brothers.

"This is Syrelle," he introduced the female guard to David and Nick in turn. "She is a senior officer, but has volunteered for the duty of escorting her kinsman's body home with the honor guard. The normal contingent is four guards and a driver, but frequently friends in the guard will join the procession as they travel on the same route, so it won't be unusual for there to be a couple of additional men. Can either of you ride a horse?"

"I've ridden a couple of times," Nick admitted, "but I'm no cowboy."

"Good. It will look less strange with you mounted. David?" Kenneth asked.

"I've never been on a horse in my life."

"Then you'll ride in the cart next to the driver."

Nick stripped out of his clothes, glad to be rid of them. It had been hard for him to put them back on after his shower, but then there hadn't been a choice.

The black trousers were of a heavy grade of what felt like wool, woven fine, they felt a little slick, as if they'd been treated with some sort of water repellant. The matching black shirt was cotton, with long sleeves and button cuffs. Both fit him well enough, but the boots weren't even close. There was no way he could force his feet into them. There was a black suede tunic with silver trim and the Guard's emblem that he pulled over the shirt. It was worn belted with a black leather weapons belt that had a frog for a sword on the right hip, and a holster for a gun on the left. There was even a pouch for additional ammo. A knife sheath buckled over each thigh, the daggers long, wicked, and deadly.

Nick knew the sword wouldn't be much use to him. He'd never

used one in his life. But the gun was a Glock 9 mm, and that was a very good and welcome thing. He checked it from habit, and found it clean, well-tended, and fully loaded. Flipping on the safety, he slid it back into its holster with a sense of satisfaction. He really hadn't realized how naked he'd felt running around un-armed until now.

His final bit of clothing was a hooded cloak, also black, with a silver wolf clasp. It was heavy as hell, delightfully warm, and treated with the same stuff as had gone into the trousers. While it hadn't actually been weighted to do it, it fell naturally and smoothly to Nick's knees. Still, he did wonder how useful the thing would be once they got out into the howling storm outside. Most likely it would be flapping around, getting in the way rather than keeping him warm.

Nick hadn't realized how comfortable the stable was until he stepped outside. The temperature was dropping like a stone. He could see his breath misting, as was the breath of the huge beast that was saddled and waiting for him.

Oh, shit. He had to ride a horse. Not just any old horse, either. This was a huge warhorse, a bay with long white hair on all four legs that made it look something like a Clydesdale. Its mane and tail were braided with black and silver ribbons and its saddle blan-ket was black with silver fringe. The saddle was well worn and well cared for.

Kenneth told Nick this was Dancer, who had been Haldar's mount, and assured him the animal was smart and well trained enough that even a novice should be able to ride him easily. Nick sure as hell hoped so, because a drop from a horse that tall would *hurt*.

Kenneth introduced Loog, the ogre. Loog was easily ten feet tall and nearly as wide. Heavily muscled, with thick green-gray skin covered in lumps and sores, he stank. Nick couldn't quite break it down in his mind. The closest he could come to describing it was a combination of sulfur and BO, or rotten eggs and bile, with maybe just a touch of cat piss thrown in.

The ogre's face was misshapen and ugly. His disposition worse. He had been ordered by the innkeeper to haul the cart, and he'd do it. But he wasn't happy about it.

The female guard, Syrelle, rode in the cart with David, having given her horse to Kenneth. The cart's original driver rode his own mount that had been tied to the back of the cart.

They had reinforcements, a workable cover, and, best of all, he was finally armed. If they were lucky, and they hurried, they might actually make it outside the ring before the storm broke.

Most of the Sidhe who would be looking for their party would be working spells to unravel illusions, so their group used none. The uniforms would hopefully disguise the humans; Pug rode in the back of the cart, huddled under the tarp that covered the coffin. Anyone looking closely might guess that something was amiss, but in a casual encounter they might pass unnoticed. And in weather like this, a chance encounter was unlikely. Nobody sane would willingly be out on the roads.

But the best part of the plan as far as Nick was concerned was that he and David were now accompanied by enough guards that anything less than a large group of attackers would think twice about moving on them.

"Hopefully we will get past the ring without incident," Kenneth said as he held Dancer's reins while Nick mounted. "But if we're attacked, I want you, David, and Pug to do whatever you must to get past the ring. Don't try to stay and fight—run. Once we've got you past the ring I can get you the hell out of here and we'll all be a lot safer."

They had barely gotten out of sight of the inn when the sky opened up and drenching rain began pouring down, the wind driving it so that visibility was limited.

Even in the rain, the stench of the ogre was terrible. Nick's cloak had apparently been spelled to keep it from flapping around, but the waterproofing could only do so much. It was simply a matter of time before his clothes were soaked through and he began to feel chilled.

They had traveled like that for a few miles, settling into a steady, if unpleasant, rhythm when the cart abruptly jerked to a rocking halt and Loog let out a deafening basso bellow that was cut off when arrows pierced his throat.

Nick pulled his gun, fighting to control his mount as it shied and bucked, startled by a blast of flaming magic aimed directly at its chest. From the corner of his eye he saw David pull a shotgun from beneath the cart's seat, stand, and fire into the bushes beside the road. Something there screamed in pain.

It was luck more than skill that kept Nick from being crushed when his horse fell, killed beneath him. Kenneth leapt into position above him, flames dancing in his left hand as he fired shot after shot from the Glock in his right. The whole time Nick spent scrambling to his feet, Kenneth stood there like a rock, unflinching even as an enemy rider charged straight at him—only to fall when her horse was hamstrung by Pug. The gargoyle moved in a blur of speed, disappearing up the nearest tree even as the attacker rolled to her feet. Nick shot her twice in the chest. The powerful magical strike she'd been readying to throw at Kenneth dwindled and died along with her.

David used Loog's corpse for cover as he loaded more shells in the shotgun, but Nick screamed a warning as he saw more enemies advancing on them from the rear. A Sidhe male, his face shadowed by the hood of his cloak, called out the words of a spell and made a throwing motion, but whatever he intended struck wide as sixty-five pounds of living, solid granite, armed with claws and teeth, dropped onto him from a branch overhead.

The gargoyle rode the attacker off the horse, which panicked, rearing, and blocking Nick's view for a moment. The next thing

Nick saw was a dismembered head with a long red braid flying into the night.

"Go, go, go!" Kenneth waved Nick and David toward the woods.

"Come on." David was just suddenly beside Nick, tugging at his arm. They sprinted for the woods. Nick didn't like leaving their allies in the middle of a life-and-death battle. He felt as though he was abandoning them. But his gun had already clicked empty and he had no way to protect himself from magical attack.

The brothers had barely cleared the edge of the woods when a pair of Sidhe women stepped from behind some trees. One threw a shimmering silver net over David, freezing him in place. In the next instant, a swarm of doxies swooped in, going straight for the eyes and necks of the attackers. As the Sidhe and the doxies fought, Nick pulled the net off of his brother, who drew in a huge, gasping breath.

"We have to keep moving," Nick shouted above the horrible screeches of the doxies and screams of their victims. Even with the sudden and unexpected appearance of the doxies their side was in trouble. Kenneth and Syrelle were fighting back-to-back in the middle of the road amid the burning ruins of the wagon. The enemies would appear, then disappear, illusion and the rain working to their advantage.

A war cry erupted from the throats of the remaining mounted guards. They'd regrouped, and now were thundering into the midst of the battle on horseback, weapons drawn and magics ready. One of the riders used her horse to ride down the attacker in front of Kenneth. Reaching an arm down, she helped the guardsman swing up behind her as her partner used a sword to cut off the arm of the Sidhe preparing to throw magic at her back.

Another pair of riders came up beside the brothers. "Climb up," the nearest shouted. "Their reinforcements are coming. I can feel it."

He didn't have to say it twice. Stuffing the net into his belt, Nick clambered up out of the gully behind the guard. The second he was settled, they galloped into the woods, moving faster than ever, zigzagging through the trees. Wind and rain pelted them, branches smacked and tore at them.

Lightning cracked overhead, followed by an ominous roll of thunder. Nick heard hissing just as David shouted a warning. He and the man he was riding with both ducked; a ball of flame passed over their heads, close enough to feel the heat, and smashed into a nearby tree, setting it furiously ablaze despite the storm.

"I thought they wanted to capture us, not kill us," Nick muttered.

"They can't afford to let us escape alive. Not when we could identify them."

He had to be joking. Nick couldn't see a damned thing in this storm. "I can't."

"I could," the guard said, weary irony clear in his voice. They rode into a clearing and the guard said, "Get ready."

He reined the horse to a stop. It reared, and Nick was dumped unceremoniously onto a slick, wet carpet of leaves and mud. In the next instant Sidhe and horse were galloping. Peering after them in the gloom, Nick would have sworn there were still two men on the horse and that one of them looked exactly like him. Then the rider was gone, and from the sound of things, their pursuers were following him.

Pug's claws grasped Nick's pant leg. "We need to get moving. David and Kenneth are up ahead. The illusions won't buy us more than a moment. Hurry, and be quiet about it."

"Right." Despite the poor footing and Nick's unfamiliarity with moving through a forest, he and Pug soon reached a second, smaller clearing. Shimmering in the center was a magical door, much like the one Brianna had created to bring them into Faerie. Kenneth and David were standing in front of it.

The second David caught sight of Nick, he dived through the opening.

Someone shouted behind Nick, who spun and saw a figure pointing in their direction. Kenneth, Pug, and Nick all swore and Nick broke into a scrambling run, straight at the portal. He dived through with Pug at his heels and landed with a thud on the hardwood floor of Brianna's apartment.

There was the sound of a gunshot as Kenneth screamed out the harsh words that closed the portal, then fell, his chest a mass of blood.

30

BRIANNA HAI

Brianna felt as though she'd been doused in an icy lake. Her body shook. Her mind refused to wrap itself around the truth of what was happening, even as her father's guards surrounded her, weapons drawn. They bound her with magically reinforced handcuffs and shackles, then dragged her bodily from the king's presence, through the crowded banquet hall, and down the passages that led to her father's study. It was a long, dispiriting trek. But it gave her time to gather herself enough that she regained her feet and managed to shuffle awkwardly under her own power through the hissing, whispering crowd of servants and toadies who came out to witness the spectacle of her humiliation.

Faced with a coterie of armed guards escorting a prisoner, the nobles who'd gathered outside the study melted into the shadows. A small voice in the back of Brianna's mind told her to look closely at those dark places, for those people were her enemies. They'd planned to kill her this night. She regained the presence of mind to memorize their faces. Later she would work with Pug or Kenneth to put faces to names. Because while her king may have seen fit to throw her out of Faerie, there were those few with enough human blood to cross the veil to seek her death in the human world.

She'd hoped she would be allowed the dignity of climbing through the painting on her own, but she was mistaken. She was unceremoniously picked up and flung through like so much trash.

It was instinct, more than anything that made her tuck her body into a ball and roll as she fell so that the impact of her shoulder on the floor of the hallway was lessened as much as was possible. Even so, she had enough momentum to slam hard into the far wall of her entrance hall, missing slamming her head onto the leg of the occasional table by a fraction of an inch. Her father's men, meanwhile had taken to throwing her possessions through after her, delicate and breakable items crashing against the floor to their ruin, to be buried moments later in mounds of fabric as elegant gowns that had hung for years in the closets of Abracham House were disposed of without thought or care for their value.

The noise had brought Pug and the others running to see what was happening.

"Are those . . . shackles?" Pug's voice came from the deep shadows at the top of the staircase leading down to the shop. Brianna could barely see him around the growing pile of junk.

"Do you need me to help you? We need to get you and the kittens out of the hallway before they get to the furniture."

Furniture? What was he talking about? Brianna didn't have . . . she followed his gaze to the painting, where she could see a pair of guards walking into her father's library carrying her mother's couch.

Brianna rolled over and got her knees under her. Snagging the black kitten from where he'd jumped to the floor and was batting at a strand of pearls, she dumped him into the laundry basket with his siblings atop the occasional table and staggered to her feet. Grabbing the basket, she stumbled through the mess toward the entrance to the main living area of the apartment. She made it to the doorway as the couch was flung through the portal. It crashed against the wall, breaking through the plasterboard. The wooden frame of the couch cracked from the impact.

Rage washed over Brianna, but she kept silent. She suspected that her father and the others were watching, eager to see her reaction. She'd be damned if she'd give any of them the satisfaction of seeing how much this hurt her. Aching with pain that had nothing to do with her physical injuries, she staggered unsteadily to her bedroom, carrying the kittens and trying to ignore the sounds of destruction behind her.

Brianna wanted desperately to just shut the bedroom door behind her, closing herself away from everyone and everything long enough to have a good cry. But tears would have to wait. She needed to know if David, Nick, and the others had made it back safely. She'd seen Pug, and it did her heart good to know that her best friend in the world had made it back from Faerie relatively unscathed. But what of the others?

Brianna pulled the door to the bedroom firmly closed, shutting the kittens safely inside. Only when she began to cross the living room did she realize that it wasn't empty. David was sleeping on the couch, snoring softly, oblivious to the commotion all around him.

Nick was not asleep. He lay propped up on one elbow, dark eyes taking in everything.

"Is he all right?" Brianna spoke softly as she gestured to David.

"He's fine. Just exhausted."

Brianna's muscles sagged just a little in relief. "You?"

"I'll be okay." He paused, "Are those *shackles*?"

"Yes." Brianna was surprised at how much bitterness filled that one word. *Don't think about it. You're alive. They're alive, and safe back from Faerie. It's almost more than you dared hope for. Thank the deities, and forget the rest.*

Brianna didn't elaborate. She really didn't want to talk about it. Turning her back on her guests she shuffled awkwardly over to the kitchen area where Pug waited patiently, paced across the kitchen counter gathering glasses and dishes from the cabinets. Behind her she could hear Nick moving to join her.

"You need to eat. There's leftover bread, milk, and honey in the refrigerator." Pug's voice was flat, his tone grim.

"Tell me everything," Brianna ordered.

"Sit down. You can eat while I talk. The news isn't good—but it could be worse."

"Just tell me."

"As you can see, we made it back, but it wasn't easy. Kenneth was injured, but between Mei and I, we managed to stabilize him enough that his own healing abilities will have him back on his feet in a day or two. He's resting in my bedroom."

"I should go check on him."

"It can wait. Eat. There's more you need to know."

"What?" Brianna asked as she gathered milk, bread, honey, and fruit from the refrigerator and began setting out the food and drink so that her guests could help themselves.

"I killed your brother Eammon."

Oh, fuck.

"He was part of the raiding party trying to kill us and take the humans. There was a battle. I didn't realize it was him when I first struck, but I'd have done it anyway. They gave us no choice. We were battling in earnest."

Brianna was shocked silent. Sweet deities. Her brother . . . Eammon . . . they hadn't been close, but she found her eyes filling with tears. Her throat tightened, making it hard to swallow, hard to even breathe. Suddenly, unexpectedly, she found herself being held. Nick had taken her in his arms, offering the warmth and comfort of a hug.

"I'm sorry it was him I killed, but not sorry I killed him." Pug sounded weary, but there was stubborn anger in his voice as well.

Brianna shook her head. It was hard to speak, but she knew that she had to—Pug needed to know that she understood, that as bad as this was, it wouldn't end their friendship. "Not your fault," she managed to choke out the words. Even though she hadn't been there, hadn't seen what happened, she believed that, believed him. Pug simply would not have killed a member of the Sidhe royal family unless he was given no other choice.

"Tell that to your father," Pug said bitterly.

Oh, sweet deities, her father. It hurt to even think about what he must be going through—particularly knowing that she couldn't contact him, couldn't comfort him. She was an exile now, an outcast.

"Brianna," Kenneth's voice called to her from Pug's bedroom. Just her name, but she could hear the pain in his voice.

"Coming," Brianna called. She stepped out of Nick's arms and he let her. Grabbing a dishrag from a nearby hook she wiped the tears from her face. Setting the rag aside, she prepared a plate and glass for Kenneth. If he was injured, he'd need to eat.

Plate in one hand, glass in the other, she shambled across the apartment, her steps made awkward by the short chain that bound her shackled feet.

Moving more swiftly, Nick moved past to open the door for her.

When Brianna decided to renovate the upper floors of the building to make permanent living quarters she set aside a bedroom for Pug. It was a nice room, twelve by twelve feet, with a bedroom suite made of oak that the gargoyle seldom used, and matching bookshelves that he did. His favorites, Heinlein and Jim Butcher were on the lower shelves, with samples from Charlaine Harris, Robert B. Parker, and Laurell K. Hamilton on the upper shelves. The bookends were geodes, sliced to reveal amethyst crystals. The walls had been painted slate gray, and blackout curtains covered the windows, so that there was no chance of a human accidentally catching sight of the gargoyle moving around. The hardwood floor was covered with a rug patterned in shades of gray and purple.

Kenneth lay on the double bed that dominated the room. He looked awful. His handsome features were drawn with pain, more than half of his naked chest covered in bandages through which blood was beginning to seep. His color wasn't good, either. And while it was obvious he should lie still, he was trying to sit up.

"Stop that!" Brianna ordered. "You need to be resting." She set the plate and glass onto the end table beside the bed within his easy reach and began helping him to sit up by propping pillows behind him.

"How am I supposed to manage that with all this commotion?"

He was right, of course. Brianna had been doing her level best to ignore the sounds coming from the portal in the outer hall, but it wasn't easy. *Surely they'll run out of things to toss soon. I didn't* have *that much.*

"I'm naked," Kenneth observed. "Where are my clothes?"

"In the trash. There was no saving them. But if you're looking for the envelope, it's in the drawer of the end table beside the bed," Nick responded.

Brianna moved aside, and Kenneth pulled open the drawer. Sure enough, inside was an envelope of ivory vellum stationery with her name written in her father's bold script.

With trembling hand, she reached into the drawer to pick it up. It was heavy, the flap sealed with wax affixed with the king's seal. Cracking it open she found a key, and three pages, folded neatly, with no writing visible on them.

"The key to your shackles."

Brianna stared at the key in her hand. He'd known then, before the dinner, before Kenneth had even left with David and Nick for the trip through the tunnels . . . but he still—it made no sense. She stared at the blank sheets, willing them to explain. There was a message there for her. There had to be. But how was she supposed to unlock the spell and read it?

"Did he tell you to say anything, give me any message?"

"No. He was angry with you. I know that. He had fed your friends, offered them hospitality as guests, which made it his duty as well as yours to protect them."

That was true, in its way. The laws of hospitality were taken very seriously among the Fae. But while such protection was implied, it was not certain if left unstated—the king had to have known that: had to have. So why . . . *to draw out the enemy, to let him know who he could and couldn't trust.*

"But when your sister attacked David he knew you would take matters in your own hands. It's your way—just as it was your mother's."

"And he planned accordingly." There was bitterness in Brianna's voice as she took the key and slid it into the lock at her wrists. The bracelets fell to the floor with a clank. It was worse knowing that what he had done to her had been done cold and with calculation— the pain, the humiliation, all part and parcel of some spectacle that served the purposes of the king. Bitter and angry as she was, she decided to wait to deal with his message, whatever it might be. She was simply too hurt, too angry to deal with it right now.

Her eyes stung, but she blinked back the tears, unwilling to let either Kenneth or Pug see her weakness. Bending at the waist, she undid the shackles on her feet.

Once free of their encumbrance, and again in control of her emotions she gathered up the chains and passed them to Pug. "Put these somewhere safe, but out of my sight if you would."

"And the key?"

"I'll keep it." It would be a reminder that Leu was always the king and a politician first, and her father a distant second.

As she spoke Brianna realized that the sounds from the hall-way had stopped. It was finished then, at least for the moment.

"Eat and rest. Enjoy my hospitality and my thanks," Brianna said formally.

"My thanks, *Ard Reigh*." Kenneth gave her a sad, sympathetic look. "And my condolences on the loss of your brother—and . . . everything."

Brianna's vision blurred, and she found herself having to fight back tears. She would grieve, but privately. She managed to choke out the words, "Thank you." Turning, she pushed past Nick, who laid a gentle hand on her shoulder.

"I'm sorry."

She turned to him. "You're sorry?"

He continued. "I'm sorry about your brother. I'm sorry about the mess with your father. I'm sorry for the things I said in the hospital. But mostly, I'm sorry we forced you to bring us along. You didn't want to. You knew there'd be trouble."

He was right. She had. But in the heat of the moment she'd de-cided it would be better to have them at her back. If she'd known the cost . . . but no, only the oracles were given foresight, and even theirs wasn't perfect. Things change—people change them, fight-ing to defy Fate and what she has planned for them.

"You need to eat and get some sleep," Nick said gently.

"The mess—"

"Will still be there in the morning, waiting." He gave her a wry grin. "We can work on it then."

Brianna looked over at Kenneth, who'd eaten his meal and fallen back to sleep; and over at David passed out on the couch. They might sleep through the commotion of clean up, but they might not, and they really needed their rest. For that matter so did she. And while Pug would never complain, he had to be as exhausted as the rest of them. She wondered absently where he'd gone—he wasn't anywhere in sight, but decided he probably wanted to be alone.

"I need food."

"Good plan," Nick said. "Mind if I join you?"

"Feel free."

They ate—bread and honey with milk, which satisfied their Fae sides, but Brianna also sliced up some leftover ham in the back of the fridge and heated it up, and fried up a couple of eggs to go with it.

The food smelled wonderful, and Brianna realized just how ravenous she'd been. Breakfast had been too nerve-wracking a meal for her to eat much, and she'd simply been too busy to eat anything since, and while the meal was nothing fancy, it was hot, and filling, and she found herself digging in with gusto, as did her companion.

They were too busy eating to talk at first, but when the worst of their hunger pangs had been satisfied Brianna looked across the breakfast bar at him, taking in the details of his appearance for the first time since she'd gotten home.

He was clean, and clean shaven, but battered, with scrapes and bruises visible on his arms and a long, shallow cut across his right cheek. His skin didn't have the grayish tinge it had back when he'd first been injured, but there were dark circles under his eyes, and worry lines creased his brow. The T-shirt he wore was obviously brand new, still bearing the fold wrinkles, and the sweatpants . . . his sweatpants were ill fitting and pink.

"Are those my sweatpants?"

"They are. Hope you don't mind. Pug pulled them out of the laundry for me. They were the only things in the house big enough to fit me. The T-shirt is from your stock downstairs—so I owe you for that, too."

She recognized the T-shirt. She'd designed it herself. It showed a blissed-out woman wearing a turban, sitting behind a crystal ball on a table with a moon-and-stars tablecloth. The caption: "I finally found a happy medium."

It looked good on him, stretched taut as it was over his muscular frame. He was still wearing his talisman, as well.

"Consider it a gift."

"Thanks. It made me laugh."

"Good, it's supposed to."

"Pug said you designed it yourself."

"I did."

"And you can cook, too! A woman of many talents." He grinned at her, and the worry lines disappeared, replaced by dimples that made him look a good ten years younger and a lot more like his brother than he usually did.

"Thanks." She returned his smile, warmth spreading through her. Small talk, they were making small talk, even flirting a little. And despite her exhaustion, and the emotional strain of the past few days she felt her pulse speed up just a little.

"So, are you glad to be back home?"

"Oh, hell yeah." The words popped out of his mouth without a second of hesitation. "No insult meant your home world," he added quickly.

"None taken."

"Are you glad to be back?" He gave her a penetrating look.

"Yes, I am. I wish it was under better circumstances. I hate being at odds with my father. But it is a relief to be able to just relax and be Brianna, not the *Ap Reigh* or *Ard Reigh* or Helena and the king's daughter. I cannot wait to get back to doing stupid ordinary things like running the shop and working out at the gym." Brianna began gathering up the empty dishes. There weren't any leftovers, a fact which drove home the fact that another ordinary thing she'd need to do very soon was make a run to the grocery store.

As she squirted soap in the sink and started the water running

Nick rose and came to join her. Opening the door to the dishwasher he began loading in the plates and glasses while Brianna put the frying pans into the soapy water and slid on a pair of rubber gloves. At that point he started chuckling.

"What?" She turned, raising an eyebrow in inquiry.

He shook his head. "It's just"—he paused unable to continue for a second because of his obvious mirth—"those gloves with that dress."

Brianna looked down at herself and started to giggle hysterically. The lovely ball gown she'd started the evening in was definitely worse for wear—but it *was* a ball gown; against it the gloves looked extremely ludicrous.

It felt good to laugh, and it was a wonderful way to relieve the stress of a long and arduous day.

When she finally caught her breath enough she struck a pose, saying, "Didn't you know, this is what all the best princesses wear to do housework?"

That set him off again, and it took a while for the two of them to settle down and finish the dishes in warmth and companionship.

31

KING LEU OF THE SIDHE

Leu stared unseeing into the fire. His firstborn son was dead. Eammon . . . Leu remembered him as a boy, always so serious, trying so hard to be grown up, trying so hard at everything. Proud and stubborn, not as quick-witted as the others, but good, and strong. Of all the children, Eammon was the last, other than Brianna, whom Leu would have expected to betray him.

But he had. And he'd died of it.

It was more than Leu's heart could bear.

But bear it he must. Just as he would have to bear the sorrow of what he'd done to Brianna.

"A king does what he must and the man lives with it." How often had he heard his father utter those words? Leu had thought he'd understood that long before, but he hadn't. Not really.

Perhaps if Leu had taken Eammon into his confidence? No, the plans were too delicate, too convoluted, and Eammon too impatient and clumsy. He'd have tried to help, and gotten himself killed.

Dead regardless, then.

God and Goddess, his son. Fate was such a bitch. Atropos had to have known, that night when she sat there dickering with him, but she'd never let on. . . .

Hadn't Leu paid enough? He'd lost his whole family to Valjeta's first coup attempt. Despite his grief and pain, he'd kept Faerie together. He'd done his best to rule as well and wisely as he knew how. He'd built himself a new family—his lovers, his children. And sure as the sun would rise, there would be more pain, more deaths, in the days ahead.

There was a familiar tap on the library door. Leu pushed the word, "Enter," past the lump of grief and unshed tears that clogged his throat.

Ju-Long slipped silently into the study, his expression serious. He was dressed simply, in nondescript clothing. He spoke in muted tones. "My condolences, your majesty. It is hard losing a child, perhaps the hardest thing of all."

Ju-Long would know, he'd lost several of his children. Dragons are hard to kill without using dragonsbane, but ridiculously easy to slay with it. There was a time when the Sidhe had sought to wipe out the dragons altogether. Only Ju-Long's treaty agreeing that his people would serve the king and royal family had spared those few that remained.

"Thank you." Leu walked over to the buffet against the wall and poured each two crystal tumblers of whiskey. He passed one glass to Ju-Long and sipped from the other before asking, "What is the news?"

"Valjeta is ready to strike. She has murdered enough humans with magic that she, personally, will be able to cross the veil using the magic she's stolen from them. She cannot tear down the veil to bring troops, or enough of the human weapons to sway the outcome of the battles. But you should know that she has attacked your daughter and her shop in an attempt to take Pug, the gargoyle, so it would be safe to assume she has figured out the stone trolls are the anchor to Helena's spell."

Leu swore.

Ju-Long ignored the outburst. "Brianna's shop is a fortress. The gargoyle is safe there, as is your daughter."

"You presume they will stay there."

"It would make sense for her to stay home. . . ."

Leu gave the dragon a long look through narrowed eyes.

"If your majesty wishes, when we finish here I will contact Mei and instruct her to keep the *Ard Reigh* Brianna and the gargoyle in the shop."

Leu nodded. Brianna could overrule Mei, but she wasn't likely to. It wasn't a perfect solution, but it was the best he was going to get unless he was willing to forego the protection provided her by her status as an exile. So long as her enemies believed the fiction that she was not to be his heir they would see no reason to attack her. That, too, wasn't perfect, but the best he could manage, so he moved on. "What of our troop deployments?"

"Your speeding of time on this side of the veil has been fruitful. We've accomplished much this past few days. Ulrich is in position, as are the others. The Diamond King has stationed legions of roc on all the roads heading into the city. King Moash has filled the woods surrounding it with doxies."

"The pixies?"

"Conspicuous in their absence."

"I should've fried them all when I had the chance," Leu grumbled. "Next time I won't be so merciful."

Ju-Long declined to comment on that, continuing his report instead. "The gates have all been activated and are ready for orderly movement of troops. The courtiers know something is afoot. I've put word out that the troop movements and such are a show of force based on recent events. I don't believe anyone suspects that you've caught wind of Valjeta's plans."

"What else? There is something you're not telling me, Ju-Long."

Leu watched the dragon over the lip of his glass. They had known each other a long time. They'd seen, and done much together. So while Ju-Long's face was an unreadable mask to most, it was not to the king.

"There was a raid on Eammon's estate. Ruala and the boys are dead."

"His daughters?"

"Escaped, I think. My man found no trace of them."

Leu turned to stare into the fire. Ruala and the boys, his grandchildren, dead. He closed his eyes against the pain and accompanying rage that threatened to overwhelm him. When he trusted himself to speak he asked, "Was this Valejta's doing?"

"I don't know sire, but it seems likely. Her supporters have begun moving in from the north and the western wilderness; there have been raids on some of the outlying settlements."

"Valjeta needs killing, Ju-Long. She's twisted, evil. If she can't rule, then she'll see it all burn."

"You think that Faerie will fall without you?" Ju-Long raised his eyebrows in surprise. Leu gave a bitter laugh. "Me personally, no. But without a king or queen that the magic accepts and molds to—Faerie will end. You know it as well as I. That is why Fate spared me. There had to be a ruler, one of my family, who was acceptable to the magic. Because Faerie would not—*will not*—accept Valjeta."

"So one of your descendants will take the throne?"

"It is what I bargained for." He took another pull of his drink without bothering to turn away from the flickering flames. "What of Chang?"

"He has been working to find out more about the rumors against *Ard Reigh* Rodan. Unfortunately, he's been unable to find any witnesses. It seems every lesser Fae who might know something has met with an unfortunate accident—he's run into nothing but dead ends."

Leu stared into his nearly empty glass. "So, there is no proof. It could be a setup, meant to make me doubt him."

"It could, but you should know that the lesser Fae fear and hate Rodan. Should he take the throne, they will not support him."

"Well, it doesn't matter now. I've made my choice. Have Chang stop what he's doing. I want him to find Paria and Ilsa and bring them to Brianna. She can shelter them, and offer them as much safety as can be had in the human world."

Ju-Long didn't say anything, but Leu felt his stare even though he watched the flickering firelight reflected in the trace of amber liquid that remained in his glass. "The nobles all would have supported Eammon, had he lived." It was true. Eammon would not have been a great king, but the Sidhe would have supported him—if only so they could use him.

"I'm sorry, sire." Ju-Long's words were gentle.

The silence grew long between them. In the end, it was Leu who broke it.

"I loved Eammon. I would never have imagined he'd betray me." Leu downed the rest of his drink in a single gulp before throwing the crystal tumbler into the fireplace. It shattered with a satisfying crash, sending shards of glass spewing outward. One or two struck the king and Ju-Long, cutting them. Neither man moved nor flinched.

"I will stand beside you, until the end," Ju-Long said softly.

"No, friend, you won't. That is the very last place you will want to be."

32

NICK ANTONELLI

Nick slipped the cabbie a twenty and told him to keep the change. He'd hated to borrow money from Brianna, but hadn't had a lot of choice. His truck had been towed from in front of the shop and was currently in impound, his wallet, keys, and cell phone were all missing—probably lost somewhere in Faerie along with the clothes he'd been wearing. . . . God, had it only been yesterday? Really? It felt like a lifetime had passed. He was tired, sore, and desperately glad to be back home.

There wasn't a news crew camped out in front of the apartment complex anymore—that was a blessing. And he was able to break into his apartment with very little effort—too little. He really needed to spend some time working on home security. How embarrassing would it be for a cop to have to report a break-in? And he did *not* want to have to explain having his weapon stolen.

But that was another worry for later. Now he just wanted to find out how Juan was doing and get back to the real world.

Nick called his mom first. She'd be worrying about him having a bad reaction to having shot the kid, and Juan's injuries, and everything else. She was his mother, after all.

She picked up on the first ring. "Oh, Nick, thank God. I was worried."

He didn't laugh, just shook his head. Some things never changed, his parents were among them. "I'm fine, Mom," he lied. "I needed to get away from the press and the phone. No big deal. Everything okay with you and Dad?"

"The news people keep calling, looking for you, wanting an interview."

Nick groaned. "What did you say?"

"Your father talked to them."

Dear God, that was even worse. His dad, the hardhead. Nick loved him, but he had opinions and wasn't afraid to use 'em. "What did he say?"

"That you're a good cop and a good man. You did what you had to do and everybody should just leave you the hell alone."

Wow, for his father that was actually pretty mild. Unless, of course, his mom was doing a little editing. "Mom?" Nick made it a question.

"Well," she admitted, "maybe he used stronger language. But that was the gist of it."

That's my old man. Nick shook his head, chuckling with wry amusement. His family might drive him crazy, but he loved and trusted them: trusted them to be annoying as hell and occasionally embarrassing, granted. But trusted nonetheless.

"Nick? Did we lose connection?"

"Sorry, Mom. What did you say?"

"Juan's wife called. Maria says he's awake and talking, asking for you. The doctors say he'll pull through," Nick's mother added, with warmth in her voice. "She wants you to please come by the hospital as soon as you can."

Nick's knees almost gave out from relief and he nearly fell into a chair. "Oh, thank God." A load of tension he'd been doing his best to ignore was suddenly gone and he felt giddy. Juan was going to make it. "I'll head over to the hospital as soon as I can."

"Good." There was a long pause. Nick knew what she was going to say, but waited for her to work herself up to getting the words out. "When you see David again, tell him we love him."

Nick pretended not to hear his father's growl in the background. "I'll tell him, Ma."

They hung up after that and Nick went into the bedroom to change clothes. He smiled as he stripped off Brianna's sweats. He liked her a lot, she was sexy, smart, and surprisingly enough, sweet. She had a sense of humor and a sense of honor. In fact, she was pretty much the full package, everything he found attractive in a woman. He knew that pursuing her was probably a bad idea—oh, hell, no probably about it. The feds thought the woman was a killer, and that was the least of her problems—talk about your family issues! But it didn't matter. In his own mind he was now convinced that the feds were wrong. Given the chance, he'd prove it. Once he did . . .

"Think positive," Nick told his reflection in the mirror above the dresser. "Things are looking up." They really were. Juan was going to make it. His statement would probably clear the decks with IAB. Then Nick would just have to go through the mandatory counseling sessions and he'd be back to work.

Assuming he *cleared* the counseling. Probably best if he didn't mention anything about fairies and venom-spewing bat monsters. The shrink might look poorly on that sort of thing.

Chuckling at his own joke, he pulled open the top drawer and grabbed some cash from his emergency stash. There wasn't a lot there. He'd be hurting for money if he wound up on unpaid leave for a while. And, oh, hell, he didn't even have his credit cards. Damn it anyway. Replacing the contents of his wallet was going to be a real pain in the ass.

———

The cab dropped Nick off at the front entrance to the hospital. A quick stop at the front desk let him know that Juan was not only awake, he'd been moved out of ICU and into a regular room. It was such great news that Nick was grinning like a loon when he stepped out of the elevator and almost ran into Martin Brown from IAB looking like someone had made him eat live worms for breakfast. As usual, his suit was the same unremarkable gray as his eyes. His hair was a sandy shade somewhere between blond and brown. Nick would have bet money Brown had chosen a red tie because he'd read somewhere that red was a "power" color. Brown was all about the power.

Nick knew there were good guys in IAB. They wanted to keep everyone on the force honest. Nick could live with that—it was an admirable goal, in fact. But Brown wasn't one of those men. Nope, he was an ass, pure and simple. Most everyone called him "Brownnose" behind his back. Some even did it to his face. He'd earned the nickname.

Currently the bane of Nick's existence, Brown had made it clear that he hoped to find something wrong with the shooting. Since Nick hadn't done anything wrong, he shouldn't have anything to worry about—as long as Brown didn't screw with the evidence.

Nick gave the other man a wide, if not entirely sincere, smile. "There's not a thing wrong now that Juan's getting better. I guess you've taken his statement?"

Brown's face reddened until it was almost the same shade as his tie. "Yes. I wanted to get to him before you had a chance to coach him."

Like he would; or needed to. Bastard. Nick's smile showed lots of teeth, but it wasn't friendly, and it didn't fool the other man for an instant.

"And?"

"He backs up your story."

Oh, Brown hated that. Nick could tell. This time his smile was more sincere. "Which means?"

"There are still some loose ends to tie up, and you'll have to be cleared by the company shrink. But it looks as if you'll be back to work by the end of the week."

"Thanks, Brown." Nick almost meant it.

"You're welcome." Brown didn't. Turning on his heel, he shoved past Nick to jam a furious finger against the button to the elevator. Nick watched until the elevator doors closed and Brown was out of sight, then headed down the hall to visit his partner.

Juan looked like hell. Normally a warm brown, his skin had the grayish-green hue that Nick had previously only seen in the dying. But Juan's smile when his partner came through the door lit up that small, grim room.

"Nick. 'Bout time you got here. Out chasing skirts again?" Juan's voice was a breathy wheeze, barely audible over the hiss of the machine pumping oxygen through the tubes in his nose. He was propped up by pillows and the head of the bed had been adjusted so he could sit up. He was hooked to a lot of machinery, which took up most of the space around the bed, leaving just enough room for a hard metal and plastic visitor's chair. Maria was sitting there. Someone—probably Maria—had taped brightly colored children's drawings to the windows. They were the room's only bright spot.

"Something like that." Nick grinned.

Maria rose to greet him. Her embrace nearly cracked his already-sore ribs and Nick felt the wetness of tears against his chest. "Thank you." The words were a fierce whisper, pitched so her husband wouldn't hear. "Thank you." She'd said it before—said it every time she'd seen him since Juan had been shot.

"Easy, Maria. Don't hurt the man. I'm going to be fine," Juan teased.

"Of course you are," Nick said heartily. "And when you get out of here, you owe me a beer."

Maria gave a choking laugh and released him, moving back to her seat. "Better than that, I think. You'll have to come over to the house. We'll fix steaks on the grill."

"I'll hold you to that."

"Good." She took her husband's hand, careful of the IV tubes attached to his arm. "You just missed Martin Brown."

Juan scowled.

"I ran into him in the hall," Nick said. "It looks as if IAB's going to clear me."

"They should!" Maria answered fiercely. "You didn't do anything wrong!"

"The politicos won't like it," Juan said. "I've seen the way the news has been playing." He grinned. "I also got to see your dad on News 4. That was a treat."

Nick laughed. "Let me guess, they had to bleep half of it out?"

"Not half," Juan said.

"More like three fourths." Maria grinned.

Nick had only been in the room a couple of minutes, but he could see Juan was tiring. It was time to go. "I can't stay. Gotta check in at the office, make sure no one's stolen my stapler. I'll be back tomorrow." Nick worked his way carefully through the maze of cables to stand next to the bed on the side opposite Maria. He held out his fist.

"I'll be here." Juan bumped Nick's knuckles weakly. By the time Nick reached the door, his friend was already drifting off to sleep.

Maria followed Nick out into the hall. "You shouldn't worry. He does that. It's the drugs. But he's getting stronger all the time." Her voice cracked, and Nick pulled her into a hug. She was trying so hard to be strong, but she was exhausted and still looked terribly frightened. This was the worst nightmare of every cop's wife.

"How are *you* holding up? Have you gotten any sleep at all? Who's taking care of the kids?"

"I'm fine. I've slept a little. I didn't want to leave until they were sure . . ." Her voice caught, then she got control of herself. "Once they said he'd be okay and moved him out of ICU, I was able to rest. Relatives are taking care of the little ones."

"Is there anything I can do?"

"You already did it."

"He would've done the same for me."

She nodded, unable to speak. For a couple of minutes Nick just held her. When she pulled back, he let go. "If there's any change, call me."

"I will."

It hit him as he was climbing into the elevator that she couldn't call his cell phone—at least not until he replaced it, and he probably wasn't going to be home much. Shit. He needed to get a new cell phone soonest, and get his truck out of hock, report his credit cards missing, and replace his driver's license . . . it gave him a headache just thinking about it all.

He stepped out of the elevator, and saw Tom Reynolds coming into the lobby from the front doors.

Tom was a senior homicide detective. He'd been on the force long enough to have seen everything at least twice and it showed. He might only be fifty-something, but he looked older, his thinning hair was gray and his wrinkles had wrinkles. His suits were worn, and didn't fit all that well. But he was a good cop, and a nice enough guy. Nick didn't know him well, but he liked him, and he'd never heard anybody on the force say anything bad about him.

"Antonelli—figured I'd find you here."

"You're looking for me?"

"Yeah. I hate to be the bearer of bad news." Reynolds gave a big sigh. "It's your brother. I need to talk to him about a case. I've been trying to reach both him and the other woman who works at Helena's, but they seem to have fallen off the map. The shop's been closed, too, which is weird. Any chance you could help me get in touch with him?"

Shit. Reynolds wanted to talk to David? "You want to tell me what this is about?" Nick hadn't meant there to be a growl in his voice, but there was, and Reynolds heard it.

"We just want to talk to him, Nick."

"Why?"

Reynolds sighed again. "Look, I'm trusting you here." He spoke softly and quickly, with just a hint of nervousness. "This morning I got called to a crime scene that matched some open serial killer cases. We don't suspect your brother, but we think he may have some information that could help. We need to talk to him. It'd be nice if he came in on his own."

Oh, fuck. This was so bad. Nick's stomach roiled and his head started pounding in time with his pulse. *Think Antonelli. If it's a fresh scene, it couldn't have been either David or Brianna, they were with you. But I can't exactly say where we were.*

He had a flash of inspiration. The FBI was interested in Brianna, interested enough that they'd asked him for an in, and had arranged for his uncle's gym to be closed for "remodeling." That meant they were watching her. There'd be lots and lots of pictures of him, his brother, and Brianna taking stuff out to the Dumpster, moving around in the apartment. Maybe audio, too. God he hoped not. Just the thought was pretty damned disturbing all things considered. What would the feds make of the doxie raid? And what had they all talked about when they got back?

"Nick?"

"Reynolds, if it was a fresh scene, David won't have any information. We were both at Helena's with his boss. I stopped on the street to help him with a painting they were carrying, and wound up getting drafted into helping them clean out their storage area. The feds are probably watching the place—they'll have lots of pictures of us hauling stuff out to the Dumpster."

"Seriously?"

"Absolutely. Give the Fibbies a call, ask for an agent name of . . ." Nick had to search his mind for the name. "Jesse Tennyson."

"We're still going to need to talk to your brother. The vics were friends of his. Neighbors saw your brother and his boss in and out of there quite a few times, and there was one of her checks at the scene."

"You want me to bring him in?"

"Yeah, and sooner is better than later."

"I'll see what I can do. I'm stuck without a vehicle or phone right now. My truck got towed and I think my phone is in it."

"You want me to give you a ride to impound?"

"You mind?"

"Nah, no problem." Reynolds jingled his keys as he led Nick through the lobby and out into the late-afternoon sunshine. "You realize that the feds are going to be pissed at you for hanging out with the Hai woman. They're going to want to ask you all kinds of questions."

Of course they were.

33

The good news—Nick's phone actually was in his truck.

The bad news—his grandmother Sophie was at Helena's when he went to pick up David and she was standing toe-to-toe with a Chinese woman, both of them in a fine fury and in full view of the display window.

He pulled the truck into the loading zone and jumped out, hurrying into the shop in hopes of stopping what looked to be becoming a fight.

"You will *not* be tampering with my grandson's mind."

"You dare speak to me thus?" The last *s* was a bit sibilant, and the other woman, too, began to glow. The temperature in the room dropped abruptly so that Nick could see his breath misting in the air.

"Enough!" The word cracked like a whip through the room. Brianna strode down the steps, her black hair pulled back in a ponytail. She wore a tattered housecoat, but she stood so straight and with such an air of power that it could have been a royal robe.

And while Nick could see the faint tracks of tears on her face, there was no hesitation to her command and no question that it would be obeyed.

"*Ard Reigh* Brianna." The Asian woman inclined her head marginally, but did not take her eyes off Nick's grandmother, who had dropped into a deep and graceful curtsy—without taking her eyes off her opponent.

"Explain yourselves."

Sophie spoke first. "Mei wishes to alter my grandson's memories, erasing everything he learned of Faerie. If she does this neither you, nor David, will have a credible alibi when the police arrive—which they will. More to the point, it will render impossible things that must happen. And, because of his nature and the strength of his will, Nick will fight the magic used on him until it eventually destroys his mind."

"Nobody's messed with my mind and nobody is going to," Nick said firmly. "And I've already talked to a homicide detective named Reynolds—told him the truth, that David and Brianna were both here with me last night."

"A *homicide* detective?" Brianna turned to Nick. "Who died?"

Before Nick could answer, his grandmother spoke. "Valjeta has been murdering humans and stealing their magic. She killed the painter and his lover last night."

Nick winced.

"Ed and George are dead?" David's voice was breathy and much higher pitched than usual when he said it. "But we . . . we just saw them."

"I know. So do the police. They want to ask you some questions. I told them I'd bring you down to the station to talk to them."

"Do I need a lawyer?" David sounded scared, and his eyes were very shiny, as if he were fighting tears.

"Yes," Brianna and Sophie chorused.

"It wouldn't hurt," Nick admitted. "I have a guy on retainer from the shooting. It doesn't look like I'll need his services. Maybe we can have him work with you instead. I'll have him meet us at the station. But we've got to go."

"But I don't know anything? I can't believe they're dead. Are you sure it was them?"

Nick didn't answer. Reynolds hadn't told him the names of the victims, just that David and Brianna knew them.

"It's them," Sophie said firmly. "I saw it. That's why I came here, to warn you, and to keep *her*"—she glared at Mei—"from making things worse than they already are."

Mei let out a hiss of displeasure.

"Enough!" Brianna snarled. "Whatever the problem is between the two of you, now is not the time. David, you'd better go with your brother and give your statement." She turned to Nick. "Do I need to go, too?"

"Reynolds didn't ask for you. He said he'd been trying to reach David, and the other woman that works for you—"

"Maxine," she furnished.

"And couldn't get either of them, so he came looking for me, to see if I knew where my brother was."

"Why would they want Maxine?" David asked. "She doesn't even know Ed and George."

"Because they suspect me," Brianna answered.

"But . . ." David turned to look at Nick, who wasn't able to deny it.

"I think," Sophie said seriously, "that someone has gone to a lot of trouble to bring Brianna's name to the attention of the authorities and keep it there."

"Valjeta?" Kenneth stood behind Brianna on the staircase. Nick hadn't seen him arrive.

"It would stand to reason," Mei said. "Not only would it cover her own tracks, it could cause no end of problems for Brianna— and should she be convicted, this state has the death penalty, so that she would be forced to flee to Faerie—where she faces a death sentence as an exile, or stay here and risk execution."

"You're assuming," Kenneth said, "that she knows about Brianna's exile. It only just happened."

"I think"—Mei bared her teeth—"that Valjeta knows everything that goes on in Leu's court."

Brianna looked pensive. When she spoke, her voice was calm, controlled. "Mei, what day is it?"

"Monday the twelfth. Why?"

"It's three in the afternoon on Monday. Maxine should be here. Where is she?"

34

BRIANNA HAI

Riding in Sophie's silver BMW was like being carried by a cloud—a fast moving, silent cloud that smelled faintly of leather and Chanel No. 5.

The seer was patently unhappy to be taking Brianna to check on Maxine. There had been no message from her calling in sick, and she hadn't answered either her cell or land line when Brianna tried to call. Under the circumstances, Brianna had insisted on going to check on her employee—despite the fact that Sophie and Mei had both said it wasn't safe.

Safe or not, Brianna was going. Maxine was her employee and her friend. She needed to be sure that Valjeta hadn't harmed her. So, she'd left Kenneth with Pug at the shop and drafted Sophie into driving her to Maxine's. Mei was flying up separately.

Despite her worries for David in his interview, and for Max, Brianna couldn't help but be curious about the woman behind the BMW's wheel. She'd heard a lot about Cephia, back when she was in the guards, from her mother, and of course from court gossip. This woman had given up a position of power to save Brianna's father—and had been exiled as a result.

"Before you ask," Sophie said, without turning her gaze from the road, "I loved Leu. I also love Faerie. I believed . . . I *still* believe . . . he was our best hope. I don't regret what I did. In fact, I'm proud of it. Valjeta had to be stopped."

"So you and Fate . . ."

"Two of her aspects, anyway. Atropos wanted no part of it." Sophie's voice changed to an impersonation of the crone's voice, "All things end. Everything dies. Including Faerie."

"And you couldn't accept that."

"Of course not," Sophie snapped. "Could you?"

Brianna considered that for a moment. Even with everything that had happened, could she just let Faerie cease to be, doom her people to die or live in permanent exile here among the humans?

No. She couldn't. Damn the cost. She'd save them if she could. Just as Sophie had.

"I've made a good life for myself on Earth," Sophie continued. "But I still miss Faerie. Every single day."

Until that moment Brianna hadn't noticed any resemblance between Sophie and her grandchildren. But in sadness she could see it, a cant to the eyes, the curve of a strong jaw. David had those, as did Nick.

Thinking of them made Brianna's stomach knot with nerves. The police were investigating a murder and she and her friends had been dropped right into the middle of it. Fury tried to rear its ugly head, but she fought it down. Emotion would only cloud her head, and she needed to be clearheaded.

"My father met with Fate the other night."

"Did he?" Sophie smiled. "That must have been interesting. What did they tell him?"

"I don't know. He's not spoken about it much."

"Your father always did know how to keep a secret. He's a canny one—and clever. We chose well."

Brianna didn't know what to say to that, so she remained silent, watching the scenery pass swiftly by.

"Tell me, have the aspects changed positions yet?" Sophie asked. "Atropos had been in her role a long time even back then. Has she stepped down and moved on?"

"If she has, I haven't heard it."

Sophie shook her head. "Stubborn old hag."

It was another statement to which Brianna could make no comment. She had never met any of the aspects of Fate. She wouldn't know. Still, she recalled her lessons. Fate was unique. She had three distinct personalities, three souls, sharing a single body. When the aging aspect, Atropos, chose to move on, stepping back onto the wheel of life and death, Lachesis moved to take her place. Clotho replaced Lachesis and the two elder aspects sought a new soul from among the dying to become the youngest aspect.

Once, long ago, Brianna's tutor had forced her to memorize the original names of every woman who'd assumed an aspect of Fate. But that had been a long time ago. She couldn't remember any of them.

They were getting close now; their exit was just ahead. Brianna closed her eyes and muttered the words of a spell before sending her power outward, seeking.

"I'm surprised you can do that in a moving car," Sophie observed.

"You need to take the next exit," Brianna said, then added, "My human mother's blood helps me. I'm surprised you can drive a car."

"My talent isn't so much active magic as an altered state of being. Humans can come close to it with the right drugs—but they usually overdose when they try."

Brianna's power returned in a wash of warm air.

"Well?" Sophie asked.

"Go left. Max is home, and she's in trouble." Her expression grew grim.

A few more directions had Sophie pulling the BMW into the driveway of Maxine Taylor's suburban, split-level house.

"Where's Mei?" Sophie asked, looking up through the windshield. "Flying, she should've been here before us."

"I've no idea, but I'm not waiting for her."

Brianna was out of the car before Sophie could respond. She hurried up the sidewalk, past beautifully tended beds of orange and yellow flowers and brightly painted lawn gnomes scattered among chunks of sparkling quartz, climbing up to the front step.

Despite its pale yellow walls, white trim, and forest green shutters and door, the house looked grim. Every window was shut, the curtains pulled tight. Brianna could *feel* darkness and despair radiating outward and thought she heard whimpering coming from inside.

Tears filled Brianna's eyes. Closing them, she extended her hands, using her power to check the wards that should have protected Maxine's home and finding only shattered shards of disintegrating power, melting like icicles in the sun.

She knocked firmly on the door, calling, "Max, are you in there? It's Brianna, and I've brought David's grandmother with me. We're here to help."

"Go 'way. Can't talk." The whisper grew panicked. "Can't, can't, can't. Mustn't tell."

"We're here to help."

"She'll be so angry!"

"Max, it's okay. I'm not going to hurt you."

"Not you. The *other one*."

"It's going to be okay, Max, I promise. Just let us in and we'll take care of it. Trust me."

After a long, tense moment, Brianna heard movement behind the door, heard it unlock and Max scurry away again. Sophie pushed the door open and gestured for Brianna to precede her.

The place was dark. No hint of light leaked in through the drawn drapes, and none of the lights in the house were on. Once Brianna's eyes adjusted, she looked around for Maxine, normally a large, no-nonsense, earth mother type who kept her iron-gray hair in a single long braid that hung past her shoulders and whose makeup was always understated but perfect. She generally wore loose, flowing cotton skirts and plain T-shirts in various shades of brown and green. She kept her person, and her home, neat, cheerful, and comfortable, which made the change in her all the more shocking.

The woman curled in a ball in the darkest corner of the living room had wild, red-rimmed eyes. Her hair stuck out around her head and her filthy nightgown was pulled over her knees so that only the tip of her manicured toes peeked out from beneath the fabric, their perfect red polish oddly incongruous with the wreck of the rest of her appearance.

She saw them looking at her and covered her face with her hands, whimpering piteously.

"I'll call an ambulance," Sophie said.

"Wait," Brianna answered, choking out the word past the lump of anger in her throat.

"It's gone too far." Sophie shook her head sadly. "She needs more than magical help."

Brianna was furious. Someone had used and abused her friend, leaving her mentally and emotionally damaged. Brianna would dearly love to get her hands on them, deal out a little retaliatory abuse of her own. But now was not the time. Max needed her.

Moving slowly, she approached the whimpering woman with the care she would use for a frightened child or a wild animal. She whispered soft, reassuring words as she knelt before Max and began gathering her will until her entire body sang with power. When she was sure Max wouldn't bolt, Brianna laid a gentle hand against the bare skin of her friend's ankle.

There was a sound like a sonic boom and a flash of pure white light bright enough to blind. Brianna spoke firmly: *"Let her go!"* Her voice had an odd, echoing quality that filled the room like water fills a cup.

"She is mine!" A second female voice came from everywhere and nowhere. With each word, the temperature in the room dropped, until their breath misted in front of them and gooseflesh crawled across exposed skin.

"She is her own. You cannot have her." Brianna's voice was harsh now, grown rough with pain and exertion. Every inch of her body was straining, the cords of her neck showing stark against the skin.

A cold wind, smelling of fresh snow, blew through the closed room. Maxine's teeth began chattering and the tears on her cheeks began to freeze.

"A quaint conceit, little one. I take what I want, unless someone is strong enough to stop me. You shouldn't have gotten in my way."

"The hell you say," Brianna shouted in defiance, her features twisting in a feral smile. "Bring it on, bitch."

She knew she was being stupid, knew she should be afraid. She'd been injured more than once in the past two days. It didn't matter. The enemy was here, before her. All the anger, hurt, and pain of the past few days hardened into raw determination. She *would* bring this creature down, punish her for the harm she'd wrought. Once a guard, always a guard. Brianna had worn the uniform. She was a protector of her people, *all* of her people, on both sides of the veil.

The smell of putrefying flesh began to fill the room, thick enough to coat the tongue and make Brianna gag. Darkness swirled, beginning to take form—a woman's form, and one Brianna recognized.

"Valjeta!" Sophie's voice was a perfectly timed distraction.

The woman turned, hatred twisting her features. *"You."*

It was the perfect opportunity, perhaps her only chance. Brianna kept her right hand pressed against Max's skin, keeping the link to Valjeta open, while her left moved with practiced speed to the hilt of the dagger tucked into the top of her boot. She shifted her grip until only the tips of her fingers touched Max's ankle and used the knife in her left hand to slice open her right palm.

Blood flowed over skin and Brianna began to chant. She flung the bloodied knife, point-first, into the wooden top of the nearby coffee table. As the words built, the power growing with them, stars swam in her vision. Her ears popped as the air pressure in the room became a crushing pressure.

The smell of death began to recede, then grew even stronger. Darkness and light swirled about each other. Maxine gave a long, piteous wail. Brianna continued to chant, heading toward a crescendo. She reached into her blouse and yanked at the crystal she wore on a chain around her neck.

Darkness surged forward, trying to swallow her whole. For a single, terrifying moment Brianna couldn't see, couldn't feel anything but hopelessness and death. She fought off the despair, refusing to let anything interfere with the spell she was casting. Blind, gagging, with a last, triumphant gasp, she finished.

At the same instant the chant ended, the chain broke and the rose quartz talisman lay free in her bloodied palm.

It was a good thing that Brianna was kneeling, for she would surely have fallen down as the stone inexorably sucked both her light and Valjeta's darkness into its depths. The air pressure in the room plunged, leaving her ears aching from the need to pop.

A shriek of rage and pain tore through the room. The darkness pulsed, then shattered with a crash like breaking glass, and the light broke right along with it.

Brianna had nothing left. She toppled sideways into a graceless heap onto the floor with barely enough energy to breathe.

35

"I'm calling an ambulance," Sophie said. "No arguments." She rose to her feet a bit shakily, then crossed the room to pick up a telephone.

Brianna wasn't going to argue. She didn't have the energy.

Her hand was throbbing in agony. The quartz, formerly a lovely pink and white, had turned a dull black, laced with pus yellow and green. It was abnormally heavy, and hot to the touch. It was a struggle to find the strength to stuff it in her pocket. When she did, immediately her hand felt better.

So much power jammed into such a small bit of rock. Some of it was hers, which explained her terrible weakness. But most had come from Valjeta. Brianna had hurt her, no doubt about it. And while she felt a certain grim satisfaction at that, she also knew that she'd made a powerful and ruthless enemy utterly furious.

"You should have killed her." Max's voice was a bare whisper, her gaze intent despite the tears that traced steady lines down her cheeks before dropping, unheeded, onto her nightgown.

"I wasn't strong enough." Brianna didn't like admitting that, but it was the truth. "She had too much power. And it felt strange, wrong somehow."

Sophie returned to Brianna's side, squatting beside her. "The ambulance is on its way," she announced. "It's not a surprise that she was too strong for you—it wasn't just her own power you were fighting. Valjeta has murdered many humans and stolen their abilities. You weren't fighting one woman, you were fighting a legion."

"I'm amazed that you survived. I'm even more amazed that she hadn't already murdered your friend here."

"She was saving me." Maxine's voice was a little stronger and saner than it had been. Maybe in time, with the right treatment, Brianna's friend would recover. "She said that when the time came, she'd use my magic and the gargoyle to break the spell." Her eyes locked on Brianna's. "I didn't . . . don't want to help her. She's going to do something terrible."

"I'm sure you're right about that," Sophie said, and Maxine wept harder, probably in response to the conviction in the older woman's voice.

———

A doctor in green scrubs stepped through the patterned cloth curtains that offered Brianna a semblance of privacy. She was hooked up to IV lines that were feeding her antibiotics and pain medication. Very good pain medication apparently, since her hand was no longer screaming in agony and the world was starting to have lovely soft edges. Sophie was sitting beside her bed.

"The receptionist tells me that you came in with Maxine Taylor." He looked at each of the two women in turn.

"We are," Sophie agreed.

"Which of you is Brianna Hai?"

"I am," Brianna said.

"Ms. Taylor signed a HIPAA release and asked that I let you know what was happening."

Brianna nodded.

"I'll step outside for a moment if you like," Sophie offered. When the doctor nodded, she got up and walked away, her retreating footfalls sounding a staccato beat on the floor tiles.

When he was certain she was out of earshot, the doctor began briefing Brianna on her friend's condition. "I've had to give Ms. Taylor a sedative. She was quite agitated—terrified that someone was out to harm her."

"She has been in actual danger," Brianna told him, trying to figure out, between the pain meds and the basic unreality of the situation, an explanation that would be palatable to the doctor. In the end, she said, "She has a stalker."

"I see," the doctor said grimly. "So it's not just paranoia."

"No," Brianna said firmly, "it definitely isn't."

"Well, we'll be transferring her to our mental health facility on a forty-eight-hour hold as soon as we can get the paperwork finished and arrange for transport. It's a secure facility. She'll be safe there while we determine the extent of her psychological problems. I have to tell you, I'm quite worried about her. I think we need to keep her under close observation so that she doesn't harm herself."

Brianna nodded, feeling grim. Magic might have caused Max's condition, but though the doctors' treatments might be hindered by their lack of belief in magic, they should still be able to do her some good. Hopefully the facility's security would be good enough to protect her, at least from most human threats.

There were all sorts of things Valjeta could still do to Maxine if she put her mind to it. But while Brianna was badly injured, she was sure that Valjeta hadn't escaped unscathed. She might still come after Max, depending on how important the woman was to

Valjeta's plans. But that might not be Valjeta's next course of action.

Damn it! Brianna wished she knew what the Sidhe was planning. She already intended to change the wards on the shop so that Max wouldn't be allowed in. But what did Valjeta really want?

"Pug."

"Excuse me?" the doctor asked.

Brianna blinked stupidly. She'd forgotten he was there. The drugs were definitely having a major effect on her.

"Sorry. It's the medicine."

The doctor picked up her chart and checked it before putting it back on the counter and coming to look at her hand.

"You should have come in sooner," he said severely. "The infection in your hand is quite advanced. I don't think we'll have to amputate, but if there is bone involvement, that might become a possibility. I've sent the nurse out to arrange with surgery for a consult, just in case."

"I'm an excellent healer. Give the drugs time and I should be fine." Brianna smiled up at him. Actually, the drugs might not be enough. But she wasn't giving up her hand. Besides, the Fae had healers that could do amazing, miraculous things. One of them would be willing to help her, even in exile . . . for a price.

He was getting ready to argue when she heard a woman cry out. Maxine—Brianna recognized her voice despite the terror in it.

The doctor dropped her hand and raced away. As he pushed through the curtain, Brianna caught a glimpse of what was causing the disturbance: Valjeta.

She was inhumanly beautiful, skin glowing pale and perfect, eyes blazing with power, long blonde hair fanning out behind her in a breeze that smelled of death and corruption and held the shifting shadows of faces, each one screaming in soundless agony.

"Give me Maxine." The words sounded odd, as if she spoke with not one voice, but the roar of a crowd. The temperature in the room dropped until Brianna could see her breath. She forced herself upright. Steadying herself with the IV post, she walked toward her enemy.

"Maxine, come to me." The order was backed with magical compulsion. Brianna heard her friend moan and struggle to obey. When the woman did not appear, Brianna assumed her friend was restrained in some way.

"Stop." Brianna's command was irresistible. The spirits that had been circling Valjeta froze in place, their eerie gazes locked on Brianna.

"You." The blonde Fae's smile made Brianna's blood run cold. But she gathered her strength and courage, steeled her spine, and gave her opponent a look of evident disdain.

Valjeta spoke. "You're not looking nearly so well as you did in your shop the other day, and the injury to your hand looks positively lethal."

"You wish."

"Bold words, let's see if you can back them up, shall we?" The blonde raised a hand. Flames danced on the end of her fingertips.

"Let's not." Kenneth appeared in the doorway behind her. He was smiling and swinging a sling. He loosed it, sending a cloud of what looked like rock salt and nails flying toward Valjeta.

The Fae woman screamed, as much in rage as pain, and hurled a fireball the size of a softball straight at Kenneth. He dropped and rolled and the fireball soared through the door to splatter like napalm against one of the trees outside, instantly setting it ablaze.

As Valjeta turned to face her once again, Brianna heard Mei's voice, ringing out clearly from behind a pair of interior metal doors marked RADIOLOGY. The dragon was chanting a spell.

Valjeta spun toward the door. Using the air around her she gathered the weapons Kenneth had attacked her with, flinging them in a wide arc. There was so much power behind the blow that the tacks embedded themselves in the surface. But there was no blood, no scream of pain, not even a pause in the chanting, which now seemed to be coming from everywhere and nowhere, a second voice, Sophie's, having joined in the chant.

Valjeta hissed, her body hunching in seeming pain though there was no sign of a blow having struck her. "This isn't over, child of Leu. Tell your father, I *will* have what is mine." Then, with a blur of speed too fast for eyes to follow, she was gone.

36

"Put that down." Sophie appeared in the empty air in front of the doctor, who'd rushed across the room and grabbed the phone to call for help.

"The hell I . . ." He stopped speaking, his face smoothing into bland blankness as she shone like a star in front of him. The receptionist, equally affected, stared slack-jawed at Sophie, her eyes blank. "*Ard Reigh*, how do you want to deal with this?" Sophie asked.

That was a good question. This situation was a complete and total disaster and Brianna couldn't think straight. She felt loopy from the drugs, her mind wandering from one thing to another, seemingly without her control.

"Your grace, you need to sit down." Mei put an arm around Brianna's waist before guiding her into the nearest chair. "You're not well."

No, she wasn't. Although she didn't feel bad. Was this what Rihannon felt when she took the drugs? There was no pain or worry, just lovely apathy. The drugs had blunted everything, including her ability to reason.

"Sophie, what do you see in our immediate future?" Mei asked.

Sophie's expression grew distant. "We need to leave. The police and fire department are about to arrive and there's too much we can't explain. We can take the *Ard Reigh* with us, but not the other woman—she's too damaged. Unfortunately, we can't leave her unguarded."

"I'll stay," Kenneth offered.

"You'll need to convince them you're her family. Otherwise they won't let you near her." Brianna paused. "Not that I'm complaining, but how did you get here?" Brianna asked.

"I carried him," Mei answered. Her expression was defiant, as if daring anyone to comment.

Brianna saw Sophie's eyes widen in shock and felt like gasping herself. Dragons were proud and prickly. Never in her entire existence had she heard of one willing to be ridden like a beast of burden.

"Fine." Mei turned to Kenneth. "Stay, guard the woman until you hear otherwise. I'll see to it that none of the employees remember our being here and that they delete Brianna's records."

"Videos, too." Brianna smiled at the three Sidhe, who stared at her blankly. She pointed to a camera in the corner.

Mei swore. "Fine. That, too." She turned to Sophie. "Take the *Ard Reigh* and go. I'll meet you back at the shop."

The shop. Yes, Brianna definitely wanted to go home. There was something she was supposed to do . . . something about the wards, and Pug. The Sidhe . . . Valjeta, she'd wanted him. That couldn't be good.

Swiftly but with care, Sophie removed the IV lines from Brianna's hand. The discomfort was enough to distract Brianna from her thoughts.

"*Ard Reigh*, can you walk?"

"I don't know," Brianna answered truthfully. Weariness was beginning to creep up on her again.

Sophie muttered something under her breath as she helped Brianna to her feet. The older woman half carried her through the doors to radiology before steering her out an emergency exit.

"Why this way?"

"Because the police and firefighters will come to the main door and we don't want them to see you," Sophie explained.

"Oh. That makes sense," Brianna said. And it did, for a moment or two.

Brianna could hear sirens approaching as Sophie helped her stagger across the parking lot. She slumped into the passenger seat of the BMW; Sophie reached across to fasten her seat belt, then rushed around to the driver's side. They were out of the parking lot and a block away when the police and fire vehicles passed them, going in the other direction.

"I hope it'll be all right," Brianna said as the clouds in her mind began to clear again.

"Kenneth and the dragon are very capable. They can handle things at the hospital."

"Not there. At the shop."

Sophie gave her a long look. "*Ard Reigh*, are you sensing something?"

"It's Pug she wants."

"Why?"

"He's the only one on this side of the veil. So it makes sense she would need him." It was obvious from the other woman's expression that she wasn't getting the point, so Brianna tried again. "Valjeta wants Pug. She needs him if she wants to open the veil wide enough for more than just herself to pass through."

"Why?"

Brianna wanted to curse the woman for being obtuse. Sophie was a seer, after all—why couldn't she understand?

"I saw it in her mind when I called earth and air. She believes my mother used the stone trolls as the ground for her spell. Pug is one of their royalty."

Sophie slammed on the brakes hard enough to throw Brianna forward against her seat belt. The car behind them swerved, its driver laying hard on the horn as Sophie steered the BMW onto the shoulder. With a muttered word and a gesture of her hand, smoke began pouring out of the engine compartment.

"Stay here," she ordered.

Brianna didn't argue. She was too tired to move anyway. She watched Sophie walk into the tall grass beside the highway. The seer squatted down and Brianna felt a soft warm wave of power wash over her. Illusion magic, strong, but subtle.

Interested, her mind fighting the drugs that her body wanted to give into, Brianna shifted in her seat to get a better view of what Sophie was doing and pressed the button to lower the electric window, curious to hear Sophie's words. The older woman drew a circle in the air before her. Her sibilant whisper carried clearly to the car even over the sounds of traffic passing by on the highway.

"Leu, Leu, King Leu of the Sidhe, I must speak with you."

A shimmer of light appeared in the air six inches in front of Sophie's face. Brianna was both surprised and not surprised to see her father looking out at the seer. *"Cephia?"* he said.

"Your majesty, we have a situation." Sophie swiftly explained what had happened, including the injuries to Brianna and Maxine.

Her father turned toward Brianna, his eyes locking with hers across the distance. To her shock, he suddenly looked *old*. And though she knew she should be angry with him, that wasn't what she felt. Sad, hurt, worried, yes, but not angry.

Leu's voice was harsh as he spoke over his shoulder. "Clear the room. Send for one of the mages with human magic and my personal healer. She will be going through the veil to tend Brianna

Hai. *Move!*" When the last of the courtiers and servants had left the room, he turned back to the women. "Tell me everything."

Sophie did, speaking swiftly as she could to take advantage of the brief moments of privacy he'd bought for them, concluding with "Brianna says that the stone trolls are the anchor for Helena's spell, and that Pug is one of their royals. Is she correct, or suffering from delusions brought on by human medications?"

"She is correct. Helena gave them speech in exchange for permission to use them as the anchor." Leu stared at his daughter. There was pride in his smile. "So, you figured it out."

"Nope. Overheard it in Valjeta's mind. Did you approve?" Brianna asked. If she'd been in better shape she wouldn't have dared. The king would not be pleased to be questioned, even by one of his daughters. She wasn't sure he would answer. But he surprised her.

"Of course not," he snarled. "Nor did she consult with me. It made me furious, but at the same time, it served my purpose not to stop her. Trapping Valjeta on the human side of the veil separated her from her allies and bought me time."

"I understand."

"Yes, I think you do." He sighed. "That time is almost up, Brianna, whether we are ready or not. And while I would gladly kill the gargoyle myself, we cannot let Valjeta have him." The bitterness in Leu's voice cut like razor blades.

Brianna sighed. "I am sorry for Eammon's death."

Leu gave his daughter a sharp look. His voice was cold and hard. "Are you? The two of you never cared for each other."

Lying was for weaklings, and while she was injured, she was *not* weak. "No, we did not like each other. But he was my brother, and I find I am sorry just the same."

Leu's expression softened slightly and he gave her a long, searching look before finally saying, "I believe you." There was a moment of comfortable silence between them. "Protect the gargoyle."

"I'd do that anyway."

"I know."

She didn't mean to close her eyes. She couldn't help herself. She was tired now, so tired.

"Brianna Ard Reigh!" Her father's voice cut through the mists fogging her mind like nothing else could. She fought for consciousness, crying out in pain, but it was too much. She was too far gone, too weak. Velvet darkness embraced her.

It was an odd dream. No, not a dream. The colors were too bright, too intense to be a dream. A vision, then. Or perhaps the afterlife.

She was in the clearing from Ed's painting—she recognized it at once. The soft sunlight of an early summer morning filtered through flickering leaves of every color of green to speckle the forest floor. The air was warm, thick with the scents of flowers. She could almost feel the life throbbing through the loamy earth beneath her hands. She looked down at those hands—whole, unharmed.

She sensed movement in the brush and looked up. There was nothing to be seen, but she heard the whisper of leaves, a faint footfall. A shadow fell on the ground in front of her—the shadow of a man, but with no one to cast it.

As she watched, the shadow writhed and twisted. She heard a faint moan that became a sibilant whisper: "Murderer . . . thief . . ."

Pain, breathtaking and immediate, centered on her injured hand, ripped Brianna from the vision, dragging her back to the reality of the front seat of a BMW.

"What the hell?" Sophie gasped in shock.

"Sweet deities, Brianna, what have you done?" Morguenna whispered at the same time.

Brianna's eyes fluttered open. She was still strapped into her seat, but her injured arm was stretched out over the window frame and held firmly in place by Morguenna, who also grasped a scalpel smeared with blood and pus. A dark mist hovered in the air above Brianna, swirling and seething with restless energy.

"Tell me now, *Ard Reigh*, what you've done. For king or no, oath or no, if you've taken to working death magic I will *not* use my talents to heal you." Morguenna's face was filled with a terrible rage and her words rang with both power and fury.

37

NICK ANTONELLI

Anyone who has ever bothered to watch a police procedural on television knows about the two-way mirrors. Thing is, they're still effective. You may know somebody might be behind there, but you can't be sure, and you don't know who.

Right now the only person in the room behind the mirror was Nick. It wasn't large, and was dimly lit, but there were a pair of chairs with a small table between them to hold your copy, and with a pencil cup and scrap paper in case you wanted to take notes.

Nick stood, restlessly shifting his weight from one foot to the other, watching his brother be interviewed by Reynolds and some unknown fed, the lawyer watching over the proceedings, making sure nothing untoward happened.

"You and your friends like to LARP?" The fed made it a question.

LARP? Oh, yeah, Live Action Role Playing . . . like Dungeons and Dragons. Why—shit, they were listening at the shop, had to be. What else could they make of all that shit about seers and dragons?

"Occasionally." David looked at the mirror and gave an odd

smile, which was weird. It was almost like he'd heard Nick's thoughts. Only other person Nick had ever seen do *that* was Grandma Sophie, and it was spooky as hell.

The door to the room opened quietly and Jesse Tennyson stepped through. He wasn't wearing the jacket to his suit, his tie had been loosened, and his sleeves were rolled up to show well-muscled forearms. He glared at Nick, eyes blazing, his expression holding equal parts anger and scorn. Taking a seat, he gestured for Nick to do the same, then slammed a file folder onto the table between them.

"What in the *fuck* did you think you were doing?"

Flipping open the file he showed Nick a photo taken with a telephoto lens showing him carrying one half of a damaged settee to the Dumpster wearing his borrowed sweatpants and tee.

"Getting you an in to the gym." He didn't say "asshole" but his tone definitely implied it. "I had to work my ass off to get it, too."

"Explain."

"I was driving to the hospital to visit my partner when I saw my brother and another idiot wrangling this huge painting. The wind had caught it and was dragging them into the street. The other idiot was Brianna Hai. I offered them a ride back to her shop to keep them from getting themselves killed and wound up getting roped into helping them sort through a bunch of her mother's stuff that her father had dumped off on her." It was the truth—almost literally.

"You went into the building wearing jeans and a different shirt. Those are women's sweats."

There wasn't a question there—just an implication. Nick waited for him to ask the obvious question, keeping the upper hand by remaining silent.

"Did you sleep with Brianna Hai?"

"Nope. As you probably heard, judging from the fact that you have her under heavy surveillance."

Tennyson didn't deny it. "Why the change of clothes?"

"I was moving furniture." Which was a non-answer answer.

He could've moved the furniture wearing jeans—probably would've. But they probably would've gotten ruined. Which was exactly what happened anyway. "Mei is the one who owns the gym, but Brianna said she'd talk to her about letting you in."

"Brianna," Tennyson sneered.

"Yeah, *Brianna.* And for the record, I think you're wrong about her. She seemed okay. But you were listening, so you know I didn't blow your cover. But she does think you're a cop."

Tennyson growled.

"All my friends are cops; so's everyone who hangs out at my uncle's gym. You want them to think you're something else, you should've come up with a different cover story."

"Right." Tennyson leaned back in his seat, looking at Nick through narrowed eyes. "So, who's the dragon?"

"That would be Mei, the little Chinese woman. Scary bitch." Nick shuddered at the memory of how casual she'd been about rearranging his gray matter.

"Scarier than Hai?"

"Oh, hell yeah."

"She the one in charge?"

"Of the gym, yeah."

"Of the operation."

"I don't think there is an 'operation'," Nick responded. "But if anybody's in charge, it's Brianna." Nick leaned back in his seat.

"What was your grandmother doing there anyway?"

"She's the seer—prophet, psychic. Whatever."

"Part of the game?"

"I guess." Nick sounded bored and more than a little irritated. The last, at least, wasn't acting. Tennyson was definitely getting on his nerves and, no doubt as planned, had kept him from hearing what was going on in David's interview.

The logical conclusion: he suspected Nick of being involved. Shit.

38

KING LEU OF THE SIDHE

Leu dropped the long braided length of black hair onto the fire and watched it burn. The stench of it filled the strangely empty library; much of its contents had been hidden in secret rooms down in the tunnels or passed "accidentally" to Brianna. Valjeta would not get his treasures easily, if at all, and he would rather they were lost for all time than have them fall into her hands.

War.

The initial raids and feints had begun. Valjeta's people had begun attacking those living in the outlying areas, the ones the most vulnerable. Leu's people were as ready as he could make them, his warriors in place and armed with the best hand-to-hand weaponry available on either side of the veil. He'd also had the king's gates closely guarded, prepared to send refugees to Earth should it come to that, where he had quietly been preparing places for them since the day he took the throne.

Leu had made sure that his people had been exposed to the language and customs of the modern world. The Sidhe would blend in with the humans. The lesser Fae would not be so shocked by the changes to the human world that they would choose to fade. He'd seen to that.

The healers had been given both human and magical training and equipment. It would serve them well both in the war effort and on the other side of the veil.

Leu's courtiers had believed he'd made changes to their world because he was besotted with human ways. He'd encouraged that belief, for it had served his purpose. Even Ju-Long had not known or guessed the full extent of his plans.

Ruling was a lonely business.

Leu stared down at his hands. On his hand was a ring, but not *the* ring. This piece of jewelry was a replacement. On Leu's finger, it looked exactly like the king's seal. Removed from Leu's hand by a traitor, the magic Leu had put into it would summon a bolt of pure energy that would simultaneously consume Leu's corpse and the traitor. It had been Leu's idea, this last death blow, and he hoped and prayed that it would rid his daughter of Valjeta. Brianna would still have to deal with her other enemies but Leu believed her capable of handling them. Valjeta was something else entirely. He wasn't sure *he* could handle Valjeta, but damned if he wasn't going to try.

I am so sorry, Brianna. I know you don't want this, nor do I want it for you. But like it or not, it is your fate to rule as it was mine.

Morguenna was a brilliant healer, but Brianna's wound . . . he could smell it through the portal. He knew that smell, and what it meant. Brianna might lose that hand, or even her life.

Damn Valjeta. Leu was Sidhe, he didn't believe in the Christian notion of hell, but at this moment he wished he did, so he could send his aunt there for eternity. Deities knew she deserved it. How many deaths? How many? And for what? Power? A crown?

Leu turned at the sound of booted footsteps. A guard approached.

Leu recognized his face but couldn't put a name to it. He frowned at himself; he should know the names of the men and women who'd sworn their lives to protect his.

The guard went down on one knee and waited for the king's acknowledgment before saying, "Your majesty, the *Ard Reigh* Rodan is at the door and awaits your pleasure."

"Send him in."

The guard backed away. A moment later, Leu's son strode into the room.

Rodan wore a tunic and trousers in traditional mourning gray, for despite the fact that Eammon had betrayed him, Leu was allowing the family to honor his passing. The younger man had pulled his hair back in a long braid. The severe style suited him, and Leu reflected that his son had inherited no small part of his mother's beauty.

"Your majesty . . . father," Rodan said softly. His expression was a perfect mask of sorrow and grim determination. Or, perhaps not a mask. For just an instant Leu wished he had his own ring on his finger, so that he could test his son as he'd tested Asara.

"My son."

"You have cut your hair, as have mother and the guards. Are we at war, then?" His voice was steady, but there was a thread of eagerness in his words and a tension in Rodan's body that betrayed his excitement. But then, Rodan was a young man, who had never experienced the horrors of battle, the blood, the stench. He'd never heard the screams of the injured and dying. It was normal for him to be eager to test his skill and training, to want to prove himself.

Deities, how old he made Leu feel. "It is a matter of hours."

"What would you have me do?"

You are my son. Given a choice I'd have had you flee to the north with your sister. But that would shame you, and I need every skilled warrior I can get. "Take a message to Brughan. He is to take a company of men and secure the tunnels. When that is done, join Ulrich at the first king's gate. He will be expecting you."

"Of course, your majesty." Rodan bowed low enough that his braid swept the floor before backing to the door.

Leu watched him go, his heart filled with sadness and dread. He knew that Rodan was skilled in magic, that he practiced regularly with all kinds of weapons, including handguns and rifles as well as the Sidhe's traditional knife and sword. His grasp of tactics wasn't what Leu would have it be, but Ulrich was battle seasoned and a fine commander.

Assigning him to Ulrich meant that while Rodan would have a part in the fighting, he would also be able to escape through the gate when the palace fell. Rodan would live, and could take the throne should Brianna die of her injuries.

"Your majesty." A feminine voice interrupted that particularly grim train of thought.

Leu looked over at the new head of his guard as she bowed to him. Kenneth had spoken well of Syrelle. Her record was impressive and when they spoke, Leu could tell that she was decisive and possessed a keen mind. It had been hard for him to choose between her and Gwynneth. In the end, the fact that she had taken part in the action that had seen Brianna's friends safely to the human side of the veil had decided him.

"Yes? What is it?"

She straightened, her gaze meeting his. "Maybelle broke under questioning, sire. She knew more than I expected. We have names and specific times, but not a location."

Leu strode over to the desk. At a muttered word, a three-dimensional map of Faerie appeared like a mist, floating six inches above his desk. Another murmur added the veil and Earth to the image.

"The timing?"

"Seven hours from now."

"Our time or theirs?" Since the ball, Leu had changed the way time ran in Faerie, as was the king's prerogative. By speeding time in Faerie relative to Earth, he'd given himself more time to prepare—and his opponent less.

"Our time."

He nodded. It was much as he'd expected, thanks to the intelligence gathered by Ju-Long.

Syrelle passed the king a list of names. "These are the people she named. She did not know the current location of the traitor Valjeta."

Leu didn't answer. His features darkened, his eyes going from silver to steel gray as he scanned the sheet of paper. In the distance, thunder rumbled ominously. Most of those listed were people he had suspected. But there were many unpleasant surprises as well.

"Shall I send troops to make arrests?"

Leu picked up a pen and put check marks by all but three of the names, then handed the list back to Syrelle. "Arrest those I've checked. Contact Ju-Long and have him put his best people on the others. I want them followed, discreetly, and I want frequent, detailed reports about their actions over the next six hours."

"And after that?"

"Take them alive if you can—although I doubt they'll cooperate."

She gave a firm nod. Bowing, she backed from the room to follow the orders he'd given.

"Syrelle," Leu said. She paused in mid-step, waiting. "I don't need anyone to give us Valjeta's location. We already know."

"Sire?" she asked, the tilt of her head showing her curiosity.

Leu pointed to the portion of the map showing where Faerie and the veil intersected with the northwestern United States. "Valjeta is here—or was as of a few minutes ago, when she fought with my daughter. Brianna is injured, but alive, and I daresay

Valjeta is worse for the wear as well." Leu bared his teeth in a caricature of a smile.

He continued, "She has a means of regenerating her magic that, while abhorrent, is quite effective. So we should expect her to be at full strength when she attacks." He blew out a single breath.

"It is time to move my base of operations to the throne room. Have the guards handle it," he said with a pointed glance at the list in her hand. "It seems that quite a lot of my personal staff will be unavailable."

"Of course, sire. I'll take care of it."

"Thank you, Syrelle. You may go." Leu watched her until she left the room, then moved back to the fire.

Seven hours.

39

LUCIENNE

Lucienne followed Gwynneth through dimly lit halls that echoed with each step. By the time they reached the doors of the throne room, she was shivering, from the chill and from fright. Brianna had been exiled and Eammon killed. Troops were being moved around the country. Nobles she'd known her entire life had been arrested. Her father had vanished behind closed doors, in meetings with his generals and most trusted advisors.

Now, in the middle of the night, Lucienne had been rousted from her bed by a summons from her father, delivered not by a page or minor functionary, but by Gwynneth herself—who had cut her hair to an unflattering, short bristle. Nor had Lucie been allowed to properly dress herself; her thin sleeping gown did nothing to ward off the cold.

At a nod from Gwynneth, one of a pair of armed guards opened the huge brass door just enough for Gwynneth and Lucienne to pass through, then pushed the door closed behind them.

She froze just across the threshold, shocked by what she saw.

It was as she had feared. The kingdom was going to war.

The throne room was awash with people. Tables were scattered throughout the room, laden with maps and other papers. A large map, made of magic and mist, hung in midair in the center of the room, being closely studied by generals and advisors; the sound of their debate echoed from the vaulted ceiling.

Her father sat above it all, on his throne. Affixed by magic to the nearest wall was the picture that normally adorned the library—the painting that had served as a portal to the human world. Even from this distance Lucienne could see the spells of prohibition that had been carved and painted into its frame, making it impossible for anyone to cross the veil through the picture. Apparently it still showed what was happening on the other side of the veil, for her father was watching the painting the way a human would watch a television.

"The lady Lucienne *Ap Reigh,* your majesty."

Lucienne made her obeisance. Her father rose and strode down the steps to meet her, saying, "Rise."

She rose, and raised her eyes to meet his.

She managed not to gasp at his appearance, but he was so changed in the last few weeks that it was hard to keep her countenance smooth. Leu looked old, tired, and very, very angry. Like Gwynneth and the guards, indeed, like every man and woman in sight, the king had cut his hair short. No doubt he'd burned the cuttings himself, to be sure they could not be used against him. He traded the gray of mourning for the black of the guards—the plain fighting uniform, the tunic woven with spells of protection and lined with Kevlar.

"What can I do to help?" Lucienne didn't hesitate. She didn't have much to offer. She'd never trained with the guard and her lessons had taught her that she was not a stellar tactician, but she was a fair hand at magic, and willing to do whatever was necessary to serve her king, and her people.

The king smiled at her. "Are you certain? I have a task for you, but it is a thankless one, and while less dangerous than some, particularly with Ju-Long at your side, it is still not without risk."

"Whatever you need, if I can do it, I will." She tried to put her heart in the words, to make him understand that she truly meant it. Eammon had betrayed him. Lucienne would not. Politics be damned, he was her father. And however belatedly she'd come to realize it, she loved him.

"Thank you, Lucie. That means everything to me." He took her hand and escorted her to the top of the dais, gesturing for her to take a seat on the small stool that had been moved to the level just below the throne.

"As you can see, we are about to go to war. The traitor, Valjeta, is returning, to supporters who have waited eagerly for her." His voice was bitter, but he waved her protests aside with impatience. "There is to be a civil war. I am surrounded by traitors. The outlook is . . . not good."

This time she cried out in earnest.

"It's Fate, Lucienne. She spared me once, to save our people. I am doing everything in my power, but—"

"I'm so sorry." Tears ran unheeded down Lucienne's cheeks.

He gave her a sad smile. "So am I. But I've made my peace with it. And as we are going to war, I must choose my heir."

Lucienne met his gaze, knowing, without being told, what that choice must be. "It's Brianna. It has to be. We're at war—she has the training and the support of the guards and the lesser Fae. They've seen that she values all of our people, all life—a gargoyle is her dearest friend, as was a dryad, she's chosen to live among the humans. All that makes the folk willing to follow her as they wouldn't any of the others."

" 'The others,' " Leu said with a brief chuckle. "You don't count yourself among the candidates? Don't you wish to be queen?"

She gave him a smile as sad as his own. "In peace, I could be a good queen. Not now. I'd be signing my own death warrant, and I might take Faerie down with me. No, it has to be Brianna. Even the nobles who dislike her will see the sense of it."

"You're not the idiot you pretend to be. And yes, in peacetime you would be a good choice."

"But not now."

"No. Not now."

"What do you want me to do?"

"Ju-Long will give you my ring, the King's Seal. Take it to your sister."

"Of course. And what of the others?"

"Asara has sent Rihannon to her family in the northlands. Neither she nor Rodan know I've chosen."

Lucie had her doubts about that. Her father might not have told them, but they would have guessed, just as she had, and they would not be happy about it. Still, she didn't comment. There was no point.

"By now Rodan should have joined Ulrich and his troops. You and Ju-Long must pass through the ring of protection that surrounds the city. Take the ring, and my decision, through the veil to your sister. Stay with her. She'll need your support should I fall."

"When do I leave?"

"Now. Ju-Long has appropriate clothing for you, and supplies. Is there anything you need before you go?"

"Scissors."

Leu raised an eyebrow in inquiry.

"I need to cut my hair."

40

The supplies Ju-Long provided were from the human side of the veil. Lucienne stepped into a pair of thick denim jeans that draped easily over her fur-lined boots. The heavy, cream-colored sweater knitted in an elaborate pattern was sturdy and covered most of her neck. It was so bulky that she had a bit of trouble pulling up the zipper of the leather jacket she was to wear over it.

A knitted cap and gloves completed the outfit. Small as she was, and with her hair cropped short, she looked very young, and nothing at all like herself. Which was, she supposed, the whole point.

Ju-Long had to show her how to put on the strapped bag he referred to as a backpack, first explaining that it had been spelled shut and booby-trapped to protect its contents. If anyone but Lucienne opened it, and even if she opened it without using the right password, it would detonate, turning everything within twenty feet to dust.

Knowing that didn't help steady her nerves, but when her father came over to them, she managed to pretend to be calm.

"A moment alone with my daughter, if you please," the king said.

"Of course, your majesty." Ju-Long bowed low, moving with deliberate haste to a table where Gwynneth was arguing loudly with a general of the King's Guard.

Leu stepped close. Leaning down, he kissed Lucienne's forehead. Pulling her into a rare hug, he whispered, "Before you go, I just wanted to tell you. I love you, Lucie. And I'm proud of you."

Lucie's throat tightened painfully, tears choking her so that she could barely breathe, let alone answer him, but she managed to gasp out, "Love you, too."

Leu squeezed her so tight her ribs hurt, before reluctantly letting her go. "You'd best leave, before your king forgets his dignity." He raised his voice and called to Ju-Long, who hurried to his side.

"Yes, sire," the dragon said.

"Take good care of my daughter."

"I'll guard her with my life."

"I know you will, old friend."

And with that, Leu turned away to join the discussion at the map table. Lucienne was glad that he did not look back. If he had, he'd have seen his daughter weeping, and that might have unmanned him.

———

"Something is wrong," Lucienne whispered, laying a hand on Ju-Long's arm to get his attention. He turned to her, his dark eyes guarded.

"There should be traps and deadfalls in these tunnels, but we've been walking for hours and I haven't seen one, or felt any magic signature that might indicate that something is hidden. Have you?"

"No."

"We have to warn the king."

"My orders are to get you and the ring safely to Princess Brianna. The king was very clear. Nothing else was to take precedence."

Lucienne's eyes darkened and her jaw thrust forward. She spoke softly but passionately. "Ju-Long, we can't just let this go. If it comes to it, my sister will be queen, with or without the ring, and Faerie and my father are more important than my personal safety. Either we go back or we leave the tunnels and find a messenger, perhaps one of your agents, and send word. Where does the nearest exit let out?"

"Not anywhere you want to go," he said firmly, and kept walking. Lucienne followed. She could tell that he was thinking over what she'd said. "Nor can we take the turnoff your sister's men used. Our enemies will look for us there.

"The sacred grove. It's not far from the ring—only a few hours walk. It's hallowed ground, close to the deities. Even Valjeta's people might hesitate to attack us there. And"—he gave her a wry smile that transformed his face, making him suddenly quite handsome—"no one has ever accused you of being religious. They won't expect us to go there."

Lucienne nodded. "Take me."

It was a long hike and not a pleasant one. The way was narrow and dark, the air musty from disuse and lack of circulation. Still, it was breathable, if only just. Lucienne had not noticed the slight downward slope of the tunnels, so did not realize just how far below the surface they were until faced with a steep staircase. The narrow treads lead sharply upward between bulging walls of iron-colored stone. The steps were barely wide enough for one thin person to pass and there were spots where Lucienne's bulky clothing forced her to turn sideways and remove her backpack. Ju-Long wound up stripped down to little more than his pants and bore deep scratches on his chest after passing through a particularly narrow point.

She was exhausted, filthy, and out of breath by the time they reached the top landing—which appeared to be a dead end.

Lucienne eased herself to the ground to rest, leaning on the wall, while Ju-Long probed the rock wall.

"I need to work out more," she muttered.

"You did fine," he assured her. "Better than I thought you would."

That wasn't exactly flattering; Lucienne gave him a half-hearted glare even as she admitted that she couldn't really argue. Her efforts at fitness were sporadic at best.

With a whisper of magic and the grinding of stone, a wall of seemingly solid rock simply vanished, leaving Lucienne blinking against the bright glare of the late afternoon sun.

She shielded her eyes with one arm as she sucked in lungfuls of gloriously fresh air and listened to the sounds of songbirds and water rushing over stone.

When her eyes adjusted she found herself looking out from the mouth of a cave through the fine mist of a waterfall, each drop sparkling like a diamond in the sunlight. About three feet below was a large pond or small lake, bedecked with water lilies. It was lovely, the water mirroring the reds and golds of the sun sinking behind the circle of standing stones on the far side, the light tinting the sandy brown stones a rosy hue. Tiny winged creatures flew across the water and gathered in the grassy area between the standing stones: butterflies and pixies, with rainbow-colored wings; dragonflies and nyads; tiny water Fae with shimmering, translucent wings.

"Oh!" Lucienne stared in wonder. "How beautiful."

"Yes, it is. I've always loved this place." Ju-Long smiled, and lines of tension she'd never noticed before melted from his face, leaving him looking years younger. "If you'll follow me, there's a dry path down to the worship area." As they walked, Lucienne forced herself not to swat at the flying creatures who were now swarming around her head. The host of winged bodies made it difficult to see, and the buzz of wings was as annoying as the drone of a fly.

"Watch your step!" Ju-Long snapped. "To step off of the path is to die."

Lucienne stopped short. He was right, of course. Nyads were small, and might appear harmless, but they loved to lure travelers into the water—so that their larger cousins, the kelpies, could wrap their legs around the limbs of the unfortunate, drowning them and feasting on the corpse.

"Enough," he growled at the tiny beings, who hissed at him in response. "Shall I change forms? Flame you from the air?"

The threat seemed a bit excessive to Lucienne, but it was effective. The nyads and pixies vanished as one, disappearing with a flash of light and sprinkle of pixie dust. Ripples moved on the surface of the water, as if something large was swimming away from the shallows.

They walked the remainder of the path unmolested, but when they stepped into the clear grass beyond the last reeds the air directly in front of Ju-Long's face began to shimmer and sparkle, and the largest pixie Lucienne had ever seen appeared.

She was at least nine inches tall, and her perfect, naked loveliness was accented by the tiny gold circlet she wore on her lavender hair, and only slightly marred by the scowl on her face, that showed tiny, sharp teeth.

"Was it really necessary for you to threaten my retainers?" she snapped at Ju-Long.

"Evidently it was. I have your right of free passage here."

"You, not your guest."

"She has *my* right of free passage here. I brought her, she is under my protection."

"She would be," the pixie spat. "What do you want, Ju-Long? You obviously didn't come here to pray."

"I need to get a message to High King Leu."

"The High King cares naught for the pixies. Were the price

right, I *might* send your message, but it would never be received, for he would not deign to speak with such as mine. Not now."

She had a point. Much as Lucienne hated to admit it, her father believed the pixies to be little more than annoying, dangerous pests. "I can give you a token that will get your messenger past the guards and in to see the king," she assured the pixie.

"Were we speaking to *you*? I don't believe so. Nor, I notice, has Ju-Long shown proper manners and introduced you to us. Give us your name."

"Is that the price for delivery of the message? Would that be your bargain?"

The little faerie hissed in displeasure. Names had power, which was why she'd demanded it. Her eyes narrowed and she stared at Lucienne for a long moment.

"We nearly had you on the lake—so I'd thought you a fool. Perhaps I misjudged you." She flew past Ju-Long and began examining Lucie closely. "Not human, despite the clothes, the ears, and the eyes, too Sidhe. You have a token that could get a message directly to the High King and your lovely red hair has been chopped short."

She flew back to Ju-Long. "It's war then, is it? And you've brought the king's daughter here with you, dragging my people into the middle of a mess that will get us all killed, more than like."

"You and yours are subject to the High King's rule, Violet."

"I swore no oath!"

"Yet you live on his lands and eat the food you can glean from them at his tolerance. Did you think there was no price? Are you Fae?"

The pixie queen rocked back as sharply as if he'd slapped her. If looks could kill, Ju-Long would have burned to ashes in that moment. After a long moment of silence, Violet settled onto the grass. "Fine, then. Though I regret the bargain, it has been made. I owe King Leu for the sustenance of my people. That buys you a few moments of my time and the consideration of your errand. The errand itself will have its own price."

"And that price would be?" Ju-Long inquired.

"Royal blood is sweet. I want hers."

"No," he answered, his tone iron. Lucie rested her hand on his arm, trying to counsel him to patience.

"One drop," Lucienne offered. "And not from the source."

Violet smiled greedily. "Not from the source? Where's the fun in that?"

"I know my lessons. I won't be having you mark me." More than one unwary soul had been so marked, and later, hunted and devoured by swarms of tiny Faeries. "One drop—and *not* from the source. That is the offer. You'll get no more from me."

"Not even to save your precious father?"

Lucienne didn't respond, didn't react at all. She'd give her life to save her father and king, but knew she wouldn't have to. She could see the longing in the little queen's eyes. She'd take the bargain. Lucie only had to hold fast to her offer.

For a full three minutes, they stared at each other in silence. In the end, the pixie's appetite won out. "Fine. One drop, not from the source. And I will send your message, and your token, to your king, immediately and without delay."

That last was a gift that Lucie hadn't bargained for.

"Done and done," Lucie agreed. "Ju-Long, your knife, please."

He passed it to her. With exquisite care Lucienne used the very tip of the knife to puncture the pad of her left index finger. She kept the knife in her right hand, in case the pixie lost control. She knelt, then, and pressed against the small wound on her finger until a single drop of blood welled forth. The pixie let out a little moan, leaning forward, a tiny trickle of drool sneaking past her lips.

Lucie leaned forward, turned her hand, and let her blood drop onto a flat pebble.

The pixie lunged. In a blur of speed she devoured the blood.

She began to glow; tiny, starlike motes of dust spread out from her in an explosion of light.

Lucienne quickly got to her feet and handed Ju-Long his blade, handle first.

When the pixie rose into the air again, she was wiping her mouth with the back of her hand. "Oh, that was marvelous, daughter of Leu. I'd give much to have more."

"No," Lucie said firmly. "The deal has been made."

"Very well." Violet sulked. "Dandy . . . Dandelion, come to your queen. I have a task for you."

There was a soft popping noise and a male pixie appeared. At perhaps six inches tall, he was smaller than his queen, his features more delicate. His body was a pale green, his hair the vibrant yellow of a dandelion in full bloom. He swept into a low bow before his liege, who smiled broadly, obviously enjoying the view.

"How can I be of service?" he asked.

"These two"—she gestured to Lucienne and Ju-Long—"have a message for you to deliver to High King Leu of the Sidhe. They will give you a token to ensure you're allowed in his presence."

Lucienne stripped a ring from her finger. A single white pearl in a swirl of gold, with diamond chips on either side. Her father had given it to her mother, Mara, upon learning that she was carrying his child. He'd bestowed it on her publicly, so the servants and retainers would recognize it. Lucie handed the ring to the pixie with some regret, but while it had great sentimental value, she'd give up more than a ring to see her father warned of his danger.

"And the message?" Dandelion asked.

"Tell him," Ju-Long answered, "that the tunnels have not been secured."

The pixie nodded once, then disappeared in a puff of sparkling dust. Lucienne prayed that the message would get through, but she very much feared that the effort was too little, too late.

41

It was midday, hot and muggy, the air close enough that Luci-enne felt like she was swimming in slow motion as she moved through the last stretch of woods. Ten more yards and they'd be past the ring and Ju-Long could open a passage through the veil. It felt like miles.

It had been a very long time since her weapons master had taught her to move in stealth through the woods using illusion to hide her passage. As a child it had been an adventure—a challenge. Now, with her life depending on it, it was just nerve wracking. Still, she said a silent prayer of thanks to the deities for giving her a teacher who was so insistent on her getting it right. Baja had been an old curmudgeon, but he had made damned sure she was capable of defending herself if she had to, or of running if it came to that. The only reason Ju-Long could see her was that he kept his hand on her arm at all times, sharing his power to fuel her illusion.

Deities bless his soul. By now Baja had been reborn—and was up to who knew what.

Five yards now.

Ju-Long squeezed his hand upon her arm in a silent signal to wait. Sure enough, less than a minute later an enemy scout passed by. Less than a foot from them, he didn't have any notion that he wasn't alone. Lucienne was surprised he couldn't hear the frantic beating of her heart. Not her breathing—she was holding her breath. She only let it go when he was twenty feet past.

Still Ju-Long held her back. And well he did. A pair of guards erupted from the ground, engaging the enemy scout in a noisy, brutal battle.

It was the perfect cover and they used it, moving more swiftly now, because the noise of the fight would bring reinforcements.

Damn it.

Lucienne felt the thrum of power through the soles of her feet. They were past the ring. Any time now he could pierce the veil—if they could just get out of sight of those fighters.

Twenty feet to the left there was the beginning of a downslope. In the distance she could hear the river. They could use the sound of the water to cover any noise they might make, and the dip in the land would keep them out of sight . . . from this group at least.

Apparently Ju-Long had the same idea. He tugged her arm in that direction. She nodded her assent.

They moved together to the edge of the river Lythos. Standing on the muddy bank the sounds of the fight carried clear, but faint to her ears. Again, Lucie strained her senses, searching for any sign of unwelcome company.

They were alone.

She felt the stir of energy as Ju-Long gathered his power. With a gesture, he opened a passage through the veil, from their reality to the shadowy alley behind Brianna's shop.

Lucienne didn't hesitate. She stepped through, her feet moving from mud to trash-strewn concrete in a single step.

Ju-Long was right behind her. As she turned to thank him she heard a sound not unlike a man's cough, and fell to the ground in agony as a bullet tore through her chest.

Time stopped. In a single frozen instant she saw Ju-Long, fire dancing on the fingers of his left hand, gun drawn in his right and aimed into the deep shadows behind a Dumpster filled to overflowing. She saw a man, silenced pistol drawn and aimed at the dragon's head. But mostly she saw a tiny white spider sliding down a silver thread—the only moving object in the entire tableau.

The spider dropped to the ground where it resolved itself into the form of an old woman, back bent from years of care, wrinkled features wearing an expression of utter weariness. Still, her black eyes were sharp and alert, their gaze penetrating.

Atropos.

"Hurts doesn't it," the old woman observed.

Lucie didn't bother to respond, she wasn't sure she could anyway. Just drawing air into her damaged lungs was pure agony. The old woman bent slowly, and painfully down to lay her hand against Lucienne's cheek.

You don't have to do this.

Clotho is right, this mess was our doing. You shouldn't be the one forced to pay the price.

Hush, both of you. This is my choice. It is time. And while painful, it will at least be quick. I'd hate a slow death.

Atropos gave Lucienne's cheek a gentle pat. "Are you ready, child?"

Ready for what? Death? No. She wasn't. But really, was anyone, ever? Didn't we all fight and claw for that one last breath?

The old woman laughed. *Well, most do anyway. Not me.* With that she bent forward, laying a tender kiss on Lucienne's forehead.

At that feather-light contact, the pain vanished, replaced by a strange sensation that she could not fathom. One moment she was dying. The next she stood over a body—her body.

"What . . ." she gasped.

"You are one of us now, Clotho."

42

KING LEU OF THE SIDHE

Leu stared at the painting on the wall beside his throne, ignoring the bustle in the room as last-minute plans were put into place. His advisors were good at their jobs, so he let them perform without undue interference.

His daughter slept. To his great relief, Brianna's health had improved dramatically once Morguenna had been able to treat her and get her fed. The gargoyle had escaped. The enemy did not have him. Valjeta would cross the veil. But she would not have an army of humans with her. Nor could she bring across any of the hugely destructive weapons available on the human side of the veil.

Some of his people would die. It was inevitable: but not all of them and, deities willing, not his children.

Valjeta was evil, twisted, and had never been entirely sane. She had committed ritual murder, using blood, pain, and death to steal enough human magic to pierce the veil. Every bit of that magic was still tangled with remnants of the souls of the dead humans—souls that would not rest until freed.

The power Valjeta had stolen was formidable. But it was not *hers* and therefore would not be easy to wield—in fact, the human magic would actively resist her. And she could only regain her strength after more ritual human deaths.

He knew Valjeta wouldn't hesitate to kill whoever she had to. But thanks to Helena Jefferson, there was a singular lack of humans on this side of the veil. Leu gave a wolfish smile. He'd been furious with Helena much of the time, but she'd been an amazing woman. In the end, whether she'd meant to or not, she'd served him well.

Valjeta would try to take Faerie from him. But were she to succeed she wouldn't keep it. The magic and the land itself would not accept her. His descendants would sit on the throne, beginning with Helena's daughter.

Civil war: It was the last thing Leu had wanted. But Fate would have her way, bitch that she could be.

"Your majesty," Asara said softly behind him.

Leu turned to face her. She was lovely, as always. With her long hair gone, the fine bones of her face were more noticeable, and the armor she wore did not disguise the gentle, feminine curves of her body. She sank into a low curtsy.

"You should have gone," he said as he gestured for her to rise.

Standing, she gave a snort of derision. "And go where? I made my choice years ago. I am yours."

He might have answered her, but a horn sounded in the distance. Furious activity erupted in the throne room.

Doxies flew in, reporting on the battles and the movements of non-combatants. The shimmering, floating map reflected the information: ground held by Leu glowed a brilliant silver; ground lost to the enemy, a sullen red.

In the field, the loyalists were winning, thanks to the brilliant tactics of Ulrich and Leu's other generals and battle commanders—and the abilities of his warriors. The carnage was horrific. Images of individual battles flickered in the air as the doxies made their reports.

It made no sense.

"Your majesty." Leu could feel Moash's eyes upon him; the old doxie seemed to see through the calm exterior Leu presented to the assembly. "A word in private, if I may?"

At Leu's curt nod, his other advisors stepped back. Moash quickly used one claw to etch a circle just big enough to contain the two kings. He spit on it, the acid saliva burning into the marble tile, and at the same time sending flickering green flame racing around the circle. When it closed, the kings stood in a bubble of silence so complete that their very breaths sounded loud.

"We are winning," Moash observed. "But you do not seem well pleased. Why? Where are the dragons? And where are your children? They should be fighting beside you. Brianna would not willingly leave your side at a time like this."

"Not willingly, no." Leu looked down at Moash, smiling at the old doxie. Moash was no fool. It was a shame about his son. The prince was a proud idiot. Then again, the same could be—had been—said about some of Leu's own children. He felt a spasm of grief at the loss of Eammon, but forced his mind away from the pain.

Moash pressed harder. "Tell me. I can't help you intelligently without knowing what we're up against."

Leu gave an exasperated sigh. He wanted to trust Moash—needed to trust *someone*. "I met with Fate the other night. I *know* I am betrayed, that I am to die this day at a traitor's hand."

Moash took a sharp step back, and was brought up short by the power of the circle. A calculating look came into the Doxie King's eyes. "Which is why the palace is so lightly defended—and none of your children at hand." Leu could see the calculation running through the doxie's eyes as he looked at his High King's plans with this new information in mind. He saw awareness, and admiration dawn.

"If I die," Leu said quietly, "and the ring is taken from my finger, you'll need to stay as far back as you can." He gave a wolfish smile.

Moash arched a single eyebrow. "I'm surprised you would trust me with this information, sire, but I am glad to hear it. I probably won't be alive to see it. But I suspect it will be—"

"Electrifying," Leu promised. "And I do trust you. Ju-Long found no evidence that you were aware of your son's plots.

Moash gave a nod of satisfaction. "Of course not. There is none." He turned, looking at the map floating nearby. "With this new information in mind, may I make a few suggestions?"

"Suggest away."

Moash reached down, deliberately breaking the circle. He and the High King strode over to the map. The King of the Doxies raised a claw, pointing at a particular spot on the map, and said, "Here is what I have in mind."

43

JU-LONG

He had failed. He knew it the instant he heard the shot—saw the human assassin in the flash of his weapon, standing in the shadows behind an overstuffed garbage Dumpster. He tried to shout a warning, drew his .45 and his magic, but it was already too late. Lucienne staggered as the bullets impacted her chest. The entrance wounds were small. The exit tore out half of her back and chest. She crumpled to the ground, blood frothing from her mouth and spurting from a severed artery to pool on the filthy cement.

He fired, and missed, his first shot taking a chunk out of the brick wall by the assassin's head, making him flinch, causing his shot at Ju-Long to go wide.

Ju-Long's second shot caught the man in the throat, and with the heavy caliber of his gun severed the assassin's spine. Head and body fell separately to the ground.

He turned, intending to rush to Lucienne's side, and found Fate standing in his way. The crone bent down, her words a sibilant whisper just beyond Ju-Long's hearing. She laid a gentle kiss on

Lucienne's forehead and the dragon watched in shock as the old woman's soul slid into the dying body and Lucienne's essence flowed upward, becoming a new aspect of Fate.

Sirens blared, close and coming closer: Brianna's shop, being downtown, was close to the main police station and ambulance dispatch.

"You need to go now, before the authorities arrive." It was Lucienne speaking, standing over her own corpse.

He just stared. Behind her the back door of the shop opened. His daughter Mei stood there with Morguenna and the *Ard Reigh* herself.

He turned to Brianna, said, "I'm sorry," before stepping back through the still-open portal and sealing it closed behind him.

Standing on the bank of the river again, tears stung his eyes. He'd failed her, failed his king. And Lucienne had paid the price. As Clotho her soul would live on, but she was not, would never again be *Lucienne*.

Fate would give the ring to Brianna, and perhaps that was as it should be. But what of him?

Listening, he heard the fighting in the distance. Could it be? Had the king synched time between the two worlds again for the day of battle?

Ju-Long felt a surge of hope. Perhaps he could still do his king some good, could still redeem himself in others' eyes, if never in his own. And perhaps he could take his revenge on the woman responsible for placing the assassin behind Brianna's shop.

In a rush of power he transformed into his true form and launched himself skyward. It was time he joined the battle.

He flew through the air of Faerie, through the clouds, cold and wet against his scaly skin. He was looking to see where he could do the most good. Looking down, the earth was small, the creatures on it tiny ants, only visible at all when he strained to see them. His destination was the royal city. But before he reported to the king he wanted to see the lay of the troops, the progress of the many battles. Only a dragon could fly fast and far enough to get a true overview.

Cloaking himself in illusion he dropped down in altitude. Now he could see individuals as bodies, though not faces.

Everywhere he looked the fight was on—outside the city farms had been set ablaze, fields of grain turned to battlefields muddied with Sidhe blood, corpses drawing the inevitable circling of carrion birds.

In the forest he glimpsed enemy forces. The wild men of the west, Valjeta's allies, creeping forward, their mottled green clothing making it difficult for him to see them clearly. The doxies, in the trees above them had no such problem. Waiting until the perfect moment they dropped down from the branches on top of their enemy wreaking death and devastation with unholy abandon.

On the road leading into the east gate of the city he saw mounted troops galloping forward to attack a knot of guards seemingly pinned down—then watched as the ground itself seemed to erupt and thousands of rocs, the gargoyles tiny kin, swarmed up and over the horses, covering them in a squirming mass of grinding rock; devouring horse and rider with abandon.

On the wall above the west gate he saw Teo and Nama'an, working together using a grenade launcher, to devastating effect, though where they'd gotten it and how they'd learned its use he had no clue.

No one here needed his help.

He circled, debating where to go, wondering where the bitch Valjeta had gotten to. She was the enemy's leader. She was in the field somewhere. He *knew* it. But there'd been no sign of her.

And then he remembered: the tunnels. If Lucienne's messenger had failed to get through they were unguarded. It felt right.

Using the tunnels Valjeta would be able to get into the palace itself—fight her way to the very throne room.

Ju-Long snarled. The enemy might even now be sneaking into the palace unhindered by the fierce battles raging above ground.

He circled back to the Guardsman Tavern and found it under attack. Enemy troops had it surrounded. The inn itself was ablaze. Still, guards fought on, raining magic down on the enemy from entrenched positions, mounted cavalry harrying them, then slipping away.

Ju-Long waited, choosing his moment with care. The riders came in on the attack, wreaking havoc on the enemy, who fought furiously, aiming both weapons and magic to take down beast and rider, with some success.

One third less cavalry returned than had set out. But as they turned, when their beasts were far enough away not to be terrified by his presence, Ju-Long swooped down, shedding his veil as he went, drawing air deep in his lungs then sending it blasting down on the enemy troops in a wide swath of destruction.

The guards cheered as the enemy was forced to draw back in sudden disarray.

That was what Ju-Long needed. Rather than rise back in the clouds he pulled illusion around himself, shifting forms as he landed. Invisible to friend and enemy alike, he was at great risk of getting caught in the crossfire. The knowledge drove him, and he dashed at a full sprint to the entrance to the tavern's stable and the tunnel entrance.

44

KING LEU OF THE SIDHE

The enemy had come through the tunnels.

The palace was overrun. Chaos reigned. Smoke and magic filled the air and bright blood slicked the black-and-white marble of the throne room. In the crowded, confusing space, using projectile weapons was nearly impossible, so battle was being waged in the traditional way, with swords and spells.

Petros had fallen, victim of a fire bolt that had been meant for the king. His body was only one of many, many fallen, attacker and defender alike.

Leu and Asara were fighting back-to-back, swinging blades and slinging spells in an instinctive rhythm. They did it well, easily holding off any attackers who managed to force their way through the ring of defenders surrounding them.

Gwynneth was engaged in a vicious battle with a warrior whose face was hidden in a hooded red cloak. They seemed well matched, trading blow for blow and feint for feint. Viktor had slain Alaric and was cutting a swath through the defenders, while continuing to shield Valjeta.

A dive by Moash forced Viktor to the floor. On the second balcony, a gnome saw his opening. He grabbed a roc from the group waiting at his feet, loaded the little creature into his slingshot, and sent spinning toward the would-be queen's head. The roc shrieked a shrill war cry as it flew. It struck Valjeta's forehead and clawed out her eye.

The usurper shrieked in pain and agony as blood and worse flowed from her eye socket. She grabbed the vicious little stone troll. In the instant before she flung it from her into the nearest marble column, it bit her hand, stone teeth shredding skin and crushing bone. Throughout the room, more rocs swarmed down from the balcony, rolling like a moving carpet to cover enemy soldiers, who screamed in agony as they were eaten alive.

The vicious duel between the red-cloaked form and Gwynneth ended with a well-placed thrust of the enemy's dagger into the guard's armpit as he was recovering from a swing of his sword.

Leu heard Asara gasp, felt, rather than saw her falter.

It was a fatal mistake.

Leu turned in time to see a red-cloaked Rodan pulling his bloodied sword from the corpse of his mother, a fierce, vicious expression of joy contorting his face into something monstrous.

Leu called lightning, from the air. It struck Asara's corpse, immolating it, melting the metal of Rodan's sword to slag, cracking the marble where it hit in a sound that was lost in the roar of thunder that deafened everyone in the room.

Eyes streaming from the intensity of the light, Leu found it hard to see, but he sensed that while many, even most of the throne room's occupants had pulled away, leaving an open area around the king, one had not.

He spun in the direction of a moving shadow, sword moving in a slicing arc, and found himself victim of the same illusion that must have killed Gwynneth.

Pain, such incredible pain.

Leu felt his knees give and he crumpled to the ground, his lifeblood pumping in spurts from the severed brachial artery. His hand still gripped his sword, but he was too weak to move it even before Rodan's booted foot slammed down on the flat of the blade, pinning it to the floor.

Leu's vision was fading. Breathing was hard, physical labor. Almost over: it was almost over. Soon, soon he could rest with his family, his lover.

Leu's world narrowed to the two of them. Rodan squatted down, bringing his face close to his father's. "I'll take what's mine now."

Leu felt his son's hand on his, prying his grip loose from the sword, working the ring from his finger.

The explosion was just as spectacular as he had planned.

45

BRIANNA

"The king is dead. Long live the queen." Lucienne/Clotho dropped to one knee, the ruler's ring extended in her hand, offered up to her half sister, Brianna Hai, High Queen of the Sidhe.

Brianna felt empty. She'd weep if she could, but had no tears. The ring in her hand was heavy, but not nearly as heavy as the weight of the stares, the expectation in those eyes. Hope. They looked at her with desperate hope, where she had only despair.

She accepted the ring, sliding it onto her finger. "In one hour I want a status report. I need to know which lands we hold, and what has fallen, and I need to know if the veil needs to come down, and our people be evacuated. One hour." She turned to walk away. From the corner of her eye, she saw Pug move toward her, and Adam's small shake of the head as he reached a hand out to stop the other man.

She was glad. Pug meant well, they all did. But she needed to be alone now. An hour wasn't nearly enough time for her to assimilate the vast changes in her life—not nearly enough time to grieve for her father. But it was all there was—and even that more than should be risked. There would be advisors to meet with, plans to make—and while the police were gone for now, along with the corpses that had been Lucienne, and the assassin, Raymond Carter, they'd be back.

A queen does what she must, and the woman pays for it.

She closed the bedroom door softly behind her. Dropping to her knees she did something that was rare for her. She prayed. "Deities, help me."

Peace, soft and silent as falling snow, descended on her. It didn't erase the sorrow of her loss, nothing could, but she felt warmth envelope her, as though she were held by strong and loving arms. In that gentle, invisible embrace, the walls holding back her emotions shattered.

She wept.

It seemed no time at all before there was a light tap on the bedroom door. Brianna wiped her eyes with a tissue from the end table, blew her nose, then rose. When she reached the door she was in control of herself. She felt . . . better, strong enough to take up the burdens awaiting her. She silently thanked the deities for their gift and opened the bedroom door.

She found herself face-to-face with, not Adam, but King Moash. The doxie was very much the worse for wear, his wings and fur heavily singed and smelling of smoke, rents in his hide still bleeding sullenly despite having been stitched closed. Still, he was upright, and moving, which was surprising giving what she'd seen of the fight in the throne room.

"Your majesty," Moash said as he bowed low before her.

"Your highness," she replied in acknowledgment, and he rose. "What word of the battle? And where is the Diamond King?"

"He awaits you downstairs. Your workroom was the best place to lower the barrier again, and the only space large enough for the war council. I hope we were not remiss in using it?"

"Of course not." She followed him down the hall where the statue her father had sent her—just days ago—still stood. Magic gone now, it was just a statue, and a painful reminder of how much had changed in the past few days.

"Ju-Long retook the tunnels, so most of our people in the palace were able to retreat to safety. But, Valjeta lives," Moash said grimly as he made his way awkwardly down the stairs. Graceful in the air, the small space and his injuries made his body cumbersome and awkward. "She has lost one eye and was badly burned in the strike that killed your brother, but the bitch lives." He turned, his gaze locking with Brianna's. "She will not have the crown. Nor will she sit on the throne. When the High King died, they were sealed away from her by the magic of Faerie itself. She can see them, but she can't touch them. According to the reports, she is near maddened with rage by this."

"Good."

"We need to evacuate our people from around the city, to regroup. Your father had prepared well. There are locations all over this side of the veil that were made ready for just this eventuality."

They were passing through the front of the shop now, and Brianna could hear the sound of vigorous debate through the door that divided the shop area from the back.

Moash nodded. He opened the door to the back room and held it open so she could enter, announcing as he did: "Her majesty, High Queen Brianna of the Sidhe."

She stepped through the door and silence descended. Every person in the room dropped to one knee in obeisance before her. Brianna stood still, taking in the room and its occupants.

On the table was the four-dimensional globe, with motes of glowing red showing on specific spots of the earth where it was overlapped by Faerie. These, she presumed, were the places where the refugees would be encamped. Hovering above the table was a translucent map of Faerie similar to the one that had been in her father's war room.

She glanced around the crowded room, looking for specific faces. Adam was there, and Mei with her brother Chang, Morguenna and Ju-Long, and others. But where was Nick? Sophie, too, was missing.

"Rise," she ordered. "Syrelle," she said to the woman who'd so recently served her father, "Moash has told me some of it. I will need to hear the rest once the spell is cast. Everyone but the Diamond King, clear the room until I send for you."

They left.

It was suddenly so quiet. Just her, and Adam.

"Are you ready?" he asked.

He was speaking of the spell, of course, but there were so many things she was facing for which she needed to be ready. Her father had put his faith in her—her people were counting on her.

Steeling her shoulders, she met Adam's gaze steadily. "I am."